LOVE IN A NUTSHELL

is

"SEXY . . . [Like] a Fred Astaire and Ginger Rogers classic performance, [the authors] mixed their expert maneuvers with graceful precision to create a fun read with the right amount of humor, suspense, and romance."
—*USA Today*

"A REFRESHING READ that will keep readers smiling—whether they are brew fans or not . . . Sassy, laugh-out-loud humor, vastly appealing characters, and an intriguing setting make this fast-paced, suspenseful romance one to imbibe."
—*Library Journal*

"CLASSIC ROMANCE . . . with an edge of mystery."
—*Kirkus Reviews*

"A STORY SURE TO PLEASE . . . Evanovich and Kelly skillfully combine comedy with romance and suspense."
—*Booklist*

Love
IN A NUTSHELL

JANET EVANOVICH
& DORIEN KELLY

St. Martin's Paperbacks

This is a work of fiction. All of the characters, organizations, and events portrayed in this novel are either products of the author's imagination or are used fictitiously.

LOVE IN A NUTSHELL

Copyright © 2011 by The Gus Group, LLC.
Excerpt from *The Husband List* copyright © 2012 by The Gus Group, LLC.

All rights reserved.

For information address St. Martin's Press, 175 Fifth Avenue, New York, NY 10010.

Library of Congress Catalog Card Number: 2011033804

ISBN: 978-1-250-01039-1

Printed in the United States of America

St. Martin's Press hardcover edition / January 2012
St. Martin's Paperbacks edition / August 2012

St. Martin's Paperbacks are published by St. Martin's Press, 175 Fifth Avenue, New York, NY 10010.

10 9 8 7 6 5 4 3 2 1

In loving memory of Bubba Gimp,
the coolest special needs coonhound to walk this earth.
And also of Ceili, his wonderful Westie mama dog.
There will never be another pair quite like you!
—Dorien

ONE

Kate Appleton needed a job. Again.

Actually, *need* didn't come close to describing the hunger and sharp bite of desperation speeding her steps across Depot Brewing Company's parking lot on that crisp October afternoon. Just as the town marina to the right of the microbrewery was growing empty of boats, Keene's Harbor, Michigan, was growing empty of tourists and their cash. And, at this moment, Kate needed cash. She had moved to Keene's Harbor a couple of weeks ago, eager to change her parents' dilapidated lake house into a thriving bed-and-breakfast. They had moved to Naples, Florida, and the harsh reality was that it hadn't been used in years, except as a nut storage facility by a family of industrious squirrels. Ironic, since a homemade plaque proclaiming the house "The Nutshell" had adorned the front entrance since before she could remember.

In any event, the house needed a lot of work, and her parents were less than enthusiastic about pumping tens of thousands of dollars into a home that was already underwater on its mortgage. To make matters worse, they'd gotten a letter from some lawyer last week that the bank had gone into bankruptcy and the mortgage had been sold to some private investor. He'd offered to release Kate's parents from the debt in exchange for the property. It was actually a fairly generous offer, considering the market, but Kate was trying to build a life for herself in Keene's Harbor. And dammit, her family home wasn't for sale. Depot Brewing wasn't just Kate's last shot at employment. It was the last shot at her dreams.

Crimson maple leaves crunched beneath her leather boots as she marched toward the handsome yellow brick and sandstone building and checked off her plan of action. She would be firm, yet polite. Honest, yet not to the point of over-sharing. And she would go straight to the top, to the guy who could make her, or— Forget that. She wouldn't consider the possibility of someone breaking her. And she wouldn't consider walking away without a job.

Kate drew in a breath, pulled back her shoulders, and wrapped her hand around the hammered-bronze door handle of her new workplace.

Matt Culhane sat holed up in his small and admittedly cluttered office behind Depot Brewing Company's taproom. He wanted one last look at his inventory spreadsheet before the afterwork crowd showed up. Not that he begrudged his customers their fun, but he should have chosen to stay put in his dungeon of an office in the back of the microbrewery rather than move into the portion of the building housing the newly constructed but noisy restaurant. He was deciding whether to work out a trade with one of his brewer buddies for some Chinese hops when he heard Jerry, his hospitality manager, greet someone in the taproom.

"Is Matt Culhane in?" a woman asked Jerry. "I need to talk to him. His office is in the back, right?"

"Yes," Jerry replied. "But . . . Wait, you can't—"

"Thanks so much for your help," the woman replied. "I can find my way."

Kate knocked once on the open door and swept into the office, closing the door behind her and leaving Jerry standing on the other side open-mouthed and clearly flustered.

Culhane's first thought was that she was a

woman on a mission. His second thought was that he was intrigued. She was just over five feet tall, and had short-cropped blond hair, big hazel eyes, and a wide mouth that he suspected would light up a room when she smiled.

Matt rose, rounded his desk, and extended his hand.

"Hi, I'm Matt Culhane."

Kate took his hand and gave it a firm business-like shake. "I know. I'm Kate Appleton. I don't have a job. And it's your fault. Twenty minutes ago, I was fired because of you."

"Because of me?"

"Yep. From Bagger's Tavern, down on Keene Avenue. It was all because of your skunky beer."

Before he could respond, she planted herself in the one guest chair that didn't have files stacked on it.

Cute but crazy, Matt thought, following her lead and returning to sit in his chair behind his desk. And oddly enough, it did nothing to diminish his attraction to her. "Harley fired you?"

"He did," Kate said.

"Did he say why?"

"Apparently, I'm no longer to be trusted behind the bar, because bad beer passed from tap to lips. I don't think that's fair. And when I look at the whole mess, I figure it's your responsibility. It was your beer," she replied in a patient tone. "I moved to Keene's Harbor three weeks ago and lobbied like crazy to get even that part-time bartending job. Then I lost it over bad beer. Now I have nothing. Every store downtown is owned locally, and every owner runs their place alone in the slow season."

Matt smiled. "That's to be expected. A town built to hold several thousand summer visitors can be pretty empty come the cool weather. Why'd you move here in the off-season?"

"Well, let's just say my options were extremely limited. I needed an inexpensive place to stay, and the mortgage payments on my parents' lake house are a heckuva lot less than any decent rental."

Actually, she was a few months behind on the payments. Between her crapola job at Bagger's and the endless repairs on the house, her savings were pretty much gone. She'd talked to the bank and they'd agreed to let her catch up over the next six months, but that was before they'd gone belly-up. Kate drove the thought from her mind, replacing it with the happy memories that had inspired her to move to Keene's Harbor in the first place. "I'd spent summers here as a kid and loved it. I thought I could come up with some sort of job."

Apparently, she had some history around town, and she also looked to be in the general ballpark of his age. Still, it was no surprise their paths hadn't crossed earlier. He'd stuck with his townie pack. In his high school days, the summer girls weren't worth the snobbishness some of them had thrown at the locals while sunning on Lake Michigan's long stretch of beach.

"So you're a summer person," he said. He wasn't into line-drawing anymore, but he couldn't resist teasing just a little, trying to provoke the same little flush of emotion to her cheeks he'd seen when she first walked into his office.

"Thanks, but I think of myself more as a Citizen of All Seasons."

"Works for me. Where's your parents' place?"

"It's on the lake about two miles north of town. It's old, big, and drafty. And it's a huge money pit, which brings us back to the aforementioned skunky beer," she said, obviously trying to drive the conversation to a set destination.

Matt was curious enough to give her the room to run. "I'll agree that Harley serves my beer, but I'm not going any further than that. The keg could have been bad for a lot of reasons, including dirty tap lines, bad tapping, or the fact that it was past its expiration date. But the bottom line is that I didn't tell him to fire you."

"Just the same, honor compels that you give me a job."

Another surprise bombshell. "A job?"

"Yes. And I'm available to start immediately."

Lucky me, he thought. The woman was clearly crazy, and yet strangely appealing in her overly earnest, convoluted reasoning.

"Supposing, for the sake of discussion, that we were hiring right now," he said. "Other than a couple of weeks at Bagger's, what's your work experience?"

She folded her hands in her lap, a gesture more appropriate for a navy blue interview suit than jeans and a puffy, off-white down jacket still zipped up to her chin. He wondered what she was going to wear when it *really* got cold around here.

"I have a B.A. in Drama from a small college in Ohio."

This time he couldn't fight back a smile. "I didn't ask about your education. I asked what you can do. Before you came to Keene's Harbor, did you have a job?"

"Yes."

He waited for more, but it didn't appear to be coming.

"And?" he asked.

"I was an assistant editor at a business magazine headquartered downstate, outside of Detroit."

"And?" he prompted again.

"I moved here."

"As you said, with very little in the way of options. What happened to the job?"

"The skills aren't relevant to what you do here, but if you really need to know, I was let go."

"Why?"

"It wasn't directly performance-related, so again, I don't think it's all that relevant."

He was hooked. He had to know. He was sure it was something worth hearing.

"Spill it," he said. "Lay it on me."

Kate bit her lower lip. "I had a little incident changing the black ink cartridge for the printer I shared with a couple other people. Maybe it was because we'd switched to a generic brand, or maybe it was because someone—perhaps with the name of Melvin—had messed with it, but whatever the case, I got ink all over the front of my dress. And then while I was in the bathroom trying to soak what I could from the dress, the fire alarm went off."

"Sounds like something you'd see on Cinemax after midnight."

"Let's just say that when presented the choice between potential death and a bit of semi-nudity smack in the middle of downtown Royal Oak, I let the skin show."

"You didn't have much of an option."

She raised her right shoulder in a half shrug. "True. As it turned out, someone—perhaps with the name of Melvin—had pulled the fire alarm. There was no fire, but between the scene on the street and the fact that the video from the building's security camera somehow hit the Internet and went viral, my boss let me go. He said I had become a liability to the magazine. No one could take me seriously. And so someone with the name of Melvin got my job."

"That stinks," Matt said.

Kate nodded in agreement. "It did. But I learned a few good lessons, including always use brand-name ink and watch out for guys named Melvin."

Matt laughed. Kate Appleton might be an involuntary exhibitionist, but so far she'd shown herself to be smart and quick with an answer, and she wore her emotions on her face. His gut told him she was possibly a little nutty, but beyond that a decent person. And Matt generally went with his instincts.

"Now, about that job?" she asked.

He leaned forward, elbows on desk. "I'll start by saying that the bad beer at Bagger's was a problem on his end of the system. Granted, there's a remote possibility it happened here, but that part of the process is under tight control, so I'm not talking to you to redeem my honor or anything like that."

She nodded. "Okay. So long as the talk involves a job, I'm listening."

Kate Appleton did not appear to be a believer in the theory of leverage, in that he had it and she did not. Still, she was bold. He appreciated that about her. And, at the moment, she might just be exactly what he needed.

"There have been some incidents over the past

few months," Matt said, lowering his voice. "They didn't start out as anything big or all that awful. In fact, for a while there, I just kind of put it down to a streak of bad luck."

"What kind of bad luck?"

He leaned back in his chair and considered when it all started. "Well, call it ego, but I'd like to think that last spring, my first failed batch of beer in years was more than just a slipup on my part. Since then, it's been small stuff . . . misrouted deliveries, flat tires on the delivery trucks . . . that kind of thing."

"All of which, pardon me for saying this, could be put down to employee screwups."

Matt nodded. "I know, but they're happening more and more often. I really think one of my employees is trying to sabotage my business."

Kate leaned forward in her seat. "What makes you think it's an employee?"

"Access. Whoever is behind it knows my schedule and my business. And most of the incidents have occurred in employee-only areas, where a customer would be immediately noticed."

Kate raised her eyebrows. "So you want me to help find some deranged lunatic with a beer vendetta."

"I'd hire a private investigator, but this time of year, it would be nearly impossible for a stranger to go unnoticed for more than a day. You, on the other hand, are not a total outsider. And between the impressive performance you just gave convincing me to hire you and your degree in drama, I'm guessing you can act a part if you have to. That makes you a great candidate for the job I have in mind."

She tilted her head. "And that would be what?"

"I'd be hiring you to be a floater. If someone is out sick or there's a crunch in a certain area of the operation, you'd be the one to step in."

"Even though it's likely that eighty percent of the time, I won't know what the heck I'm doing?"

"I get the sense you're a quick study."

"Absolutely. Definitely. I'm your girl. And since I'm so smart, I get the sense that I'll be more than a floater."

"Your job will be to tell me what's going on around here. What am I missing? What don't people want to say to my face? Who have you seen that shouldn't be here?"

"You want me to be a *snitch*?"

"How about a secret agent?"

She sat silent a moment, trying on the phrase for fit. "I like it. I'm Appleton. Kate Appleton. Licensed to Snoop."

"Good. You'll be my eyes and ears. If someone in Keene's Harbor has a grudge against me, you'll let me know."

"Sounds doable. From what I heard behind the bar at Bagger's, folks around here still do love to talk."

"Well, don't take the buzz too literally. The colder the weather gets, the bigger the stories around here grow. Town is pretty quiet after Labor Day, and we need something to keep life interesting."

"Fair enough. How much are you offering for the position?"

"Minimum wage," he replied.

"I'm sorry, but don't think so. I'm desperate, but not shortsighted. Sooner or later, someone is going to figure out that I'm bringing gossip back to you, and at that point, I'm not going to be worth anything."

Matt grinned. "So what do you suggest?"

"How about minimum wage and a $20,000 bonus if I'm directly responsible for finding your saboteur?"

"You're kidding."

"Nope."

Matt considered his options, and they were limited. He couldn't hire a full-fledged townie any more than he could a PI. If word got out that some crazy was targeting Depot Brewery, it could scare away a lot of customers.

Kate smiled. "Hey. It's no more than you'd pay to a PI, and I only get paid if I actually solve the mystery. And it could end up costing you a lot more to just ignore the thing and hope it goes away."

Matt paused to consider her argument. The truth was, the "accidents" were starting to add up and had already cost him more than $20,000. "Okay, deal."

Kate beamed. "I promise I'll be the best secret spy you've ever hired."

At a quarter to nine on Friday morning, Kate parked at the far end of Depot Brewing Company's lot. She exited her ancient, beloved green-and-slightly-rust-spotted Jeep and pocketed her keys. Since she had the luxury of a handful of minutes, and Mother Nature had granted Keene's Harbor yet another blissfully sunny day, she checked out in more detail her new place of employment.

If Kate could whistle—which, sadly, she couldn't—this place would merit a nice long and low one. Small wonder the tourists flocked here like it was nirvana. An outdoor patio, now closed for the season, was surrounded by evergreens that must have cost Matt Culhane a fortune to have transplanted onto this sandy spit of land. She could picture the patio full of people, laughter, and music in the summertime. And she could picture Culhane here, too.

As the microbrewery's name implied, this had once been Keene's Harbor's railroad depot. Kate's dad, who was a history buff, had told her that this town had been built on the lumber trade. In a few decades, though, most of the area was logged out. A few decades after that, the rail spur to the harbor was abandoned. All that had been left was a wreck of a building that Kate recalled as a prime spot for the underage summer kids to drink a few super-sweet wine coolers.

Since she hadn't been alone at this party spot, she'd bet she wasn't the only one who got a kick out of Matt Culhane turning it into a micro-brewery. He'd obviously added on to the small depot, but whoever had come up with the design had made sure that the original architecture still shone through.

Kate was unsure whether it was okay to go through the "employees only" door near where she'd parked, since there was a huge semi backed up to an open garage-type door next to it. She opted for the public entry.

Now that she wasn't wrapped in a haze of determination and desperation, she noted the mosaic in front of the entrance. Set into the concrete was the Depot Brewing logo—a steam locomotive surrounded by a bunch of whimsical items, including what looked to be a happy three-legged dog.

Kate stepped over the image, feeling that the dog had suffered enough without being trod upon. "You're a pretty cool dude, three legs or not."

"His name is Chuck, and he's my dog," Culhane said, suddenly standing in the open doorway. "Well, the real one is. That one's tile, so I don't think he'll be answering you."

She couldn't work up a single word in reply. The man was flat-out gorgeous. A muscled, dark-haired, blue-eyed, one-dimple-that-he-could-apparently-produce-at-will kind of gorgeous. She'd noted this yesterday, too, but anxiety had kept her on her game. If she'd babbled in the face of male hotness, she would have walked away empty-handed. Today, she had a job and her words were fleeting.

"I—I like dogs," she finally managed. She thought of her former dog, Stella, and felt a little lump forming in her chest.

"Good. And I like dog people. Why don't you come on in?"

Kate did, trying hard to cut back on the staring. She was sure he was wearing the same slightly faded chambray button-down shirt and pair of well-fit jeans as yesterday afternoon. New to his features was the shadow of a beard. His dark brown hair looked either tousled with sleep or the lack thereof.

"You're seriously tall," she said.

He laughed. "To you, maybe."

Pull it together, Appleton, she thought. Get a grip!

"Point taken," she said. "From the vantage point of just over five feet, pretty much every guy's a giant. You look tired, too."

Matt ruffled a hand through his hair. "We pulled an all-nighter."

"An all-nighter doing what?" she asked, immediately wishing she hadn't, because the answer might be personal. Her long-dormant libido stirred at the possibilities.

"Come this way and I'll show you," he said. "It's not all that exciting."

Cross orgy off the list.

"We just got into bottled beer in addition to kegs and growlers, so we don't have a regular bottling line yet," he said. "That means we have to rent a portable line every couple of months until I think sales justify the expense of a permanent one. It will take another addition or a move of the whole facility to do it, so for now, we make do. And we also do it after hours so that our regular business can cruise on."

Matt ushered her past his office, through a set of glass doors to a room with enormous stainless-steel tanks, and then through another door into a brightly lit storage room with a truck well. The kind of industrial orange, temporary lighting she'd seen sold in building warehouse stores shone up the ramp and into the back of the semi.

"A bottling line on wheels," Matt said.

"Very cool," she said, thankful to have something other than Matt to focus on while she regained her business manners. That done, she turned her attention to the people busy checking her out. About twenty exhausted-looking souls sat at tables someone must have dragged in from the taproom.

"Everyone, this is Kate," Matt announced. "Kate . . . everyone."

"Hey, Kate," a few of them said. Most just raised a glass of beer in a weary greeting.

Kate fought hard not to gag at the thought of beer as a breakfast staple. She liked the idea of herself as a yogurt-and-fruit girl, but the reality was she was more the cold pizza type. Especially when she was PMSing.

"Kate's coming to work with us as a floater," Matt said to the assembled crew.

That brought on a little more enthusiasm.

"Good, a new victim," a midnight black–haired young woman said.

Kate thought the employee looked too young to work with beer, except for the tattoo of a bare-chested cowboy riding a neon-colored dragon wrapping its way from her wrist up her arm. Either she'd forged her mother's signature for that beauty, or she was at least eighteen.

"Does this mean that Hobart and I are breaking up?" the young woman asked Matt.

"For this weekend, at least."

She squealed, then ran and hugged her boss.

"It's up to Jerry if Kate stays there, Amber," Matt said, gently unwinding her and taking a step back. "But you worked hard last night, and I know you're sick of Hobart."

Who the heck is Hobart? Kate thought, scanning the crew for a guy who looked remotely like he might have the misfortune to be named Hobart.

Matt turned to Kate. "Let's go to my office. We might as well get the paperwork out of the way. Then you can report to Jerry."

"So he'll be my direct supervisor?" she asked as Matt ushered her back the way they'd come.

He nodded. "He manages food services, which will include you for the time being. He's the guy you met out front during our unscheduled job interview yesterday afternoon."

"Oops. I sort of bulldozed right past him. I probably didn't make the best first impression."

"Jerry can be pretty forgiving, and you'll like the rest of the crew, too. About half of the people you saw back in the storage room work for me, and the rest are temps who come in for the bottling. We finished up over two hundred cases just a little while ago. Most of the other employees, except the summer staff, you'll meet today."

Matt opened his office door. "Come on in. It

shouldn't take long to get this squared away, then we'll get you a uniform."

Kate glanced around, taking in the framed photos on the cubicle-style walls, which didn't quite make it all the way to the ceiling.

"My family, mostly," Matt said. He waved one hand toward another shot of a pack of helmeted and uniformed men bearing sticks. "And my hockey team."

She smiled. "That, I'd figured out."

Kate pulled her driver's license and social security card from her wallet and handed them to Matt. "You need these, right?"

He settled in behind his desk. From its front, she guessed it was a vintage oak piece that had been left to molder in the closed-down depot. Its top looked as though a file cabinet had disgorged itself onto it. Working in a measure of chaos definitely didn't throw this guy.

Kate sat and watched as Matt studied her license.

"Turn it over," she said, knowing exactly what he was thinking. "I'm divorced. My name is changed back to Appleton on the back."

He glanced up at her. "Divorced? Sorry."

"Don't be," she said. "It was for the best."

Except for that messy little glitch whereby both she and the ex, Richard, had lost their savings. The McMansion he'd so desperately wanted had turned out to be worth less than a soggy chicken patty when they'd gone to sell it. Even tougher on Kate had been handing over their poodle, Stella, to the ex because he'd ended up in a place more suitable for dog ownership and the court had awarded him guardianship. Kate had fought hard to keep Stella, but the truth was, Richard had a more expensive lawyer, and she lost. She couldn't bear to think of Stella too much these days.

Matt pulled a form from one of the stacks of folders covering his desk. "Yeah, well, from what I've heard from friends, it had to be a pain to go through."

"Well, it's survivable, but let's just say I'm convinced that if you look in the mirror and say *Richard Slate* three times, he'll magically appear and kill you with annoying small talk. Although that wasn't what ended the marriage. I trusted him completely, and he cheated on me. Even after I caught him, the weasel denied the whole thing. You know what he said after I told him I wanted to leave? Nothing. He just shrugged his shoulders and went back to his sudoku puzzle."

"So your married name was Kate Slate."

Kate winced. "It seemed like a good idea at the time. How about you? Ever married? Dating anyone?"

He glanced up. "Why? Interested?"

"Not a chance. I've got enough complications to handle without dealing with men."

"What kind of complications?"

Kate pushed her hair back. "Well, for start-ers, my parents have given me four months to turn our broken-down lake house into a B&B, or else they're going to turn it over to the jerk who bought the mortgage. I have a $10-per-hour job and $15,000 worth of repairs. I'm going to be a homeless dishwasher if I can't make this work."

Matt admired an entrepreneurial spirit, espe-cially when it was nourished by an impractical dream. Everybody had rolled their eyes when he announced he was going to build a brewery.

"I know you've got the stuff," he said. "And the lake is a great place for a bed-and-breakfast. Just put one foot in front of the other."

Easy for him to say.

"Knock, knock," a guy said from behind Kate.

Matt looked over and gestured him in.

"This is Jerry," he told Kate. "But then, you've already met."

"In passing." She gave Jerry an apologetic smile.

Jerry looked tired and overworked, though he was a good-looking guy. He was probably some-where in his midthirties, and of medium height, with dark brown hair and a goatee. But at the moment, even that goatee was slumping, and his brown eyes looked worried.

"She practically knocked me to the ground," Jerry said. "It was sort of embarrassing."

For both of them. Kate didn't believe in flattening guys, except when strictly necessary. And even though Jerry-as-a-victim had been unavoidable in her quest to get to the big boss, she could still feel the Appleton Curse of a neon blush rising. When she'd been little and playing Go Fish with her mom on The Nutshell's back porch, the blush had been the tip-off to a fast move on her part. And now it only grew brighter under Matt's steady gaze.

He smiled at her. "Kate, why don't you wait for Jerry out in the taproom? He and I have a couple of things to cover."

Kate recognized a gift when handed one. She said her thank-yous, saved her fence-mending with Jerry for later, and beat a hasty retreat.

So Kate Appleton blushed. Matt liked that about her. There was something fascinating about being bold enough to run over a guy and yet a day later, be contrite enough to blush.

"She's presentable and all that, but kind of pushy, don't you think?" Jerry asked Matt as soon as Kate had cleared the room.

"I think she's going to do great. And you're twice her size and her supervisor. If she can pull one over on you again, you deserve it."

Jerry looked a little brighter at that thought.

Considering the matchup, Matt wasn't one hundred percent sure he should look so happy.

"So Amber says you want Kate with Hobart this weekend."

"Yeah. Amber could use a break, but after that, you can move Kate around as needed."

Jerry stroked his goatee. "Huh. Anyplace."

Matt began recalculating the odds on that particular matchup. Kate might have Jerry in the gutsiness department, but Jerry was nothing if not a dogged and steady guy. And he could also be a little sneaky, in a good-natured sort of way.

"So go to it," Matt said.

After Jerry took off, Matt looked at his weekend schedule and sighed. He had just enough time to head home, shower, and change before he had to drive an hour north to Traverse City for the weekend. He was getting tired of being on the road all the time, even if it did mean his business was growing in a tough economy. Much as he was proud to keep so many people employed year-round, he wanted his life back. He wanted some romance in his life, and maybe even love. He had a good feeling about Kate. She was going to help him find his saboteur, and maybe a lot more.

TWO

By the time Friday's lunch rush hit full swing, Kate knew too well what Hobart was. Instead of being paired with an unfortunately named coworker, she stood in front of Depot Brewing's noisy, sloppy, and steamy commercial dishwashing machine. Hobart had been named for its maker. It had a four-foot-long stainless-steel prep counter running at a right angle to its boxy entry and a staging area for clean racks of dishes at the exit. The machine was bulkier than her Jeep. More demanding, too.

"Hot!" called one of the line cooks as he dropped a dirty skillet onto the end of the prep area.

"Thanks," she replied from her side of the

counter, but he had already hustled back to his station.

Every inch of the white tile—walled kitchen had been designed for food production, and the staff worked it to the max. Elbow-to-elbow, the three line cooks held their territories in front of the stove, grill, and fryer. Servers darted in to pick up orders, the barback hauled glassware, and pretty much everyone brought Kate more work. Her job was to clear the food debris and paper trash from the gray plastic bus tubs delivered to her. Then she had to rack all the dirty ware, send it into Hobart, and circulate the clean stuff back out for use.

"You've never done this before, have you?" a male voice asked.

She glanced up from her duties to see Steve, one of the servers, watching her. Tall and slender, with a dark tan and blond highlights in his hair, he looked like a surfer dude.

"Nope," she said.

"Definite bummer, but you're gonna have to speed up. We're almost eighty-six on forks."

"Eighty-six?"

"Out of."

"Gotcha," Kate said, moving a silverware rack into the cleaning line.

Jerry, who was currently MIA, had demonstrated the job to her well enough. In fact, it had seemed easy before crunch time came. But Jerry must have left something out of his instructions, because this just wasn't working out the way it should. In the battle of woman versus machine, the machine was kicking her butt.

"Do you have any tips on how I can go faster?" she asked Steve.

Steve's mouth widened into a goofy smile. "Nothing much I can say right now."

Something was up. Something no one had shared with her. Not that she could do much about it, other than feed more dishes through Hobart. Without thinking, she used her arm to wipe sweat from her forehead, forgetting that hot sauce and ketchup were smeared on that particular arm.

"Careful, there. You don't want it to end up in your eyes," Laila, the most senior of Depot Brewing's servers, said as she made room for another tub of dishes. The silver-haired woman pulled a clean napkin from her server's apron, and handed it to Kate.

Kate wiped her forehead. "Thanks."

"I've been in this business a lot of years," Laila said. "Worked most everyplace in town, too."

Kate nodded. She'd seen Laila's plump and smiling face in an old staff photo behind the bar at Bagger's, right next to Harley Bagger's vintage lighter collection.

Laila adjusted her apron and patted Kate on

the shoulder. "Over the years, I've collected some nuggets of wisdom, and I'd like to share three with you."

Kate brightened, despite the fact she probably still looked like an accident victim. "Really? What?"

"First, don't go anywhere with empty hands. There's always something that needs tending."

"Okay."

"Second, comfortable shoes are a must."

Kate looked down at her food-speckled, white leather sneakers. "Got that covered. What's the third?"

Laila grinned. "How about we let you stew on that until you get caught up?"

Yup, Kate smelled something, and it wasn't just the hot sauce she'd been wearing. The scent was that of a rookie dishwasher being roasted. But she could appreciate a little gamesmanship as much as the next girl. And when inspired, she could engage in some, too.

The clock on the wall opposite Kate inched its way to three P.M., one hour before her quitting time. The kitchen's rhythm had slowed from its earlier frantic beat to a busy yet congenial hum. The line cooks cracked jokes and laughed with one another. The servers took brief breaks, chugging soft drinks and counting their tip money. And Kate finally caught up.

"Awesome job! I can see the counter," Steve said as he approached with a heavy load of dirty dishes.

"But not for long," Kate replied. "Where was this stuff hiding?"

"Hiding?" He set down the bus tub. "Dude, it wasn't hiding."

Just like Steve wasn't hiding another goofy grin. Now, at least, she knew what was up.

"No biggie," she said. "I'm game. Bring it on."

And he did. Two more tubs soon joined the first.

"Is that the end of it?" she asked.

"Dunno. There might be more," Steve said before ambling off.

"How's it going?" Laila asked when she arrived with yet another stack of dishes a couple of minutes later.

Kate gestured at the mess. "Could be better. I'm not sure I get the rhythm of this place."

"And that, my new friend, is where the third nugget of wisdom comes in."

"Which is?"

The older woman smiled as she added her contribution to the mess. "Ask Steve once you've caught up."

Another dishwasher might have whimpered, but not Kate. She was made of sterner stuff. Craftier stuff, too. After feeding another couple racks into Hobart, she took a quick glance around the kitchen. The servers and the cooks were all out front, too wrapped up in their current conversations to be paying attention to her. She quickly stowed the three remaining unwashed tubs on the floor, in the open area beneath Hobart's exit ramp.

She'd barely had time to hide her grin, too, when Steve arrived with another load. He did a double take at the clean counter.

"Wow! Did you really get through all those dishes, Tink?"

"Tink?"

"Short for Tinkerbell. You made that stuff disappear like magic."

Tink wasn't the sort of nickname she wanted to encourage, but she'd have to deal with that later.

"Just doing my job," she said, knowing that his view of the dirty tubs was blocked. "And Laila said you'd share her third restaurant hint with me as soon as I was caught up. So how about it?"

"No can do," he said with a nod to the dishes he'd just delivered.

She'd been expecting this.

Kate gave Steve her best smile. "You know, that's one awesome-looking orange-and-white VW van with all the old surf shop stickers out in the employee parking area. It's yours, right?"

"Down to her tires," he answered with obvious pride.

"I thought so!"

"Betty's the real deal. I found her in a junk-yard when I was seventeen, and . . ." His brows drew together. "Hey, why are we talking about her right now?"

"Steve, order up!" one of the line cooks called.

"In a second," he answered without looking away from Kate.

"Now, before it's cold!" the cook bellowed.

"Betty looks like you keep her nice and neat," Kate said.

"I do."

"Then you'd probably be real sad if all these dirty dishes ended up in her, wouldn't you?"

His tan seemed to fade. "No way. You wouldn't."

If her mascara hadn't already been sweated off, she would have batted her eyelashes. "I might."

"Yo, Steve!" the cook shouted. "Now!"

Steve briefly looked his way. "Yeah, just hang on, would you?"

"Sounds like you're pretty busy," Kate said. "I, on the other hand, have plenty of time to go out to the parking lot and bring Betty a little gift. Or you can tell me Laila's third nugget of wisdom."

The cook had started hissing something un-intelligible in the secret language of angry fry cooks.

Steve winced at the sound.

"So what's it going to be?" Kate asked.

Steve hesitated for just a second, appraising Kate with a friendly stare. "You're tougher than you look, Tink."

It was nice to hear. For so many years, Richard had told her that she wasn't tough. Her moving to Keene's Harbor and her nutty plan to turn a broken-down family vacation spot into a B&B was all about showing that she could survive— and more than that, succeed—without anyone's help. She had something to prove to herself and the world before she was ever going to let a man back into her life.

"Thanks, Steve," Kate said.

Over at the grill, the cook seemed to be speaking in tongues.

"You might want to hurry this along," Kate said.

Just then Jerry strolled into the kitchen from the taproom area. Unlike Kate, he looked well rested and free of food stains. "Sounds like you have an order up, Steve," he said.

Steve bolted for his food, glancing back over his shoulder at Kate and Jerry. "Understatement."

Jerry toured the dishwashing area, then gave Kate a crooked grin. "Looks like you have a couple of stragglers. Are they there for a reason?"

"Persuasion for Steve."

He laughed. "So I've heard. I've been getting Hobart updates out in the taproom. Those dishes you've hidden have been doing double-duty today."

"What do you mean?"

"Yesterday, you rushed by me. Today, I kept you rushing." He hitched a thumb at the bus tub still on the prep counter. "Servers are supposed to clear the trash before dumping everything else in the tub. I figured for today, that job should be shifted to you." He paused, smiling. "See, Laila's final nugget of wisdom is do unto Jerry as you would have done unto you."

Kate laughed. "Golden, all the way."

Now she got the rhythm of Depot Brewing, and she had a feeling she was going to fit right in, too.

Early Saturday afternoon, Matt stood in the parking lot of his latest purchase, a decrepit Traverse City motel called the Tropicana Motor Inn. Next to him stood Ginger Monroe, his local office manager.

"A flamingo mural? Are you sure about this place?" Ginger asked, flipping her aviator sunglasses from the top of her bright red head down to her elegant nose as she surveyed the motel's front wall.

"If I weren't, I wouldn't have bought it."

"I can't believe I never noticed the painting before. Those birds are wrong in every possible way."

Matt didn't respond. So far as he was concerned, a glam-looking twenty-five-year-old who had a burning love for 1950s fashion and B movies shouldn't freak out over flamingos. Those quirky birds and she were kindred spirits.

"Their beady eyes are following me," she said.

"Then look away."

"I can't. Trying to avoid looking at this place is like turning away from a train wreck. I don't know what you're thinking."

He grinned. "That's half the fun of working for me, isn't it? And I'm working on building a sister restaurant on the lake in Keene's Harbor. If you think this motel's going to be work, you should see that place."

Ginger laughed. "All the same, how about if I just wait for you at the truck? And much as you might want to stand here all morning admiring your buddies, remember you have a meeting back at the office in ten minutes."

"Don't let Ginger hurt your feelings," he told the fading birds after she'd walked away.

In truth, the flamingos *were* his buddies. They amused him as much now as they had when he'd been a kid and his parents would bring the family here on vacation. With five kids to clothe and feed, and a business that had never exactly cranked out money, the relatively cosmopolitan atmosphere of even sleepy Traverse City, and the Tropicana Motor Inn, had been a treat. His mom said the mural made her feel as though they were in the Caribbean instead of on Grand Traverse Bay.

Ginger was dead-on about the train wreck part, though. The city had grown in popularity and wealth, but the Tropicana hadn't been so lucky. The former owners had moved to Florida five years ago, believing they could sell water-front land to a developer in a heartbeat. Not so. The real estate market had gone south directly after them.

Matt had kept an eye on the languishing property while he'd worked to find the cash to cut a deal. Earlier this year, he'd played with the numbers and figured out how to both retain the motel's character and make it work. Last week, he'd finally been approved for a resort liquor license. After renovations and the addition of a restaurant, this place would be a gold mine during tourist season. As would the property in Keene's Harbor he planned to renovate.

Matt was all about envisioning. While he'd negotiated this deal, he'd imagined himself kicked back on the new restaurant's terrace, saluting his bird buddies with an ice-cold beer. Weird, though. Right now, as he pictured it, a small and curvy blonde named Kate had planted herself in the middle of the vision. He'd had a lot of daydreams about the brewery over the years, but they'd always been *his* daydreams. Just him and the brewery. He kind of liked having Kate there.

After checking his watch, Matt headed back toward the truck. The last thing he wanted was to be late for a meeting with Travis Holby. Like Ginger and the Tropicana flamingos, Travis was an original. A sometimes cranky original. He was also a prodigy of a master beer brewer and key to restoring this motel. For that, Matt would deal with the guy's quirks.

Nine minutes later, Matt pulled up to the office building housing his third-floor walk-up office space on Traverse City's Front Street. It was small but had a great view over Grand Traverse Bay, the long natural harbor separating Lake Michigan from the town. The largest city in the area, Traverse City was a grown-up version of Keene's Harbor, with a sleepy population of 15,000 in the off-season, swelling to the breaking point with tourists and summer people in July and August.

Travis had made himself comfortable in Matt's office, taking up residence in the reception area from the seat behind Ginger's desk. "You're late, Culhane."

Matt fought back a smile. You had to admire the kid's style. "Last I checked, this was my office. So I'm not late. You're early."

Travis gave Matt a flat stare that usually came

from the kind of man who had teardrops tattooed at the corner of his eye. And while twenty-something Travis was missing that particular mark, he did have his share of tats and piercings, including a gauged ear that made Matt wince every time he looked at it. The younger man was both wiry and wary, like a cage fighter. Sometimes he had the combative attitude of one, too.

Ginger entered the office on Matt's heels. "He's not late. And I'm betting you got here early just to snoop around."

Travis did his best to look indignant. "I'm not snooping."

Ginger cut her eyes first to Travis and then to Matt. "I really should start locking the door."

"You did," Holby said. "I just didn't feel like waiting in the hallway."

Matt glanced back at the door. No visible signs of damage. The guy was good.

Travis smiled proudly. "Don't worry, I've been keeping myself amused."

And there was plenty of stuff filling the office for Travis to amuse himself. Matt had to admit that he'd been kind of annoyed when Ginger had stuck a television and a mini-fridge in the outer office. He'd kept his mouth shut, though. She worked here forty hours a week, managing his books, taxes, and investments. He spent most of his time at the brewery, so if he made it up to T.C. three times a month, that was a lot.

Travis picked up a bag of potato chips from Ginger's desk and popped one into his mouth.

"Those were in the drawer," Ginger said.

He popped another potato chip, daring her to complain. "Jalapeño. Spicy, just like you."

Matt had no idea what was going on between Holby and his office manager, but this clearly was not the first time they'd met.

Matt inclined his head toward the closed door to his private space. "Do you want to head into my office?"

"When I've got football on the TV and your amber ale chilling in that fridge? Hell, no."

Matt looked over at Ginger. "Why don't you head on home? I'll catch up with you on Monday."

"Okay." She shot Travis another glare. "Not a single crumb or you're a dead man."

"Sorry about that," Matt said after Ginger had left. "She's not usually so—"

"Locked and loaded?" Travis said. "Don't worry about it. Actually, I'm surprised she didn't body slam me."

Matt dragged over one of the guest chairs so he was seated next to Travis. "I take it you know her?"

"Used to date her. She dumped me for cause."

Matt didn't especially want to know the cause. He was sure he'd either done it or had it done to him at one point or another.

"Thanks for coming into town and seeing me."

"No point having you drive all the way out to Horned Owl."

Which was part of Travis's problem. He'd sunk a ton of money into a brewery and taproom so far off the beaten path that visitors needed to drop a trail of bread crumbs in order to find their way back to the highway.

Matt stood, got two ambers from the fridge, and handed one to the younger man before sitting. Travis opened the top-right desk drawer and pulled out a bottle opener.

"You've got this place scoped out, haven't you?" Matt asked.

The brewer opened his beer with a well-practiced motion. "It's good to know what weapons a woman can use against you."

Matt's thoughts traveled the road south, back to Keene's Harbor and Kate Appleton. Weapons like wide hazel eyes and a mouth made to linger over? Oh, yeah. That was good stuff to know.

Travis waggled the opener in front of Matt's nose. "You coming back from wherever you are?"

Unfortunately, yes. He took the opener and dispatched his beer cap.

"I've learned there's no good way to start a conversation like this, so I'm just going to put it out there," Matt said. "Word is, you're having cash-flow problems."

Travis took a long pull on his beer. "Bull. Where'd you hear that?"

Matt shrugged. "You know how it goes. There aren't that many of us in the business, relatively speaking, and we've all got bar gossip down. They were just a couple of passing comments, but enough that I wanted to talk to you."

Silent and clearly torn between anger and embarrassment, Travis turned his attention to the television. Matt did the same.

After the Spartans completed a fourth-down conversion that was a work of art, Travis asked, "If I do have a cash crunch, why would you care?"

"A few reasons. First, I like your product. And you remind me of me, ten years ago. You've got all the enthusiasm of a homebrewer and, unfortunately, all the business skills of one, too. But I think, given some time, you're gonna kick ass."

"If I'm so hot, why didn't you hire me as a brewer when I came to you four years ago?"

"You and Bart working together?" he asked, referring to his brewmaster. "One or both of you would have been dead inside a month."

Bart was one of Matt's closest friends, and also the only guy out there who could consistently kick Matt's butt at poker. Bart's competitive streak didn't stop at cards, either. When it came to beer, he was as determined to remain top dog as Travis was to attain that status.

Travis scratched the spider tattoo on the side of his neck. "Suppose I was having money troubles, just what is it you're proposing?"

"A loan and a leg up," Matt said. "There's a niche market I think you can fill. And I also think you can help me. You have both the skills and the edgy attitude for a project I'm working on."

Travis shook his head. "So you think I'm good, but not good enough to make it big?"

"Not yet."

"You pulled it off."

"Yeah, but I also screwed up plenty along the way. Why not ride along on a little of what I've learned, like how you're killing yourself by changing up recipes so often? It's like you've got beer ADD."

"So what? I like creating."

"You probably also like keeping the lights on and heat running in your brewhouse, too."

"Yeah."

"Winter is coming. Business might be so-so at best for you right now, but in another month, no one is going to follow that donkey trail out to your place. What then?"

"I'll deal with that when I get there," Travis said.

"Wrong. Too late then. You always have to have a plan."

"I can think on my feet. It's all good."

"You can also fall on your ass. Out of curiosity, how much do you need to get through the winter?"

Travis took a swig of his beer, clearly considering the matter. "Thirty grand."

Yeah, the guy had major *cojones*. "Okay, how much do you need if you don't spend February in Mexico or whatever you've factored in there?"

"Twelve to fifteen grand, assuming prices stay stable," he said. "I don't suppose Ginger has that much cash hidden in a secret compartment in her desk?"

"No, but for the right terms, I can scrape it up."

"So, deal."

"Any money I lend you is going to come with an interest rate of five points above prime. And no complaining about the rate, because it's more than fair. It's a gift. If you're at the point I was when starting out, your equipment is leveraged to the hilt and you have no other assets."

"Close," Travis admitted. "I've got my car and my house, both of which are mortgaged."

"Okay, then. For any outstanding loan, you pay me interest only for twenty-four months, with the balance due at the end of that time. I

don't cut into your cash flow with principal payments, and in exchange, I get the exclusive right
to feature your beers in a restaurant here in
Traverse City. You can sell by bottle in markets,
but I'm it otherwise."

Travis's pierced eyebrow met his unpierced
one. "Small point, but you don't have a restaurant here. Best I can tell, you've got nothing north
of Keene's Harbor."

No shock that Travis wasn't aware of Matt's
activities. Under the radar was generally his style.
Exactly four people on the planet knew about his
Tropicana buy, and that he was already corpo-
rate angel to another struggling brewpub in this
city's warehouse district: Bart, Ginger, his lawyer, and his accountant. And Matt trusted all of
them not to spread news until he was ready to
have it spread. What Matt did outside of Depot
Brewing was his business and his way of stepping
out from under the microscope that could be
Keene's Harbor.

"I'll have a place for your beer by next Me-
morial Day," he said to Travis. Assuming spring
actually arrived in April and he could get the
footings dug. That was a dicey proposition near
the tip of Michigan's mitten.

"What happens if I can't pay you back?"

"I'm not through with the conditions yet.
You also have to agree to have Bart come up and

do a one-week consult with you on your recipes. They're original, for sure, but rough yet."

Travis pushed out of his chair. "No way am I consulting with that jerk."

Matt fought to hide his grin. His reaction would have been the same, back when. "Huh. And yet you wanted to work for him."

"I was desperate."

Matt didn't reply. Travis would do the math and see he was desperate now. To point that out would cut into the guy's spirit, and Matt liked that spirit, warped as it was.

Travis stalked over to the television set, blocking Matt's view. No problem. Travis could contemplate wherever he wanted. He drew down his beer and thought about taking the rest of the jalapeño chips. Except, as he recalled, Ginger also usually had some locally made sourdough pretzels in her stash. He leaned over and reached into the appropriate drawer.

Travis swung around and faced Matt when he was halfway through his second pretzel twist.

"For fifteen grand upfront, I can kiss up to Bart," Travis said.

"Twelve grand."

While Matt was fair, he wasn't into giving away money. "And just so you know the final deal points, before you get dime one, you need a business plan. A real one on paper and with financial projections that I have approved. And if you default any principal payment, I get a controlling interest in Horned Owl Brewery."

Travis went slack-jawed. "So if twelve grand is all you end up lending me, you think that should entitle you to run my life?"

"If you can't pay me back, maybe you need someone to run your life for a while. And at least I'm giving you a fair shot at making it."

"The last four years of my life are worth more than twelve grand."

"I can't deny that," Matt said. "But that's the price of a start-up. Hell, I did the math on what I was earning per hour after my first year and almost crawled under my bed. It was depressing and unfair. But you have to look at it from my side now. If Horned Owl fails—and I don't think it will—all that money buys me is some recipes, beer names, and label art."

"So why are you doing it?"

Travis still looked skeptical, and Matt didn't blame him. This was a big step.

"There's no scam here and no motive other than to get your beer out there for people to find," Matt said. "I'm going to have a place for that soon, and you are straight-up the best brewer for the spot. And like I said, you remind me of me." Minus the tattoos, the piercings, and the attitude. Okay, add back in the attitude. Ten years ago,

Matt had been happy to brawl for the sake of brawling, just as Travis was.

Matt gave the idea a final push. "Tell you what, think about it for the rest of the weekend, and if you're interested, give me a call on Monday. I can have my lawyer draw up the paperwork for you to take a look at. For now, let's catch the end of the game."

Travis settled in, and both men drained the last of their Rail Rider ambers. Matt had done all he could. If Travis Holby was the man Matt estimated him to be, he'd take this deal even if it chafed his pride, and he'd also pay back the money as agreed.

"No need to wait until Monday," Travis eventually said. "Let's do it."

"Okay," Matt replied.

Though he'd kept up a mellow front for Travis, Matt was feeling damn good. Someone had once bailed him out, and now he got to pass along the favor and make a few bucks in the bargain.

THREE

AT TEN ON MONDAY MORNING, KATE LOBBED AN OPEN case of uncooked chicken wings into the Dumpster behind Depot Brewing. Misfortune had sunk its teeth into Matt Culhane. Or at least into his walk-in cooler.

"I'm telling you everything was okay when I left last night," Kate said over her shoulder to Jerry.

Jerry's face was locked tight with anxiety, a muscle twitching at the side of his jaw. "Can you prove it? Someone screwed up and hit that cooler's power switch. I'm betting it was you."

She turned back to grab something else to toss from the cartful of spoiled food. Jerry wasn't looking much better than the tray of tepid slider patties. Having had her work life pass before her eyes on a couple of occasions, she knew the expression of someone staring down unemployment. And because it must suck to be him at this moment, she decided not to take it personally that without cause or investigation he'd pinned the blame on her.

He'd also called her in five hours early. Niceties such as hairstyle and matching socks had fallen by the wayside as she'd scrambled to get to the brewery.

"Jerry, I know I had the least experience of anyone last night, but honestly, my lack of experience makes me even more careful. I've told you what I saw. What happened after that, I don't know."

Before last night, she also hadn't known that Jerry was in the habit of leaving the kitchen and taproom in the hands of the crew and disappearing when Matt was elsewhere.

"Someone has to have seen something," he said.

Kate lobbed a five-gallon jug of mayonnaise that was now both heart attack and food poisoning by the tablespoon. It made a satisfying thud as it hit the bottom of the Dumpster.

"Possibly," she replied, though she had her doubts.

Jerry sighed. "I need to go in and clear more food. Just keep tossing."

Kate couldn't begin to imagine how much

money Depot Brewing had lost overnight. She couldn't put the cooler incident down to carelessness, either. Not only had the unit's power switch to the right of the door been turned off, but the door had been left open, too. From what she could gather from the brewery gossip, without both of those events, the cooler would have held its temperature within the allowable range until morning.

She also knew that the walk-in's door was tough to leave open. Kate had scared the bejeezus out of herself Saturday evening when she'd wheeled in a cart with the bins from the salad prep area and the door had shut. On the bright side, her panicked scream had made the cooks' nights. So what if her brain had shut down when the door slammed? So what if there was a latch on the inside, too? Everyone had issues, and maybe hers was a touch of claustrophobia, especially when trapped inside a giant stainless-steel refrigerator.

Her attention was drawn by the clank and rattle of a cart being wheeled across the asphalt. Steve and Amber had arrived with more spoiled food for the Dumpster, and Kate knew this was prime sleuthing time. She kept her head down and continued to clear her cart.

"So where do you think Matt is?" Amber was asking Steve.

"I'm thinking more about what he's gonna do when he gets here. Someone is dead meat."

Amber grimaced. "I'm glad I got cut early. I'm off the hook."

Steve nodded. "And the dude trusts me, for sure."

"So where do you think he is?" Amber asked again.

Steve shrugged. "Maybe he has a secret girlfriend. Like a married one."

"I'm sure that's not the case," Amber said, turning on her heel and huffing off, back to the building.

"Another babe under the spell of Matt Culhane," Steve said to Kate. "I've been asking Amber out for weeks. She always says she's too busy, but I know if *he* was asking—"

"I find it hard to believe he would date an employee," Kate said.

Steve shrugged. "You never know in the restaurant business. Late nights. Lots of beer and parties. And he's got one or two women hanging around here who are borderline stalkers."

Kate thought it sounded a little like jealousy on Steve's part, but Matt was a pretty hot ticket. "Are you saying Amber might have sabotaged the cooler because she's obsessed with Matt?"

Steve looked shocked. "No way! She just has a huge crush on the guy. But who doesn't? I mean, every female in a hundred-mile radius drools over him."

Matt stepped forward to take a tub of blue cheese from Kate and pitch it into the Dumpster. "Talking about me?"

Kate hadn't realized he was there. She allowed herself a glance to see if his sex appeal had diminished over the weekend. She decided it definitely hadn't and looked back to Steve before she turned to stone or salt or whatever a woman did when staring into the face of temptation.

"We can handle this," Matt said to Steve. "How about you head inside?" He waited a moment and grinned down at Kate. "Interesting look you've got going on. I didn't know you were into tractors."

She had no idea what he was talking about. "Tractors?"

"Your choice of headwear. It makes quite the statement."

Kate absently touched the crown of her head. All she'd been able to find in the way of hair protection when Jerry had ordered her to the brewery had been a fluffy feathered hat of her mom's or a green-and-yellow John Deere tractor–emblazoned bandana that she'd unearthed in the linen closet. She'd chosen the bandana.

"I was short on time, and Jerry sounded borderline hysterical. Desperate times and all that.

Speaking of which, you know this wasn't an accident, right?"

"Yes. I'm just glad it's not the weekend. We've got a fighting chance to pull it together for a Monday crowd. If this had happened on a Saturday, we wouldn't have had time to prep the volume of food we'd need." He paused. "How'd you survive the weekend?"

"I have a new boyfriend named Hobart. He and I have become very close."

Matt smiled. "I'm going to hate to break you two up."

"Don't even think about moving me away from Hobart. Everyone's back there at one point or another, and all of them talk. You move me, I miss all of that."

"You'll have to tell me what you've heard."

"I will, when we can find the time alone."

"Let's step into my office when we're done here."

"Your office? The one whose walls stop about six feet shy of the ceiling? Think not."

"Then come to the market with me. I have to pick up food to cover us until the frozen stuff thaws and our replacement shipment arrives this afternoon."

"*Harborside* Market?"

"Yes, why?" He hesitated. "Are you worried about the way you look?"

"No, even though maybe I should be a little. What's worrying me is that anything I know about the locals in this town, I learned from Marcie at the market. Harborside is the place to see and be seen. If I go there with you, people will think . . ." She rolled her hand, sending him on to what she felt was an obvious conclusion.

"That we're shopping?" he asked.

"No, they'll think we're more than employer and employee."

His grin widened.

"What?"

"You *are* a summer person, aren't you? Among the locals, you don't have to do anything to start gossip. It's self-seeding. The second I hired you, it started."

"But it's unsubstantiated."

"I don't think a trip to the market constitutes a marriage proposal."

"We do need to talk, but I want it to be away from town," she said.

"How about the public parking lot in Frankfort?"

Frankfort was a fifteen-minute drive south, but worth the effort if it kept their conversation off the record.

"What time?"

"Midnight. Hoot like an owl if you think you may have been followed."

"You're making fun of me!"

"Only a little."

"Okay, we'll compromise," she said. "How about a ten-minute head start for me, and then we meet at the market?"

"So we're just bumping into each other?"

"Totally casual."

Five minutes later, Kate pulled into an open parking space near Harborside Market, which was weirdly named, since it stood seven blocks from the water. After grabbing her keys and hopping from her Jeep, Kate walked past Keene's Wine Bar/Bookshop, with its pastel-bright and cheerful Victorian façade. The sporting goods store, with its canoe-shaped sign and manly dark wood exterior, had a placard out front advertising its evening fly-tying class. She skirted around that and moved on.

Kate arrived at the quaint market, which still had an original leaded-glass panel of intertwined green vines and red roses above its broad plate-glass window. Inside, she saw the usual gathering of locals, some shopping and some just shooting the breeze.

The market's automatic door opened as she approached. Even if she hadn't agreed to meet Matt, the scent of freshly baked cookies would have lured her in. And as always, everything in the store was perfectly faced, stacked, and alphabetized. Kate had heard the occasional first-time visitor whisper that it was a little eerie, but she liked it. It gave her comfort to know that someplace in the world, everything was down-to-molecular-level aligned, because in her life, random ruled.

She grabbed a basket from the rack at the door and started down the first aisle just like a normal, non-cloak-and-dagger shopper would. She had no idea what she needed back at the house, but she had to buy something in order to maintain her cover. She reached for the first item that caught her attention and stuck it in her basket.

"It's quirky-looking, but it tastes the same as regular cauliflower," a woman's voice announced from behind her.

Kate turned to see Marcie Landon, the market's owner. Marcie had ash-blond hair cut into a sleek bob and had been blessed with classic features that left people guessing her age. Not that she held still long enough for a guess to be made. The woman zipped around so quickly that it seemed she was everywhere at once.

"What does?" Kate asked.

"The cauliflower," she repeated as she came to stand beside Kate. "It's purple, but the flavor isn't any different."

"Oh. Okay."

"Since I started carrying it a few months back, all you summer people have raved over it."

"Great," Kate replied, amused that she was still lumped with the summer people long after summer had gone. She'd heard somewhere, though, that it took three generations of full-time residency to be considered a townie, and she was well short of that mark. But speaking of townies, she wondered where Matt was.

"They're all about the same weight," Marcie said.

Kate blinked. "What are?"

"The cauliflowers. You're staring at them. I did worry that there was a certain hypnotic quality to this display. Maybe I should . . ." She trailed off and gave an appraising look around the produce aisle. "But if I move the cauliflower, then I'll have to move the peppers, and after that, it's anarchy."

"Oh, no. The display is perfect. I'm just distracted."

The market door opened. Instead of Matt, Junior Greinwold, the town's beloved but totally inept handyman, shuffled in. As always, balding, slope-shouldered, and bulky Junior carried a blue six-pack cooler. He'd been helping Kate patch up her house, fixing broken toilet seals, regrouting leaky showers, and other minor assorted broken things until she could afford to hire a real contractor. She still didn't know what he kept in the cooler.

Kate had begun checking out brussels sprouts

still on the stalk when the door swung open again. This time, it was Matt. He grabbed a cart and headed her way.

He pulled his cart even to her. "Funny meeting you here."

"Amazing coincidence."

"So what do you say we shop together?" he asked.

"Sounds like a plan."

He closed his hand around her basket's metal handle. "Here, let me take that for you."

Kate grasped her basket tightly. "No, I can carry it."

Matt grinned, "Are you sure? Letting go can be a helluva lot of fun. Good for you, even."

"Are we still talking about my basket?"

Marcie popped up at Matt's side. "Well, look at you, Matt. Aren't you the chivalrous one, taking Kate's basket."

Kate let go of the basket and Matt took an involuntary half step backward. Marcie gazed speculatively, first at Matt and then at Kate. "So how long have you two known each other?"

Matt was seemingly oblivious. "Since I hired Kate last week."

Marcie settled a hand against her heart. "So, no long-ago romance rekindled? That means you felt a spark right away. How sweet."

"There was no spark," Kate said.

A bold-faced lie, of course. But her feelings

were hers and she wasn't sharing her spark with the whole town. Or even Matt.

"Nonsense," Marcie said. "I have an eye for these things. I could tell immediately with each of Shay VanAntwerp's three husbands. There's always a spark."

"Cheese. I need cheese," Matt said.

Kate figured that was as good a change of topic as any. She whirled around and took off for the deli counter, followed by Matt.

Matt stopped dead halfway to the counter. Junior Greinwold was peeking out at them from behind a soft drink display.

"Hey, Junior," Matt said.

Apparently, Junior didn't spy often. He stammered something, grabbed a couple of plastic two-liter bottles, and bolted.

Kate turned to Matt. "You know Junior? He's been working at my place. He seems like an okay guy, but I have to say the way he holds on to that blue cooler like it's made of gold is a little creepy."

Matt resumed walking toward the display case filled with cheese. "He's a good guy. Hangs out at the brewery. The cooler's probably filled with my beer, but nobody really knows for sure. And don't worry about Marcie, either. People love to talk in this town."

She shook her head. "I don't care about the gossip. What I care about is having my job made tougher."

"Tougher how?"

"Tougher, as in nobody is going to talk trash in front of me about you or Depot Brewing if they think we're an item."

"I could give you back your basket," he offered. "You know—the symbolic handing over of the cauliflower to mark the end of our affair?"

Kate tried not to smile. "Funny. But I'm being serious here. There's no point in handicapping myself."

"True," Matt said. "I should have thought about that."

They'd arrived at the deli counter, as had Marcie, Junior, and a couple of women Kate had seen at Bagger's Tavern every now and then. Somehow, she doubted they all craved cold cuts.

Marcie hustled around the counter and nudged aside the teenage boy working there. "I'll take care of this." She gave Matt a cheery smile. "What can I get you?"

"Three pounds of Swiss and two of American, sliced medium, please."

Marcie didn't move. "It's been a while since I've seen you dating anyone, Matt."

"Work keeps me busy," he said.

"Then it's nice to have found someone right there at work, isn't it?"

Matt was unfazed. "About the cheese?"

"Sammy, three Swiss, two American, medium," she called to her helper without letting her gaze waver from Matt. "Really, I've never seen you look at any woman the way you do at Kate."

Kate tried to respond but had to pause to catch her breath first. Was that true?

"I am not dating Kate," Matt said. "I have no plans of dating Kate. She's an employee and that's all."

That might have been true, and even what Kate wanted, but darned if the words didn't feel harsh. She glanced at her watch and pretended surprise at the time. "Speaking of which, I need to go home and get cleaned up for the dinner shift." She retrieved her mutant cauliflower and focused on Matt. "I guess I'll see you at work this evening?"

"No, I have dinner with my family tonight."

"Good," she said, and she meant it, too.

Kate needed some time to get her "this is only work" attitude in place. It was that or give in to the spark she refused to feel.

Matt sat looking at the dining table, worn and scarred from decades of family dinners. Lots of happy memories were contained in those scars and, even though he and his sisters were adults with their own lives and dining room tables, there was something comfortable and special about that particular table that drew them all together for the occasional family meal. So here he was, women to the left, women to the right, and his dad at the far end.

In just about every way, Matt was a younger mirror of his salt-and-pepper-haired dad. Now, they got along great. When Matt had been in his teen years, however, there had been some friction. It hadn't been anything bad—just the usual stuff involved when a kid's testosterone level jumps ahead of his common sense.

When he was a kid, his friends had always told him he was lucky to have the "cool mom" in the neighborhood, and he agreed. He liked that she had bowled in the same Thursday bowling league for the past thirty years, walked three miles every day, and was an eagle eye of an archer. He did, however, feel that pretty soon they were going to have to stage an intervention when it came to her holiday decorations. Every year, for each holiday, she tried to outdo herself. This year, she'd added an assortment of bunny figurines dressed in Halloween costumes parading down the center of the dining table like a zombie army. And last year's creepy wrought-iron bird figures still glowered at him from the bay window's sill.

This house had been in the family since it was built in the late 1800s, back when the Culhanes had money enough to build a three-story, seriously ornate Victorian. The locals still called it the Culhane Mansion. Matt found the mansion reference to be overkill, just like his mom's decorations. He frowned at the bunny in a tiger costume lurking by his water glass.

Matt's mother leaned forward from her seat to his father's right. "Is something wrong, Matt?"

Matt opted not to insult the bunnies. "Tough day at work."

The buzz around the table quieted and Matt knew he'd made a mistake. All his sisters and his mother focused their attention on him. His father pretended to be lost in thought, abandoning Matt to his Inquisitors.

Matt's sister Maura, nine months pregnant, gave him a concerned look, implying that he lived in a constant state of chaos. Her four-year-old, Petra, sensing something interesting was about to happen, stopped coloring and gave Matt the same look.

"What happened *now*?" Maura asked.

Petra looked up at her mom and then to Matt. "Yes. What happened now?"

"The walk-in cooler had an issue last night. We lost a lot of food, and I had to scramble to make today work. Did it, though."

Maura looked relieved. "Now that Dad's sold the business, you really should have him help out at the brewery. God knows you could use it."

Matt smiled. His family might be overprotective, but they all looked out for one another. "Got it covered. I added staff last week."

Petra put down her crayons. Her face was covered with tomato sauce. "Is it a girl or a boy? Boys smell sometimes."

Matt's sister Rachel laughed. She was the family's baby and undisputed princess. She was also the only one in the family with curly hair. Matt's mother always said it was her mischievious nature that made her hair curl.

She turned to face Matt, her hand resting on her hip. "That's an excellent question. How does your new employee smell?"

Matt concentrated on chewing his food.

Petra looked around the table. "Boys have a penis and girls have a bagina."

"Come on, Matt," Rachel said. "We all want to know if your new staff member has a bagina."

"Jiminy Cricket. I'm eating pizza. Do we really have to talk about baginas?"

Rachel put her index finger to her lips and studied Matt. "You know what I think?"

She paused for effect. "I'm reading a book about body language right now, and yours is very closed. As if you don't want to talk about baginas at all."

Matt put his hands flat on the table. "That's what I just said. I said it two seconds ago."

Rachel leaned over to Maura. "Matt's always been very excitable when it comes to baginas." Everybody at the table nodded.

"Anyone I know?" Lizzie, his second-youngest sister, asked. She was his best friend as a kid and the tomboy who'd always kept up with him. Her brown hair was still cut short, and her years of playing sports with Matt and his friends had given her an athletic body that looked great in her Keene's Harbor police uniform. Matt's friends hadn't shown a lot of romantic interest in her back then, but they sure did now.

Matt grabbed a slice of pepperoni from the pan. "I don't think so. She's new to town. Her name's Kate Appleton."

"Hmmm . . . Is she Larry and Barb's youngest?" his mother asked.

Matt looked up, intrigued that his mother might know Kate's parents. "I don't know."

"Short, cute, long and curly blond hair?" his mother asked.

In Matt's estimation, Kate had also gone from cute to sexy. Not that his mom needed to know that. "Short, with short blond hair."

"I'll bet that's Kate, all grown up. And you'd know Larry if you saw him," his mother said. "He always used to have his Saturday morning coffee with the group in the hardware store."

Maura smiled at her brother. "Matt didn't like working Saturday mornings. It cramped his Friday night style."

"Well, back when we'd spend our Friday nights

together at Bagger's Tavern, I remember Barb being quite the social butterfly. Great singing voice, too," his mother said.

"As I recall, Larry was a bigwig in the auto industry," his dad added.

"Advertising," his mom corrected.

"Cars," Dad said.

His mother patted his father's hand where it rested on the table. "No matter. They were good people, though they haven't been around much in recent years. They own that big old house, The Nutshell. Sits right at the end of Loon Road, on the cusp of the lake, and has a great view of the bird sanctuary across the way."

Matt stopped eating. "That's Larry and Barb's house?"

He knew the house well. He owned the mortgage. The owner was three months behind on the loan and his lawyer had already begun the foreclosure process. He was the jerk evicting Kate Appleton from her bed-and-breakfast.

Matt wanted to ask for more details, but he knew that would tip off his family to the fact that Kate had caught his attention, and in a big way, too. Matt looked toward the front windows, where the iron crow ornaments were silhouetted in the setting sun. He pushed away from the table and went to get one.

"Mind if I take this?" he asked his mother.

"Of course not. Are you actually going to start

decorating your house? I could come over with the spare decorations up in the attic, and——"

"Thanks, but all I want is the bird," he said before she could offer up anything else.

Matt returned to his seat, moved the bunny away from his water glass, and put the crow in its place. The ornament was really kind of creepy, with feet too big to ever work and corroded spots that gave it a diseased look. No matter. Kate was either going to understand the spirit of his peace offering or think he was nuts.

FOUR

Night had fallen. Kate sat on the overstuffed floral chintz sofa in The Nutshell's circa 1976 living
room. She'd left the room's beach-facing windows open enough that a crisp breeze pushed
through them. As a teen, when she'd been feeling
a little blue, this couch had been her landing
spot. While Kate wasn't blue, exactly, she did feel
the need to decompress. Between the cooler incident, the market nonmeeting, and a wild dinner
shift that had followed, she was tapped out. A
half-eaten bag of chocolate chips and an equally
depleted bottle of white wine, along with its
glass, sat on the oak coffee table in front of her.
She'd had a decompression fest.

To make matters worse, there was something

wrong with her living room floor. The floor-boards on the western side of her house, next to the master bedroom, had buckled, bowing up-ward. She had noticed it a week ago and moved a heavy armoire to the affected area in order to flat-ten the wood. But it had only gotten worse, much worse.

Kate suddenly felt a twinge of late-night lone-liness. She picked up the telephone and dialed her friend Ella Wade. Ella answered on the third ring.

"Chocolate chips and Chenin Blanc for dinner aren't necessarily signs of a pity party, are they?" Kate asked.

"I think that depends on the hour and the quantity consumed," Ella said.

Kate rested the phone between her ear and her shoulder while she corralled a few more chips. "Started early, and lots of both."

"I'm sorry to say, then, that your meal has all the earmarks of a pity party."

Kate smiled at Ella's answer. They had be-come friends as teenagers, sneaking Strawberry Breeze wine coolers behind the then-abandoned train station. Ella had always been the brainy one of the pack. Kate had gone on to a middling college and lots of parties. Ella had cruised through Harvard and then moved on to Stanford for law school with every intention of becoming a professor. She'd changed course a couple of years ago and joined her family's law practice in town. Ella's family had been lawyering in Keene's Harbor since the late 1800s.

Kate dug around in the bottom of the bag for a chip. "I'm going to continue to think of my meal as decadent pampering."

"A handful of chips is pampering. A bag is pity-scarfing. I heard that plastic crinkling. What's going on?"

"I'm never going to get this house fixed. What do you know about warped floorboards?"

"Sounds like you've got a water leak. The water gets trapped under the wood, causing it to expand, and it buckles to relieve the pressure."

Kate sucked in her breath. "Great. A water leak. I'll call a plumber tomorrow and see if he can find the problem."

"So," Ella said, "not to change the subject, but I had lunch at Bagger's yesterday. How'd you get Matt Culhane to give you a job?"

Kate refilled her wineglass. "Equal parts desperation and determination. And the end result seems to be a whole lot of suffering on my part."

"I don't see how a person could suffer too much with Culhane to look at," Ella said.

"The suffering comes from running Hobart, the dishwasher from hell. As for my boss, I'll admit he's a stellar decorative item, when he's around. But really, after Richard, I'm not looking at men as anything more than decorative. There are good substitutes for any of their other uses."

"Ouch! That's a little bitter."

And a lot easier to say to Ella than it would've been to Matt when he was handling her cauliflower, but Kate was determined to keep her head on straight.

"I'm going to continue to think of it as a practical attitude," she said. "As a species, men are great—some of my favorite people. But I need to sort out a whole lot of stuff before I date, let alone do anything else, ever again."

"Okay, I can agree with that. I've taken the celibacy pledge until I can bring in enough work to support the salary Dad insists on giving me. Not that there's anyone around here to date, in any case. Except Matt Culhane," Ella added in a teasing voice.

"So, anyway, how's work?" Kate asked.

"Pretty much how you'd expect it to be when working with a father, a brother, and two cousins. Wonderful, except when it's not. And then, at least we all still love each other. The other day—"

Kate was distracted by the crunch of tires on the gravel drive out front of the cottage. She set aside her wineglass and stood.

"Hang on," she said to Ella. "I think someone's here."

"Out there? You're kidding."

The drive to The Nutshell was a good, winding stretch off the road just inland from the shore. People didn't end up at her door by accident.

"Wish I were," Kate said.

A ratty black T-shirt emblazoned with the words SEX AND BEER in fat white block print, and plaid flannel sleep pants so worn that they were frayed over her knees weren't exactly "meet the visitor" wear.

Then again, who could possibly be visiting her? Her wine buzz was swept away on a sea of adrenaline.

"Don't hang up," she whispered to Ella.

"Why would I? And why are you whispering?"

Kate nudged aside the lighthouse-themed curtain that covered the front door's window and peeked outside. A pair of truck-height headlights shone directly into her eyes. She let the curtain drop and turned the door's dead bolt.

Her visitor's vehicle had come to a stop. "Don't know," Kate said to Ella. "I'm just a little edgy. You're the only one who'd be out here, and you're there."

"Okay, you have a point," Ella said. "Should I dial the police on my cell?"

"A lot of good that will do when I'm way out here."

The truck's headlights were off. Kate scurried to the kitchen and grabbed the biggest knife she could find in the knife block.

"Single girl. Lake house. Mysterious midnight intruder. This is so straight out of *Friday the 13th*," she told Ella.

Kate glanced at the serrated bread knife in her hand. Great. She'd have to saw the prowler to death.

A knock sounded at the front door. Kate considered this a good sign. So far as she knew, homicidal maniacs didn't knock. Then again, she had limited experience with homicidal maniacs.

"Jeez, this is like one of those horror movies!" Ella said. "Don't go to the front door. That's the equivalent of the stupid babysitter who goes down into the basement. Just hide."

Kate approached the door. "My car is out front, Ella. The lights are on in my house. Clearly, I'm here." Funny how calm she sounded when her heart was slamming its way out of her chest.

Another knock . . .

"Do you have the knife?" Ella asked.

"Yes."

Kate ducked below the door's window. She had no intention of losing the element of surprise. Slowly, carefully, Kate moved the curtain. Inch by inch, Matt Culhane's face appeared, lit to glowing perfection under the porch light.

"Oh, no." Kate let the curtain drop.

"Who is it?" Ella asked. "Freddy Krueger? Your ex, Richard?"

"No. Worse. It's Culhane."

"You're kidding!"

Kate rolled her eyes. "Nope. He's here in all his glory."

"Really! All his glory? Nice."

Matt knocked again and called her name.

"I have to go," Kate whispered into the phone, and disconnected over Ella's pleas to stay on the line and eavesdrop. Then holding the phone and knife in one hand, Kate released the dead bolt and opened the door just enough to peek out.

Big, strong guy, eyes full of ambition, and a smile that was full of humor—at himself and the world—the kind of humor that only comes with a healthy dose of self-confidence. Yep, it was Culhane all right.

"Hey," Matt said.

Kate tried to process how best to get rid of the knife, which now seemed a little excessive. "Gosh, this is a surprise. How'd you find my house?"

"Well, that's an interesting story."

That got Kate curious.

"I don't suppose you'd consider letting me inside?" he asked.

Good grief, she thought. She was a wreck. Almost-empty wine bottle, ratty clothes, hair from hell, and she had a bread knife in her hand.

"I thought we were going to talk tomorrow?" she said to him.

His smile was crooked and endearing. "I decided I like tonight better. And I come bearing gifts." He reached into his pocket and pulled out a weirdly shaped object.

Kate squinted down at the thing, uncertain what it was.

"Is it chocolate?" she asked.

"Sorry, no chocolate. It's metal."

"Metal what?"

"A metal crow."

Kate reached to accept the gift, inadvertently brushing her hand against Matt's. A little tingle of heat rushed through her, leaving a breathless lump in her throat.

The knife in her other hand dropped to the floor, interrupting the moment. "Come in. I was having a glass of wine. Can I get you anything?"

He stepped inside. His gaze shifted from her to the knife at his feet, then back to her. He took his coat off and casually hung it on the rack. "No, thanks."

Matt followed Kate into the living room. "So, why aren't you drinking beer?" he asked.

Kate hastily cleared the coffee table of the remnants of her Not a Pity Party. "I've never been much of a beer drinker. To be honest, I hate the stuff. Have a seat."

Matt settled on one end of the sofa, and Kate took a spot on the opposite end, leaving a fabric field of poppies and chrysanthemums between them. She was glad for the space, because he looked good. Really good.

"Let me get this straight," Matt said. "I hired someone who hates beer to work in a micro-brewery?"

"It looks that way."

"I think I need a more detailed application form." He pointed at her shirt. "Should I assume you hate both the things listed there?"

She glanced down at her SEX AND BEER T-shirt, then back at Culhane, who gave her a grin.

"Neither of them are at the top of my priorities these days. But this is a song title, and the shirt's from Milwaukee 2006 Summerfest."

"You sound pretty certain about that no sex or beer thing. I think I'm going to have to take you up on the challenge."

Her heart stumbled. "You're talking about the beer, right?"

"Of course I am. I have my priorities, too."

Yeah, and not for a minute did Kate believe it was beer. Okay, truth was she *hoped* it wasn't beer.

"So what is it we *really* had to talk about?" she asked.

"First, you were right and I was wrong."

Kate laughed. "That's always a good start."

He pointed to the ornament. "And this comes with the admission. I'm not much for eating crow, so I thought I'd give you one."

She examined the weird little metal bird.

"Thank you, but it looks more like a raven to me."

"My family vote came out in favor of a raven disguised as a crow."

She couldn't have heard that right. "Your family voted?"

Matt shrugged. "Long story. It begins with my birth. Let's just skip it and move on to me saying that I was nuts to have thought we could talk at Harborside Market."

"It's okay," she said. "I think everyone in town is now pretty clear on the fact that you're not attracted to me."

"I'm not that good an actor," he said. "*No one* believes it."

Kate bit into her lower lip.

Matt studied her for a beat. "I just admitted I'm attracted to you, and I can't read your reaction."

"Flustered," Kate whispered.

He blew out a sigh. "I get that a lot. Why don't you give me a quick rundown of what you learned this weekend?"

"Well, first, I learned that Jerry doesn't seem too devoted to the concept of management once you leave town. He shows up for a little while, tells the staff to follow the usual program and call his cell should something break, burn, or blow up. Then he leaves."

Matt raised his eyebrows ever so slightly, but he said nothing, so Kate plowed on. She might as well get all the bad stuff out of the way. He'd wanted an unfiltered report, and she would deliver it.

"Well, Steve thinks you've got some secret affair with a married woman, but I think he was just saying that to enhance his own romantic life."

"I don't think I want to know how that could possibly enhance his romantic life. And for the record, married women always have been and always will be off-limits."

"I haven't known you long, but you seem like a stand-up guy to me," she said. Still, time would tell.

One life skill Kate had been working to develop was a keener eye for dishonesty. She'd missed the early warning signs with Richard, but eventually she'd caught on. Now she was at least marginally older and wiser, both of which rocked. And while she still planned to open her heart and trust, she'd do it with some initial caution. She wasn't up for another loss of love or poodle.

"Is there anyone else I should know about?" Matt asked.

Kate shook her head. "It sounds like you're golden with the rest of the staff. I didn't hear anything, except a passing mention from Laila that her son couldn't get a job with you."

"He'd have to apply for a job first, which he won't, because he likes his winters off from his marina job."

"I got the feeling Laila believes he *has* applied."

"Well, employee applications are confidential, so I won't be clearing that up," he said. "That's it, then?"

"Yep."

Matt nodded. "Any thoughts on who might have sabotaged the walk-in fridge?"

"That's tough. It could have been anyone. Laila and Steve were in and out. The cooks were there. And so were the bartender, the busser, and the barback. It could have been Jerry, until he went on walkabout, or whatever it is he does. No one saw it happen and all of them had access. Add to that, it probably happened after hours, which means the back door was open while the trash was being hauled out. The walk-in is on a straight path from that door. It's highly unlikely that the crew would have missed someone slipping in, but it's possible."

"True, but I'd rather believe the nearly impossible than think my own employees would mess with me."

"I understand. But until someone is caught pulling one of these stunts, everyone's on the list. And I know this is technically none of my business, but maybe if you shared a little info with your staff when you take off, they wouldn't pass their free time coming up with the Top Ten Bizarre Reasons Matt Culhane Is Missing."

"You're probably right," he said. "But I shouldn't have to tell everyone my every last move. For all the time I'm there, I deserve some privacy when I'm not."

"It was just a suggestion."

"I know, but I'm used to running my show my way."

"Sorry. I'm hardwired to just put it all out there."

"So I've noticed," he said. "I think it might be one of your better qualities."

They smiled at each other, and she found herself considering how it would feel to close the distance between them on that flowery sofa and kiss him. It would feel good, she thought. *Really* good.

It was like a dreadful out-of-body experience as she witnessed herself begin to lean toward him like a teenager crushing on a new boy. The lean was immediately followed by panic, and Kate shot to her feet and set the metal bird on the coffee table. "It's getting late. I'm sure you're really tired."

Matt rose and reached out to touch her hair. "I could never be *that* tired."

Holy Moses, Kate thought, the panic mingling with flat-out lust.

"Before this goes any further," he said, "I have something I need to tell you. I'm the guy who owns your mortgage."

For a moment, Kate thought she'd misheard. "What?"

"I didn't know it was your house before tonight, I swear. I'm really sorry, but I have a lot of money already invested in this, too, and I made a fair deal with you and your parents."

"You think it's fair to take my home?"

"Kate. It's falling apart and nobody would pay what I'm offering."

Kate felt her blood pressure hit the stroke zone. "It doesn't matter what somebody would pay, because it's not for sale. I'm going to get the money to fix the place somehow, and I'm going to turn this place into a home and a business."

Matt shuffled his feet and looked into Kate's eyes. "Look. I'll give you until Thanksgiving to get caught up on your mortgage. Just ignore the foreclosure papers."

Kate's eyes were as wide as saucers. "Foreclosure papers! You're serving me with foreclosure papers?"

"Not anymore. At least, not right now."

Kate turned Matt around and hustled him to the door. "I don't have much of a choice. I'll take the deal. And I'll see you at work tomorrow. The sooner I find your saboteur, the sooner I get my bonus and the sooner I can pay you. Good night!"

Kate listened to the crunch of gravel as Matt's car drove off. She hated him for taking her house, but she had to admit he'd been honest with her, and even generous giving her until Thanksgiving. She leaned her forehead against the door and gave up a sigh. The worst part of the whole hideous mess was that she had very friendly feelings for him. Feelings that might be misinterpreted now. She worried that he might have a hard time sorting out her genuine attraction from a cheesy attempt to bail on a mortgage payment.

FIVE

Matt and his three-legged dog, Chuck, had hunkered down to watch the flames dance in the large fieldstone fireplace that anchored the great room in Matt's log home.

Chuck gave his standard contribution to any conversation: a thump of his tail against a pine floor scarred from his constant quest to discover if the darker knots in the wood might actually be hidden dog treats.

Matt stretched his arms across the back of the brown leather sofa. He took in the family photos that sat on the fireplace's rough-hewn oak mantel. Chuck starred in more than one of the shots.

Five years ago, Matt had found Chuck tied to a newspaper box outside a gas station. Apparently, someone had stuck him there the prior night and no one had laid claim to him during the course of the day.

Matt liked to think of himself as a practical guy. He'd known that a three-legged hound, no matter how much he otherwise appeared to be bred to hunt, was going to be ornamental at best. But one look at that dog's chocolate brown eyes and hopeful expression, and there had been no way he could have left him behind.

"That was my lucky day," Matt said to Chuck. Chuck was a good listener when Matt needed to unload. And Chuck could be counted on for unconditional love any time of the day or night. "I don't know why I'm letting Kate get to me," Matt said.

Chuck tilted his head, probably trying to pick out words he knew, like "food" and "treat."

"But that's not what's messing me up. There's something more about her. Look at the way she took on Hobart like it was her life goal. And the way she's straight with me, too. No sugarcoating. I like her. A *lot*, if you know what I mean."

Chuck started to snore as he fell into a doze. He had been neutered a long time ago and had absolutely no idea what Matt meant.

Matt's thoughts turned from Kate to his business problems. As the old saying went, it wasn't paranoia if someone really was out to get you. The flat tires and messed-up deliveries he'd dealt with, but the open walk-in had cost him some serious money. He had been trying not to take it personally, since whoever was doing this had a certain level of insanity going on, but this *was* personal.

Matt headed into the kitchen. He opened the fridge and pulled out the orange juice jug, only to discover that at some point or another, he'd stuck it back in there empty. At least that way it matched the rest of his fridge's barren expanse. He left the empty jug on the counter and swore he'd remember to get food tomorrow. Or eat at the restaurant again.

The phone rang and caller ID told him it was Lizzie. Guess she wasn't through with him for the evening. He could ignore her, but it would do him no good. As a Keene's Harbor police officer, she'd been known to pull him over when he'd ducked the rest of the family for too long. He picked up the phone. "Hi, Lizzie."

"You blew out of the house so fast, I didn't get the chance to give you your ticket for Friday night," Lizzie said.

Ticket.

Matt didn't like that word in any Keene's Harbor context, be it parking or speeding or, far worst of all, admission. And even though this was Lizzie on the phone, he was damn certain that she was referring to the dreaded admission ticket to whatever Friday night benefit was planned at the Brotherhood of Woodsmen's Hall.

"There's a fund-raiser for Lester Pankram," she said.

Matt winced. Lester was a nice old guy, but thrift had gotten the better of him. He'd been driving his tractor along the shoulder of a road when he'd seen a beer can. Hot for the ten cent refund, he'd stuck his tractor in neutral and hopped down. Blind to anything but that shiny can, he'd failed to note the road's downhill slope and had pretty much run himself over. He'd come out of the incident with a broken leg, the sure knowledge that he'd become a Town Legend, and a Friday fund-raiser that would be held to help cover his medical expenses.

"I'm working Thursday and Friday this week," Matt said. "There's a private party at the brewery on Thursday, and we're always slammed on Friday night."

He rolled away from the nearly weekly fund-raisers the way Lester should have from his tractor. For some reason, at these events the older folks in town found it amusing to reminisce about the many dumb-assed moves Matt had made as a kid. The talk came with multiple elbows in the ribs, wry winks, and laughing. A lot of the stuff was funny when he heard it the first time of the night, but by the fifth or so time around, he found himself remembering why he'd decided to build his home deep in the woods. And why he liked to send an anonymous envelope of cash to the fund-raiser's beneficiary.

"Let your staff do what you pay them for, and come to the fund-raiser," Lizzie said. "You can meet and greet there, too."

"Thanks, but I'll pass."

"How about you don't, this time? You skip ninety-nine percent of these things. It makes you look like a hermit."

He smiled at the gap in her logic. "Only if you can find me to see me."

"I'm not joking, Matt. This is a town tradition, and we Culhanes have been part of the town forever. Dad wants you there with the rest of the family, even if he's too proud to say it."

That was the thing about Lizzie—she'd always known just how to get to his soft spot. She had none of the noise of his other sisters and ten times the efficiency. Matt didn't want to disappoint his dad. He loved the man, even if he had never been able to pull off working side by side with him.

"I'll stop by," he said. "But no way am I staying the whole night."

"That's up to you. All I did was commit to getting you there."

Matt sighed. No doubt another of his siblings had the duty of making him stay.

He wandered out of the kitchen and back to

his spot in front of the fireplace, where Chuck slumbered on.

"Anything else?" he asked his sister.

"It would be nice if Depot Brewing dropped off a keg for the event, don't you think?"

"I wouldn't have it any other way."

At least then he could be sipping some of his favorite Scottish Ale while being retold the tales of his youth.

"Great. And Matt, pick up Mom and Dad on the way to the hall, okay?"

His mom and dad were fully capable of driving to the hall, not to mention circumnavigating the globe.

"What? You don't trust me to show up?"

Lizzie laughed. "I just know you."

"Fine, I'll pick them up. But so long as we're horse-trading, do you want to do me a favor?"

"What?"

"When you're on night patrol, take an extra loop by Depot, could you?"

"Do you want to tell me why?"

"It's nothing big, just enough small stuff going down that I'd like a little extra attention."

"Define small stuff," she said in a voice that was now one hundred percent business.

"One set of flat tires on delivery trucks and an open freezer door. The first definitely took place after hours, and the second, maybe. Either way, an extra drive-by or two would help."

"Okay, I'll make sure we swing by more often. There's not as much to patrol this time of year, anyway. And I'll see you on Friday, right?"

"Wouldn't miss it," Matt said.

He disconnected and looked down at Chuck.

"Dude, I'd trade places with you in a heart-beat."

Chuck briefly opened one droopy hound eye as though to say "no way," then cruised back to napland. The canine king would not be deposed.

In bed but not sleepy, Kate reached for the phone to pick up her conversation with Ella.

"I just wanted to let you know I was alive," she said when her friend answered.

"When you didn't call back right away, I figured maybe you were putting Matt Culhane to one of the better uses God intended."

"It was briefly tempting, but no."

"Do tell."

"I'd rather not," Kate said. "It wasn't one of my better moments. How about if we take a look at my big social picture, instead? I remain in social limbo. I need to start getting out and meeting more people."

"That, I can help you fix. This Friday there's a fund-raiser at the Woodsmen's Hall. Why don't you come along with me? It's nothing all that thrilling. There's beer, potluck, and gossip, but it'll give you a chance to meet a few more people."

Kate smiled. "I think you've just given me incentive to survive the rest of the week at work."

Including Thursday's private Halloween-themed party being thrown by Shay VanAntwerp. Jerry had told Kate she'd be doing a lot of detailed prep work for the gathering. Kate didn't know what that meant, but she expected it wasn't good.

"Don't get your hopes up too high about this fund-raiser," Ella said, then yawned. Too late. Kate was primed.

Wednesday had been little more than a blur of frenzied work as the Depot crew prepared for Shay VanAntwerp's annual extravaganza. It was now Thursday evening, and Kate was exhausted. She stretched the cramped fingers of her left hand and looked at the jack-o'-lanterns leering at her from tables set up in Depot Brewing's loading dock area. Wednesday morning, she'd viewed Jerry's assignment of creating fifty pumpkin carvings as a gift. This was her fun, artsy reward for having become BFFs with Hobart. For the first dozen works of art, she'd been all about the details, shaving away paper-thin bits of rind for perfect translucent accents. Frankenstein and Dracula came to life, along with a tribute to Stella, her poodle. As she'd worked, Kate had enthusiastically separated pumpkin seeds from guts, thinking that salty roasted treats at each of the party tables would be an ideal accent to Culhane's fabulous brew. But by the afternoon, her gag reflex had kicked in, and washing slimy mutant gourd seeds had fallen off her list of volunteer activities. She had left work and taken a series of long hot showers, both before bed and after she'd woken this morning. No luck. She still smelled like a giant pumpkin.

By 5:30 P.M., Kate no longer cared how she smelled and her artistic impulses had begun to sputter. No more tiny tools for her, just a nasty, sharp filet knife.

"Almost done?" Laila asked as she entered the storeroom.

"Just three more to go."

"No time. You're going to have to put them aside and help set up. The early comers are starting to trickle in."

Kate looked at her watch, which she'd set on one of the table's edges to avoid most of the pumpkin carnage. "But the party isn't supposed to start for another half hour."

"Free beer tends to make for overly prompt guests."

"I hadn't thought of that. All the same, I'd really like a shot at finishing. I swear, with my new minimalist approach, I'll be done with the last three in a flash."

"Okay, then. I'll gather up some help to have the finished ones taken out, and you keep carving.

Everything needs to be done before Shay arrives. The good news for us is that she always arrives late," Laila said, filling a cart with grinning heads and leaving Kate alone in her pumpkin kingdom.

Figuring the time had come to kick the assembly line into high gear, Kate grabbed the big butcher knife she'd borrowed from the kitchen and stabbed it into the top of the first of the three intact pumpkins. It sunk in quickly and deeply. The act was weirdly satisfying. She seemed to be developing a very real disrespect for pumpkins.

"You look like a natural."

Kate glanced up to see Matt watching her from the doorway. She pulled on the knife, but it had gone in too deeply and wasn't coming out. She tried to rock it back and forth. No luck. "I'm not sure that's a good thing."

He approached her. "Problems?"

If one counted among them a heady overappreciation of a man dressed in something as simple as a black polo shirt and jeans, she had exactly two at the moment.

"The knife is stuck."

"Let me see if I can help."

Matt came around to her side of the table. Wow, but he smelled good. She caught a hint of woods and green fields. And, unlike her, he didn't have a bit of pumpkin slime on him.

Kate moved her hand away from the knife, but

not quickly enough. They touched, and she swore she felt an electric tingle as her hand involuntarily began to close around his. The sensation was far more satisfying than stabbing into a pumpkin. Good news on the mental stability front.

Matt wrapped his hand around the knife's handle and winced.

"Sorry," she said. "I guess everything's a little messy at this point."

With his free hand, he brushed a fleck of pumpkin from her cheek. "So it is," he said, "but it still looks good."

He turned his attention back to the pumpkin and pulled the knife free with an ease she envied.

"Tell you what," he said. "Why don't you get a bunch of these outside to line the front walk, and I'll finish up the last three?"

Kate shook her head. "No, you don't have to do that. It's my job, and I'm all about finishing what I set out to do."

"You're not just talking about pumpkins, right?"

"I moved to Keene's Harbor for a reason. To start a new life and build something I can be proud of."

"And I'm the guy trying to take that away from you? It's not personal. It's business. And it was in the works a long time before you even moved to Keene's Harbor."

Kate crossed her arms. "Look. I know that. But that doesn't mean I like it. And I'm going to find your saboteur, collect my $20,000 bonus, and buy back *my* house."

Kate didn't want to even think about the fact that a contractor had spent an entire day at her house trying to locate and fix her water leak. She didn't have the money to pay him, either. Yet. And she wasn't about to ask her parents for help. She wasn't even sure they had the money, what with her father retired and living on long-held investments.

"Right now, all I want to do is carve a pumpkin," Matt said. "Cut me a break here."

"Well, since you put it that way, I could use a break, too. I'm pretty much pumpkined out."

He smiled. "Consider yourself sprung."

Kate grabbed a cart and loaded it with four jack-o'-lanterns. She made her way to the front of the house, where costumed beer lovers had already gathered. Once there, she slowed her pace enough to check out the guests. The event, like her emotional state, was high school all over again. The women had taken the borderline bawdy path to apparel, while the men had gone for minimal effort. Among the male ranks, there looked to have been quite a run on Grim Reaper costumes. Kate counted five of them in the crowd already. Two Grims were tall and skinny, and the other three of more well-fed dimensions.

The taproom was in full Halloween mode, too. The front windows were edged with strands of orange lights that glowed warmly against the dark wood trim. Tealights adorned each table, adding to the festive look. And an appetizer bar had been draped with orange linens and decorated with absurdly grinning skulls that shone from within. Kate wished she could stay and mingle, but there was work to be done.

She thanked one of the tall-and-skinny Grims as he held open the front door for her and the pumpkin cart. A sharp blast of wind greeted her. No doubt a storm was brewing out on the lake. Chilled, she hustled the cart over the mosaic mural, then hung a left to the end of the jack-o'-lantern line that Laila had already started.

Once Kate had her pumpkins in place, she patted her pockets for a light. She had none, of course. She turned her back to the wind and headed to the bar to snag a pack of matches. Inside, she spotted Laila chatting with a Grim Reaper. Market owner Marcie Landon was with them. She was very fittingly costumed as a tape measure. The bit of tape showing from the front of the bright yellow box was probably marked to perfect scale. The tall-and-skinny Grim definitely liked Laila, hovering close enough to be in her personal space. Laila didn't seem to be objecting, either. She was laughing at something the Reaper had just said. Kate smiled, waved, and moved on.

Outside again, she hunkered down by the first jack-o'-lantern and pulled out her pack of matches. Two sputtered and died even before she could get them to the tealight waiting inside, and the next two were snuffed by a draft coming through the pumpkin's eyes.

"Okay, then," she said to herself and sat down cross-legged on the sidewalk. Clearly, she would be there awhile.

"You need a lighter."

Kate looked up past a pair of sensible white server sneakers and standard Depot uniform to Laila's serene face.

"I don't suppose you have one?" Kate asked.

Laila pulled out a rectangular silver lighter adorned with what looked to be crystals. She flipped it open with a distinctive click, bent down, and did in two seconds what Kate hadn't accomplished in four matches.

"Sometimes the old things are the best," Laila said.

Kate smiled. "Obviously, you haven't seen my house."

At eleven that night, Kate lay in bed, unable to sleep. The contractor had found her leak. Evidently, when Junior had regrouted the shower tile in her master bathroom, he hadn't inspected the shower pan. It had completely failed. Even worse, he'd reset the toilet without a proper seal, and raw sewage had swept underneath her bathroom floor. The water damage from the shower and toilet had infiltrated her living room, causing her floor to warp. The contractor was coming back tomorrow to pull up her water-damaged floor and tile. Kate had tried to call Junior several times but he wasn't answering—probably in his best interest, given the problems he'd caused.

The good news was that it seemed like a pretty simple fix, and the contactor thought he could do it for a couple thousand dollars. More than Kate had but doable, especially with the bonus money she planned to earn.

Kate set aside the magazine she'd been leafing through. An article on "Ten Ways to Drive Him Wild" wasn't what she needed to get Matt Culhane out of her head. Indulging in each of those ten with him might do the job. But she wasn't going there.

Kate's cell phone rang, and she jumped at the unfamiliar sound. She hadn't received too many phone calls since her big move away from the city.

"Hello?"

"Hey, Katie-bug!"

"Dad?"

"I know it's late, but I picked up this new phone today that does everything but clean the pool, and I wanted to be sure I had your number right."

Her father sounded pretty chipper—about

one double Manhattan's worth was her guess. She could picture him sitting in a lounge chair out back of their Florida house, with the pool lights and stars shining. He was probably wearing his favorite navy cardigan and blue-and-white seersucker trousers. And Mom was probably inside pining for the days of wholesome television and good old-fashioned family values. Kate loved her parents, but it was like they'd just been freed from a 1960s time capsule.

"You've got the number right, Dad."

But he'd never called it before, always opting for the landline when she'd lived back downstate. And she hadn't heard from either her mom or her dad since that highly uncomfortable family dinner three months ago, when she'd had to admit how broke she was. Of course, she hadn't called them since then, either.

"So as long as we're chatting, I was wondering how . . . The Nutshell is?" her dad asked.

"The house is fine, Dad."

"No issues with the plumbing? I know we're due for a new septic system."

"It's all good," she said.

"And that loose step on the way down to the beach?"

"I nailed it back down," she fibbed.

Fact was, she hadn't ventured to the water. All she'd done since she'd landed in Keene's Harbor was focus on finding a job and nailing down her future. Beach walks had seemed like a luxury she hadn't earned just yet.

"Well, that's just great," her dad said with more enthusiasm than the conversation warranted.

"Are you and Mom okay? There's nothing going on down there that I should know about, is there?" she asked.

"We're fine, Kate. Just fine! How's the refrigerator?" he asked. "Do you need any help stocking it?"

They'd finally reached the real purpose of the call. Kate was glad no one was around to witness her embarrassment. The last time her dad had asked questions like this, her brother, sister, and their respective spouses had been watching. Kate had felt like the loser-girl on a reality TV show.

"I promise I have more than diet soda and shriveled-up apples in the fridge," she said.

She still had that head of purple cauliflower, after all. But so long as she loaded up on the cheap employee meals at work, shopping was optional.

"Just checking. I know things have been tight."

"It's okay. I found a job."

"Really? What are you doing?"

"I'm washing dishes and doing prep work at Depot Brewing."

The line fell quiet for a beat.

"That's great! It's a tough job market out there. You should be proud. If you come up short, let me know and I'll slip a care package your way. Just like your old college days."

Ugh. Kate knew he was trying to be positive and supportive, but she was right back to feeling like the loser-girl. Kate wanted to be there for her parents, like her siblings were. Not the other way around.

"Thanks for the offer, but I'm doing great," she said. And it was true, if "great" could be defined as able to splurge on a fake cappuccino the next time she put gas in the Jeep.

"Just say the word, Katie-bug . . ."

She wouldn't, though. Her parents were retired, and money didn't grow on trees. They probably had a woefully out-of-date concept of how much money was needed to get the house in shape. But more important, Kate had something to prove. Not to her parents, but to herself. She could stand on her own.

SIX

On Friday night, Matt walked into Woodsmen's Hall with a parent at each elbow. The crowded room was filled with laughter and the blended smells of three dozen casseroles that probably all included crispy fried onions. This was an old-school Keene's Harbor food-and-gossip fest, right down to its location. Other than getting an occasional refresher coat of paint, the long and narrow single-story hall hadn't changed in a hundred years.

Matt felt pretty okay with being there until he saw Deena Bowen over by the beer table. In her bright blue V-necked dress, Deena was as much a knockout as she had been on the one date they'd had together. One date had been more than enough for Matt but not for Deena, and a woman scorned is a woman to be feared. Matt turned his head before Deena could catch him looking. It was the same technique he used when faced with a black bear in the woods. Deena and that bear bore a lot in common, personality-wise.

"You're dragging your feet, son," Matt's father said.

"Just soaking it all in."

"Come along, Patrick," his mother said. "I want to see what's over in the silent auction."

"Harley Bagger has offered up a couple of lighters from his collection, and Enid Erikson was donating some of those fun toilet paper covers—you know, the ones with the dolls' heads and frilly dresses?"

His parents headed to the back of the hall, Dad with less fervor than Mom. Matt stuck to the front. One of those blank-eyed dolls would be staring at him from the back of a toilet at his parents' home soon enough. Mom would probably give him one for Christmas, too. Unfortunately, Chuck could sniff out chewy plastic items the way most of his breed could raccoons. The doll would be history.

Matt stopped and talked with Bart, his brewmaster and buddy, about the upcoming hockey season. They were defending league champs, and Bart had his eye on a prospect to be sure they stayed that way. Matt gave Bart a fist bump and took the slow route toward the three refreshment tables. The first held soda and mixers, followed by high-octane punch, and then beer. He stopped and chatted with as many folks as he could. He wanted to give Deena time to move on.

Clete Erikson, the town police chief and husband to toilet paper doll-maker Enid, was manning the brew table. Clete reminded Matt a little of Chuck. Not that Clete was missing a limb. He just had the same droopy hound features.

"Hey, Chief," Matt said.

Clete returned the greeting and slid a red plastic cup of beer Matt's way. "Guess you're wanting one of these."

"Sure am."

Matt took a sip and scanned the stream of new arrivals flowing into the hall. And then he saw her. Kate was a flash of scarlet sweater and spiky blond hair, so obvious among the less vivid colors surrounding her. The night was looking up.

"It's the townie mother lode," Kate said to Ella as they worked their way into Woodsmen's Hall. The place was packed, which made it all the better to be with Ella. Kate's friend was gorgeous. She was tall, with straight black hair that just swept her shoulders. She also possessed a figure that Kate envied but didn't want to work to attain. Crowds just kind of parted for Ella.

"This is also the safest place on Earth," Ella said.

Kate could see why. She'd already spotted a handful of police officers and most of the volunteer fire department, all of whom she recognized from her brief stint at Bagger's.

As Ella and she wove through the throng toward Ella's unstated destination, Kate said hello to the people she recognized. She was pleased to even get a few return greetings that didn't come with that confused "Where do I know her from?" look in the eyes.

"Where are we heading?" Kate asked her friend over the noise of the music that had just started.

"Beer table for the first stop," Ella said.

"I don't suppose there's a wine table?"

Ella shot her a dubious look. "You're not serious, are you?"

She had been, but she'd never admit it.

Ella had a conspiratorial look in her eye. "I have a plan for you."

"And beer is part of it?"

"If you don't want a beer, just make sure you grab something to drink, because you're going to need it."

"That sounds marginally dangerous."

"If it's only marginally, we're doing pretty good," Ella said.

They rounded food tables packed with the kind of calories a sensible woman would avoid, but which Kate considered staples. She looked away from the temptation, but suddenly the evening's danger factor rose. Matt stood at the beer table, and something way hotter than hunger for ham casserole rippled through Kate.

"Hi, Matt!" Ella called.

Matt *very* slowly turned his attention from Kate. This was a first, since usually when Ella called, guys hopped to.

"He's into you," Ella said to Kate in a low voice.

Kate shook off the moment. "Punch sounds good. Really good." She moved on to the table directly to the left of Matt.

Ella lined up with Matt, got a cup of beer, and chatted a little with Clete Erikson.

Kate investigated the punch. Clearly, this was the grandma drink, complete with the obligatory island of orange sherbet slowly melting in a sea of bright pink liquid studded with chunks of melon and strawberry. Not her beverage of choice, but still about ten thousand spots ahead of beer. She ladled herself a big plastic cup, trying to avoid the fruit. If anyone was going to have the bad luck to create a scene with a public fruit-choking incident, Kate knew she'd be that person. To make up for the fruit, she added a little more punch, plus some of the orange stuff.

She glanced over and caught Matt watching her, a broad smile on his face.

"You sure you want to drink that?" he asked.

"Not really, but I'm going to give it a try, anyway."

"Note the people lining up for the beer and note the continuing absence of people at your table. What does that tell you?"

"That Keene's Harbor is a haven for beer snobs?"

He grinned. "Live and learn."

She raised her cup of sludge in a sketchy toast. "That's my general plan."

Ella, who'd been watching, fought back a laugh. Kate glanced into her cup again. It wasn't the prettiest stuff she'd ever seen, but it couldn't be *that* bad.

"We need to get moving," Ella said. "We'll catch you later, Matt."

With that, she snagged Kate by the wrist and began hauling her and her foaming punch back past the sirenlike lure of the casseroles.

"You still sing, right?" Ella asked.

The summer they were sixteen, they had nothing better to do than drive around town and sing along to the radio. Kate had a shiny new driver's license and a less shiny hand-me-down car. And when they'd needed money for more gasoline, Ella had played the guitar and Kate had sung on the street corner until they had change for a few gallons or the police told them to close up shop.

"Not even in the shower. I keep the water

temperature set too low to carry a tune," Kate replied.

They passed through what was obviously a silent auction area. Kate halted at a collection of old vinyl albums up for bid. Her parents had stuck their ancient stereo at The Nutshell. There was nothing Kate would like more than to mix a little retro Jimi Hendrix and Janis Joplin in with the Frank Sinatra and Barbra Streisand already in residence.

Ella nudged her along. "No time to window-shop. You've got music of your own to make."

Kate noticed the small stage at the back of the long hall. About a half dozen people were in a line to the stage's left, and Marcie Landon was onstage aligning a microphone stand behind a monitor of some sort. She seemed to be giving the arrangement the same OCD level of scrutiny she gave the shelves at her market.

As they came closer to the group, Kate started picking out the particulars. Junior Greinwold, with his trusty blue cooler at his feet, was flipping through an aged three-ring binder while a guy and another woman Kate didn't recognize were peering at it from either side of him. A liquor-tinged memory of a party in someone's basement and a lot of really bad versions of "Pour Some Sugar on Me" came back to her.

Kate stopped dead. "Karaoke? No way!" Ella

settled a hand on Kate's arm and drew her to the edge of the room. "You wanted to know how to become part of the town again, right?"

"Yes."

"Then rule in karaoke."

"You're kidding. I thought the only place you could still find it was in ratty college bars."

"It's become the favored competitive sport in Keene's Harbor. See those chairs?" Ella pointed to three chairs lined up at the far edge of the dance floor in front of the stage. "Judges. Olympic scoring. The whole thing. Now, come on."

Kate looked around. "Isn't there an arm-wrestling or kielbasa-eating challenge I could do instead?"

"Just get on up there," Ella said.

"What, alone? You're going to make me do this and you're not singing?"

"I still can't carry a tune, but you can. Do this, Kate. I'm telling you it will help."

When she'd asked Ella for help in being accepted as one of the locals, she'd been thinking of something that might have taken a bit less effort and potential for humiliation on her part. But she trusted Ella. And what had dignity ever gotten her, anyway?

"Okay, then. Just stick by my side until I get a song under my belt."

"I'll be your personal assistant, I promise," Ella said. "Let me hold your drink for you."

They joined the field of karaoke Olympians.

"No cuts," said a woman at the back of the line.

Kate blew out a sigh. "No problem."

Ella drew Kate back a few steps, her voice lowered. "That's Deena Bowen. She's about five years older than us, so you missed out on her when we were kids. She's also the town's undisputed karaoke queen, among a couple of other less perky titles."

"Such as?"

"Psycho revenge queen. She's always verbally gunning for Matt, and from what I've heard, they only had one date. Though I guess she lobbied long and hard even for that one."

"She's a little spooky. Do you think she'd ever do more than just bad-mouth him?" Kate asked Ella.

"I don't know. She's bitter, for sure, but I think she's just acting out over a whole lot of bad stuff in her life." Ella paused long enough to give her a teasing smile. "Why? Are you worried about being in the line of fire if you date him?"

"You don't have to be dating a guy to want to see him stay in one piece." She inclined her head toward Deena. "And you have to admit she's somewhere south of hostile. It rolls off her in waves."

Ahead of Deena, Junior was pacing back and forth, shaking his arms and repeating "ma, me, mi, mo, mu" as his apparent warm-up exercise. Deena hissed at him to shut up before she had him sedated. Junior picked up his cooler and walked away from Deena to practice next to Kate.

"How's it going, Junior?" Kate asked.

Junior glanced at Kate and hugged his cooler. "Fine."

"Don't you want to know how things are going for me?"

Junior hugged the cooler even tighter. "I guess so."

"Well, I'm glad you asked. I've been trying to call you for two days. The 'improvements' you made to my toilet and shower leaked all over my entire house. The contractor was there today. Do you know what he found when he pulled up the floor?"

Junior looked a little ashamed. Kate suspected it wasn't his first plumbing disaster. "Dooky."

"That's right. Lots of dirty dooky and mold. There were guys in hazmat suits in my house for eight hours containing the 'affected' area with plastic sheeting and setting up negative air blowers to suction all the mold outdoors."

Junior bit his lower lip and shoved his hands into his pockets. "I heard they can be a little noisy."

Kate's eyes were as big as dinner plates. "It

sounds like a hurricane is blowing through my house."

"Everyone, come line up back here," Marcie said from the stage, rescuing Junior and gathering the group behind a white wooden latticework screen that had been decorated with plastic ivy.

Not the most attractive ivy Kate had ever seen, but she was glad for whatever cover from the audience she could find. She needed to get her stuff together before facing them.

"For the benefit of the new entrant, I'm going to repeat our standing rules," Marcie announced.

Kate gave a quick wave in acknowledgment to the other contestants now scoping her out. Happily, only Deena looked like she meant to inflict bodily harm. Everyone else nodded or waved back.

"There are six of you singing. We will determine the order of competition in the first round by pulling numbers from the bingo cage." She patted the cage in question, and the balls in it quivered. "Lowest number goes first. Two competitors will be eliminated in each of the first two rounds, leaving two finalists for the kamikaze challenge."

Kate raised her hand like the obedient student she'd never quite been.

"In a moment, Kate," Marcie replied. "The

judges' scores are final. No bribes will be accepted or threats tolerated." She said the last with a pointed stare at Deena. "And tonight's winner will receive the grand prize of five pounds of venison burger provided by Harley Bagger."

If Kate was going to sing for her supper, she would have appreciated something non-Bambi-like, but she wasn't here for the chow.

"You had a question, Kate?" Marcie asked.

"What's the kamikaze challenge?"

"In the final round, a song will be selected at random for you from the playlist."

Deena snickered. "As if you have to worry."

Marcie gave Deena a glare. "And no sabotage, either. Now, if you'll excuse me . . ." She walked back out to the microphone, leaving Kate and the other singers hidden behind the plastic jungle.

"And tonight's judges, chosen at semi-random from among our guests, will be . . ." She looked down at a sheet of paper. "Starflower Creed, Shay VanAntwerp . . . and Matt Culhane."

SEVEN

MATT FLIPPED THROUGH A STACK OF ALBUMS BEING OF-fered in the town's garage sale of a silent auc-tion. Actually, if he thought he could consistently find a stash of music like this in local garages, he'd be joining his mom on the Saturday morn-ing circuit. Next to him stood Lizzie. She must have pulled the short straw in the "keep Matt here" challenge, because she hadn't left his side in the past ten minutes. And somewhere at the very back of the room, Marcie Landon was call-ing names over the sound system.

Matt picked up his head at the sound of some-thing all too familiar.

"Did I just hear my name?" he asked Lizzie.

"I don't know. Did you?" His sister's smile

was nothing short of smug. This was never a good sign.

Again his name drifted above the crowd. "Matt? Matt Culhane?"

"That's definitely your name," Lizzie said.

"It is. But I have the option of ignoring it," he said, testing Lizzie's level of investment in whatever was going down.

His little sister tried to hip check him away from the album collection. "Come on," she said. "Let's go see. Maybe you've won something."

He held her off long enough to write a bid on the vinyl collection big enough to scare off competitors. He knew that wasn't the silent auction spirit, but he wasn't messing around. There was a pile of Doors and Jefferson Airplane in that stack.

Marcie waved her hand, urging him toward the stage. "Matt, there you are!"

"What am I here for?"

She laughed as though he'd made a joke. "Ladies and gentlemen, our third judge is now taking his seat. Let the karaoke competition begin!" she said with a flourish and hurried back behind the screen.

"You set me up," Matt said to Lizzie.

"Fact. But think of judging as an exercise in civic duty. We all have to do it. It's your turn, and now that you're trapped, I can go have fun."

While thinking of a fitting revenge to eventually spring on his sister, Matt made his way to the open judge's chair. He settled between Starflower and Shay.

Starflower, one of the silver-haired elders of the Creed Commune outside of town, said, "Remember, Matt, peace comes from within."

She didn't generally offer up platitudes without a purpose.

"I take it you've judged these before?" he asked.

She gave a slow nod of her head, closed her eyes, and began humming to herself. Matt wondered if he was catching a whiff of something less legal than the scent of Starflower's lavender oil, which she sold in a shop the commune owned in town. Matt preferred to find his inner peace the way he'd been raised—family, friends, and hard work.

To his right, Shay VanAntwerp flicked her perfectly straight and shiny blond hair over her shoulders. "I was told we'd be up on the stage. That's the only reason I agreed to judge."

At least she'd been given a choice.

Besides, Matt understood Shay's stage addiction. She'd been Little Miss Keene's Harbor for four years running when they were kids. After that, Shay had been hooked. If there was a sash or crown to be won, she was in the race. Matt had always thought that if Shay redirected all that energy and determination, she could govern a small nation. Kind of like Kate. He wondered what she was making of this whole scene. If it was odd to him, it had to be downright surreal to her.

Deena Bowen was truly psycho.

"You cheated," Deena said.

"How could I cheat? Marcie drew the numbers," Kate replied.

"You came in here earlier and rigged it."

"Why would I do that?"

"Because everybody's out to beat me. But just because you get to sing first doesn't mean you're going to win. It doesn't give you any advantage," Deena said.

"Another good reason I wouldn't come in and play with a bunch of bingo balls, don't you think?"

Deena's hostility aside, Kate was looking forward to getting this first number done. She hadn't sung in front of strangers since she was sixteen, and the idea of doing it now had her a little rattled. And the idea of having Matt judge her was even more uncomfortable.

"Ready?" Marcie asked.

Kate nodded. Because her mouth was as dry as the dunes overlooking Lake Michigan, she poked her head out from the far side of the jungle screen and signaled Ella for the punch. Kate chugged half and winced. The concoction was so sweet that she swore her blood had just turned to syrup.

Ella gave her a weird look as she took back the cup.

"What?" Kate asked.

"You feel okay?"

"Nervous, and now probably borderline diabetic."

Ella waggled the cup. "That's okay. You won't be feeling anything very soon."

"What do you mean?"

"This is trash-can punch. Beneath all that sugar is enough overproof rum to pickle a sailor. All I can say is good thing I drove."

"Thanks for sharing. If I'd known about the punch, I'd have started drinking earlier."

"Kate," Marcie said. "Curtain time."

Except for the crucial lack of a curtain.

Palms clammy and heart slamming, Kate stepped out from behind the latticework jungle and walked tentatively to the microphone. She allowed herself a glance toward Matt, then wished she hadn't. As surprise and then pleasure paraded across his face, Kate had to quell a truly chicken-feathered urge to jump from the stage and chug the rest of that overproof courage. But if this was what it took to be initiated into Keene's Harbor, no way was she going to back down.

"I'm going to give you a little 'Crimson and Clover' . . . Joan Jett style," she said into the microphone.

Kate didn't care that half of the hall still

talked and laughed as the music started. All that mattered was reaching the end of the song. She hadn't lied when she'd told Ella she hadn't been singing, but more than the chilly shower had been stopping her. In the space of one year, she'd lost her marriage, her home, her dog, and her job. She wasn't exactly depressed, but she was just flat-out busy trying to rebuild her life and her identity. Most of the time, she just felt too tired to sing.

But as she eased into the song, Kate recalled one cool thing about singing. When singing, she didn't have to be Kate of the somewhat screwed-up life. She became whatever character she chose to take on. And tonight, she chose to be a rocker seductress.

Kate let herself go with the song's sensual sway and began to kick out the lyrics with conviction. This wasn't about winning Bambi meat or even town approval. It was about living in this moment. It was about feeling the slow, sexual surge that made her grip the microphone stand with both hands and make love to the crowd.

When the song finished, Kate dropped her gaze to the plywood stage and blew out a sigh of relief. She was fairly certain she hadn't sucked. Except the hall remained weirdly silent. Okay, maybe she was delusional. Maybe she really had sucked. Just when she was sure that was true, applause and a couple of whistles and howls kicked in.

Kate smiled at the crowd and said her thanks.

Then she caught Matt looking at her with an intensity she'd never gotten from any other man. Not even from Richard. She felt as though the stage was rocking and rolling beneath her feet. It wasn't the not-so-grandma punch, though. This was a punch of another kind, one of sheer hunger and absolute sexual certainty.

Matt wasn't messing around.

Now Kate got why women trailed after him as though they'd lost their favorite plaything. Still, she refused to fall for him, no matter how hot that landing might be. Without even looking at the scorecards the judges now held aloft, Kate escaped the stage while her legs could still carry her.

Matt was a goner. He was ready to serve himself up to Kate however she wanted him. Preferably naked. And even more preferably, tonight.

Matt listened to a damn fine version of "My Wild Irish Rose" by Junior and an equally scary rendition of "Do Ya Think I'm Sexy?" by Deena. But all of that was second to wondering how he could get Kate alone. He *really* liked her. Ironically, that made things more complicated. Not that he was going to let that stop him. Or even slow him down.

Marcie stepped onstage, aligned the microphone to her satisfaction, and announced the second round finalists. Kate had made the cut.

Starflower leaned over to speak to Matt. "We get a ten-minute reprieve before they start the next round."

"You mean a break?" Matt asked.

"No. Definitely a reprieve," she said. "I'm stepping outside to meditate and make myself one with the evening peace."

Or peace *pipe*.

As for Matt, he planned to meditate on how to make progress with Kate.

The overproof rum had kicked in and was burning through Kate like jet fuel. She didn't feel buzzed so much as energized. Sometime around midnight, when both the alcohol and the sugar had wreaked their havoc, she knew she'd be parched and cranky. And no doubt still sleepless. Too late for regrets, though. She looked out at the people gathered behind the judges, and Kate the Performer took over. It was round two of the Great Karaoke Olympics, and Kate was into it.

"Marvin Gaye's 'Sexual Healing,'" she said into the microphone.

Kate ripped into the song, enjoying her time in the spotlight, loving the lyrics, loving the music, thinking that life was full of moments just like this. Unexpected, surprising moments. And Kate realized that unless you put yourself out there, you could very easily miss them. Maybe it was time to take some more risks with her life.

A low howl drifted into the room from somewhere outside. The sound slowly raised in both pitch and volume, and people began to turn and head toward the door. Kate knew her voice wasn't chasing them off. She'd witnessed this scene before at Bagger's Tavern. The place could go from full to empty in sixty seconds flat when the town's volunteer firefighters heard the alarm sound.

"Fire," Ella mouthed from the base of the stage. She pointed toward the door, and Kate nodded in acknowledgment. Ella was one of the handful of women who served on the town's fire department.

More people filed out, but Kate kept singing. Now she knew how the band on the *Titanic* had felt. A woman who looked kind of like Matt leaned over his shoulder and said something to him. He stood. Kate didn't like the grim look on his face. She finished, skipped her bow, and made a moderately graceful jump from the low stage.

"What's going on?"

"There's a fire at the brewery," Matt said. "Could you come with me?"

"Of course," she said, because she'd decided not to let herself lust after Matt Culhane, but she darned well liked him.

*   *   *

Matt looked at the crowd gathered in his parking lot. In Keene's Harbor, the only thing that drew a bigger crowd than a Friday night fundraiser was a good, old-fashioned Dumpster fire. There was such a weirdly festive atmosphere that he half expected to see the spectators pull out marshmallows and start toasting them. Of course, the spectators would have to fight their way through the most massive contingent of first responders that Matt had seen since the Independence Day fireworks debacle of '90. Since he'd been intimately involved in the accidental early start to that annual celebration, he'd watched that group from afar.

"Is the whole town here?" Kate asked.

"More or less."

He found a spot for his truck, and immediately noticed an ambulance parked at the brewery's employee door. The vehicle's back door was open and the interior was lit. Inside, a familiar figure lay on a stretcher.

Matt sprinted over to the ambulance. He'd barely reached it when Kate joined him. For a little thing, she had a long stride.

"Give me a second," he said to her.

"I'll be right here."

Matt didn't recognize the two paramedics working on Laila. All the same, he climbed into the back of the ambulance.

One of the paramedics was inflating some sort

of air cast around Laila's ankle. "You'll have to get out, sir," she said.

Laila tried to prop herself up on her elbows, despite the paramedics' orders to stay still. "He'll stay right where he is. Work around him."

"What happened?" Matt asked.

"Twisted it hard." She winced as she tried to settle more comfortably on the stretcher. "I had stepped outside for a second to use my phone when I saw the fire. I called 911, but the fencing around the Dumpster was already burning. I tried to run a hose from the loading dock door. The hose ran me, instead, I guess. Broke my phone when I went down, too."

"Don't worry about the phone. I'll get you another one," Matt said. "Let's work on getting you fixed, okay?"

Laila had been with him since the day he'd started serving food. Yeah, she could be a little bossy, but he'd learned more from her than he could have from any number of highly paid consultants. She was family, plain and simple. And he felt sick that she had been hurt trying to help him.

"We're ready to roll," the larger of the paramedics said.

Matt touched Laila gently on her shoulder. "Can I do anything for you?"

"Get ahold of my son, Joe. Tell him where I am and that someone's going to need to come get my car."

"No problem. And I'll be over to the emergency room in just a while."

"Don't you dare. You've got enough to deal with right here. Clete already shut you down for the night."

At that news, Matt bit back on a couple of his favorite curse words.

"The Dumpster was too far from the building for a spark to fly. And even if one did, the roof's metal," he said.

"I know," Laila replied. "But you know Clete. And Steve went to look for Jerry to argue the closing, but Jerry was nowhere to be found."

"Don't worry," Matt said. "Just focus on getting yourself better and let me deal with the rest of this, okay?"

"I will."

He gave her hand a squeeze, which was about all the affection Laila would accept

"Hang in there," he said before climbing out.

Kate still stood watching the firefighters spray down the smoking Dumpster and fence.

"Arson is a definite buzzkill," she said without looking his way.

She'd voiced what Matt had been thinking since they'd pulled into the parking lot. If not for all the other incidents, Matt would have attributed it to Steve sneaking a cigarette by the trash. Matt had snagged him doing that countless times.

"It is. And I know I'm lucky it wasn't worse. Laila's fall was bad enough."

"She'll be okay, though, right?"

"I don't know if her ankle is sprained or broken, but she'll recover." He paused. "And probably demand to come back to work long before she's ready, too."

"Speaking of which . . . Besides Laila, who was on staff tonight?"

"The usual. Amber and Steve were in the dining room. Ruby was busing dishes. Pat, Renaldo, and Manny were in the kitchen. And Jerry was supposed to be here, not that he is." He paused a second. "Before I left for the hall, Nan and Floyd were in the brewery working on one of Bart's new beer recipes. I don't know if they're still around. So what it comes down to is any one of my own employees could have done this to me."

"Or maybe just a random firebug. I'm betting Keene's Harbor has a pyro or two," she said. "What's frustrating is that I'd like to say everyone at the fund-raiser can be dropped from the suspect list but it's too easy to make it here from the hall to say that for sure."

Matt understood frustration. He was frustrated that his night's business was literally going up in smoke. He was angry that someone had made jerking him around their new hobby. And he was furious with himself for permitting them to mess with his ability to coolly sort through the facts.

Kate briefly settled her hand against his arm. "Hey, this isn't going to go on forever. It's going to be okay."

"Now would be a good time for it to end."

"Agreed," she said. "Should we talk to the fire chief?"

"That's up next."

"Mind if I come along?"

"Not at all. A set of objective ears is good. But you should know that Norm's more about putting the fire out than any kind of investigating. That's one of the quirks of having a volunteer fire department."

"Still, if you tell him about all the other things that have happened, he'll have to see a pattern."

"You and I might, but unless you've been living through it, it's a tough pattern to see." He led her to the back of the fire truck, where Chief Norm stood talking to Clete Erikson.

"Sorry about this, Matt," Norm said as they neared.

The fire chief had been of average size in his active days as a charter fishing boat captain. Retirement had caught up with him, though. Now he was shaped like his favorite bowling ball. Still, he remained surprisingly agile.

"Thanks for getting the fire put out," Matt said.

Norm nodded. "A few of us are going to stick around awhile in case any hot spots flare up."

"Great. Will you start your arson investigation tonight or wait for first light?"

Norm looked surprised. "It's a Dumpster fire, Matt. What makes you think it's arson?"

"The fence was burning. You can't believe that the entire enclosure sparked and went up without an accelerant."

"Son, what does a Dumpster hold but trash?" Clete asked, but gave no time for an answer. "The ember from one cigarette butt could have set it off. I'll interview your employees, but I don't see any point in rattling the whole town with talk of arson."

"The town will be talking anyway," Kate said.

The police chief turned his head. "What did you say?"

"I said that the town will be talking anyway. That's what Keene's Harbor does, especially when the topic is as high-profile as Matt and Depot Brewing. They bring more money to this town than any other five businesses combined. Failure to investigate won't make the talk go away. It will just get worse."

Clete moved a step closer to her. "Well now, little lady, I'm not sure what business any of this is of yours."

She looked up at Matt. "Little lady? Did he just call me *little lady*?"

Yeah, that had been a critical error on Clete's part, Matt thought. And Matt was happy to urge her on. If anyone could help him quickly shake loose an investigation, it was Kate. "I believe he did," Matt said.

She turned back to Clete. "I might be little and I might also be a lady, but I am *not* a little lady any more than you're the ghost of John Wayne. And even the ghost of the Duke playing a sheriff blindfolded would know this is arson. If you and Chief Norm aren't interested in investigating it, I'm sure someone is."

Clete was more puzzled than annoyed. "Didn't anyone ever tell you that you can catch more flies with honey than you can with vinegar?"

"She's right, Clete," Matt said. "If you don't step up, I'm going to have to call the county sheriff's office and bring them in. You don't want that."

There wasn't enough light to catch the look in Clete's eyes, but Matt was betting it wasn't a happy one. Somehow Kate had hit his hot button without even knowing it. Or maybe she'd sensed it. Keene's Harbor wasn't flush with money. Clete lived in fear of the town cutting back on its police coverage and using county services.

Clete stood taller, probably trying to make up for the fact that he was in civilian clothes. "Norm, if you're going to be staying, could you put crime scene tape around the Dumpster area once it's cooled down?" He turned to Matt. "Could you tell your employees to stay in the restaurant until I can interview them? Site photos and talking more to Laila will have to wait until the light of day."

"Thanks, Clete," Matt said.

He glanced at Kate, who wore a victorious smile. Their methods might vary, but Matt appreciated another person of action when he came across one. And he was appreciating Kate Appleton more by the minute.

Kate looked at Matt's profile in the dim illumination of his truck's dashboard lights. The guy was wiped out, and she couldn't blame him. He turned onto The Nutshell's winding drive, then pulled up beside her Jeep.

"Home again," he said.

She took in the silhouette of her childhood home and felt comfort ease into her bones.

"I am," she said.

That much, at least, felt very right. She smiled at the thought and the man who had triggered it.

"Did you get dinner?" she asked.

"I never made it over to the food tables."

"Why don't you come in? I don't have much outside the key food groups of chocolate and wine, but I'm sure I can pull something together."

"Thanks, but I need to get back to the brewery and make sure everything's under control, then look in on Laila. How about if I take a rain check?"

"Sure," she said, even though she felt a little disappointed. She reached for the truck's door handle. "Good night, then."

Kate was about to exit the truck when Matt spoke again. "You're not scheduled for tomorrow, are you?"

"No."

"Then I'd like you to take a road trip with me. I'll pick you up around eight."

"Where are we going?"

"A motel."

"A *what*?"

He smiled. "You heard me. We're going to a motel, among other places. But it's business. You can relax . . . for the moment."

Kate was guaranteed not to sleep at all.

EIGHT

A COUPLE MINUTES BEFORE EIGHT ON SATURDAY MORN-
ing, Matt pulled into Kate's driveway. He reached
for the closest of the two travel mugs of coffee
he'd brought along. As he took a swallow, he
also took advantage of the opportunity to check
out The Nutshell in the daylight. He'd bought
the mortgage on the advice of his financial advi-
sor, and his interest had been in the land and not
the house.

Last night, when Kate had cornered Clete,
she'd invoked the ghost of John Wayne. Matt
had found it tough not to laugh, since he'd often
thought Clete purposely cultivated the look and
attitude. But if Matt were to talk ghosts and
The Nutshell, he'd have to say the Rat Pack,

with Frank Sinatra leading the charge, would hang out there.

Once upon a time, this had been a top-of-the-line cottage, but that time had passed. The Nutshell's upkeep had to be a bear by virtue of its size, not to mention its windy perch over Lake Michigan. Though Kate had limited Matt's indoor tour the other night, he'd guess the house held at least six bedrooms, and probably more.

The place's white paint was pulling away from its trim, its entry porch had begun to sag, and its silvery cedar shingles were becoming gap-toothed in places. The Nutshell had character, though. He liked that it was as quirky as its current resident.

The front door swung open, and Kate appeared. She wore dressy boots, snug jeans, a clingy red V-necked sweater, and had a huge brown leather purse slung over her shoulder. Matt slipped from behind the wheel and rounded his truck. He opened the passenger-side door for her and waited while she climbed on board.

"Was it this big last night?" she asked, clicking her seat belt into place as they pulled out of her drive.

"What?"

"Your truck. Last night is kind of a haze of stage fright, adrenaline, and punch, so my memories are fuzzy. But it's like *Land of the Giants* in here. My feet barely even reach the floor." Her smile was brief, but it still made him feel good.

"So the standard question would be: Tell me, Culhane, are you compensating for something with this monster vehicle?"

He grinned. "I've never worried about compensating."

"Really?"

"Want to check?"

"I'll take your word for it," Kate said.

That was a flirtatious warning shot across her bow, she thought. She'd set it up, and he'd followed in kind. It was fun, but she didn't want it to go further just yet. She dug through her purse and pulled out a pair of oversized sunglasses.

"I probably shouldn't talk again until I've had my second coffee," she said. "Anything before that is the insomnia speaking."

"Do you really have insomnia?"

She nodded. "I'm having a little mold problem. The place is filled with negative air blowers, and there are guys coming today to remove the damage and HEPA vacuum the place."

Matt raised an eyebrow. "Mold problems can be really hard to fix. And expensive. Are you sure you don't want to bail now? I was going to raze the structure anyway."

Kate felt her jaw drop. "Excuse me— You want to destroy my family's lake house so you can build some tourist trap of a restaurant? Are you serious? I will never, ever, ever let you get your hands on my house."

"I think I pushed a button best left alone for now," Matt said. "Would you consider coffee as a peace offering?"

She reached for the mug in her cup holder. "Coffee would be a wonderful peace offering. Sorry I snapped. If I don't catch more than three hours of sleep in a row soon, I'm going to be giving Deena Bowen a run for her money in the cranky department. And it isn't just the blowers. I wasn't sleeping too well even before they arrived. All night long the house is filled with creaks and groans and whispers. At four in the morning, it sounds downright haunted. Not that I have issues or anything." She took a swallow of coffee. "But enough of my neuroses. Why not tell me where we're going besides that motel you mentioned."

"First, we've got to head to my office," he said.

"Bad news, then. We're heading in the wrong direction."

"My Traverse City office."

She turned her face his way, and he had to focus on the road not to smile at how cute she was in the big glasses.

"Okay," she said. "So you *do* have a secret life. Are you a spy? Is this one of those 'I'm going to tell you but then I have to kill you' road trips?"

Matt laughed. "You stand a better chance of being bored to death by my secret life. All the same, it's mine and I choose to keep it among certain people. Now that I'm making you one of them, no sharing this with Ella or anyone else."

"Deal," she said. "And thank you."

"For what?"

"For letting me be in the know. I've been kind of low on friendships since I moved here, and I like having one with you. It's . . ." She lifted one shoulder in a small shrug. "I don't know, really special, I guess."

It was to Matt, also, but he didn't want to make the moment sappy. He went for one more kick of caffeine before setting the mug back in its holder. "Today, among other things, I have to pull the plug on a business relationship that hasn't worked out."

"What kind of business? Is it at least something dangerous or exotic?"

He smiled at the excitement in her voice. "Sorry to disappoint, but he's another micro-brewer. I gave him a rescue loan a few years back. The guy brews some great beer, and I didn't want to see him go under. But good beer isn't enough to be a success."

"Do you lend money often?"

"When I feel it's right. I wouldn't be in business today without the help I got when I started."

"That's pretty cool of you, actually."

"Don't let word get out. I like it better being viewed as the tough guy in town."

"So you have a full second life as a business investor."

"It wasn't in the plan, but accidentally, yeah."

"So why not at least tell the people at Depot what you're up to? It could save you a lot of grief."

"The more success I've had . . . at least, success from a Keene's Harbor viewpoint . . . the tougher it's become to have any privacy. And you have to remember that I'm the guy they've had stories about since I was eight years old and painted a bunch of the town dogs bright orange at the start of hunting season."

She laughed. "Makes sense to me."

"It did to me, too. Especially since I'd lost a family pet to hunters a year earlier. But a legend was born, and it's only gotten worse. I guess on one level, it's cool that everyone cares enough to watch me. But on another, it's tough to be under that level of scrutiny, even if it comes with a whole lot of love."

Kate had last been to Traverse City when she was sixteen. Back then, it had been a quaint place of cherry festivals in the summer and hot cider in the winter. Now, as she looked up Front Street, she saw it had become the home of bistros, film festivals, and Pan-Asian food. The city had grown up while she did, and apparently with fewer glitches than she'd experienced.

Matt pulled around a corner and then into a city parking lot behind a three-story redbrick building. Kate grabbed her bag and tried to find a graceful way to exit his ginormous, but apparently noncompensating, truck.

"I'm going to leave you with Ginger, my office manager, while I finish up business with Chet," he said as they headed toward the building.

"You have an office manager? How many people work for you up here?"

"Just Ginger, and I let her choose her title. So long as people do their work, I'm happy to call them Galactic Emperor or Most Royal of Personages or whatever they want."

Matt led her up to the building's metal security door and opened it. "I'm leasing the space from the yoga studio below. It's cheap rent, since it doesn't put out a fancy public face, but I don't need one of those."

They reached the third floor and Matt opened the door to a suite marked only with its number and ushered her in. Behind a desk in the moderately sized reception area sat a movie star–looking, twentysomething redhead. She wore a red wrap dress with a plunging neckline, red lipstick that matched the dress, and just the right amount of mascara to show off thick black eyelashes over her green eyes.

"Kate, this is Ginger Monroe," Matt said. "And Ginger, this is Kate Appleton."

Ginger gave Kate a blatantly inquisitive look. "Hi."

Kate returned the greeting, but tried to keep her curiosity under control.

"Is Chet here?" Matt asked Ginger.

"I sent him into your office. You might want to consider a bulletproof vest before you go in."

"That bad?"

"Oh, yeah."

Matt shot a dubious look at the closed door. "Then he knows why he's here. I'll be out in a couple of minutes." He paused. "Or maybe even sooner."

Kate settled into a guest chair and Ginger pulled open a desk drawer and brought out a semi-full bag of salt-and-vinegar potato chips. "Want some? They've got a good bite."

"I love them, too, but I'm all about coffee at this hour," Kate said.

Ginger nodded. "Okay." Without pausing a beat, she added, "So, are you Matt's new girl-friend?"

"No, I just started working for him last week."

Kate suddenly realized how much longer it felt, and not in a bad way. No, this was more a *What did I do with myself before all this crazi-ness?* feeling.

"Interesting," Ginger said.

The conversation was starting to feel a little

interesting to Kate, too. "So, Ginger, have you two ever dated?"

Ginger raised her eyebrows. "No! My dad would kill him. Dad was Matt's high school football coach down in Keene's Harbor. Matt was a big star, but that was ages ago. I was just a kid. And then Dad changed jobs and we moved up here."

"Matt was a football star? Figures."

Ginger grinned. "Doesn't it? He was hot stuff. I guess he had a full ride to Michigan State, but then messed up his knee during baseball season his senior year of high school. He lost the scholarship and ended up working around town before he took off for a couple of years. Everything turned out fine, though."

Just then the younger woman's eyes widened, giving Kate an instant of forewarning before Matt's office door slammed into the wall, and a short, heavy man whose skin color had risen to a shiny puce marched out of the office.

The purple man was sputtering so much he could barely choke out his words. "You'll pay, Culhane," he said.

Matt followed him out and remained admirably impassive. Kate wanted to learn how to do that, though she suspected she lacked the talent.

"I agree this is tough, Chet, but you know I've been more than fair," Matt said.

The older man's breathing was ragged, and he opened and closed his hands into fists. "Another six months wouldn't have killed you. Instead, you're killing me."

"You have four weeks before I'll be filing anything. Just work on those other possibilities, okay?"

Chet told Matt in graphic detail what *he* could work on, then stormed out.

Doing the right thing and doing the easy thing didn't seem to be lining up too well for Matt these days.

"I would have given Chet more time if I could have," he said to Kate, who sat next to him in the truck as they headed to his next appointment. "But I need to think about my cash reserves and my business. The slow season is coming on. It's going to hurt to take any more financial hits. I hate to be a survivalist, but it's better it's Chet's business than mine, especially when he's been in default for over a year."

"There's nothing else you could have done," she said.

"But there is. I should have pulled the plug on his financing last year. I built up expectations that I'd just keep letting this slide." He shook his head. "Big mistake."

Kate eyes narrowed. "Does that mean you're thinking of pulling the plug on our deal? You gave me until Thanksgiving to come up with the money, and if you try to back out, I'll make Chet look like Gandhi."

Matt laughed. "You caught him at an off moment. He's not usually so purple."

"Good news there, or he'll be among the spirits pretty soon. One little vein in the brain goes *ping*, and it's all over."

Matt knew the feeling, even if he hadn't yet achieved Chet's color of purple. All the same, bringing a measure of calm and sanity into his life was now part of his game plan.

"True," Matt said. "And the good news is that no one is purple at our next stop, though Travis is pretty tatted up."

"And tatted Travis is . . ."

"The owner of Horned Owl Brewing and my newest project. Great concepts, but bad business decisions. Bart is spending today and tomorrow with him to go over his beer recipes and maybe tweak 'em where they need tweaking. Nothing too big."

He wasn't about to clue her into the other activity about to take place at Horned Owl. One that had occurred to him early this morning. Matt wasn't totally up to speed on it, but he knew that surprise was crucial. . . .

NINE

KATE FELT AS THOUGH HER FILLINGS WERE GOING TO FALL out as Matt's truck slammed and rattled down a pitted gravel road in the middle of nowhere. "Are you sure this is really the road to the microbrewery?"

"Positive," Matt said. "It's also the first of three issues that have been tanking Travis's business."

Kate couldn't wait to see the other two.

"Do you think maybe you should slow down a little?"

"No way. Then we'd feel every rut in the road."

Being airborne didn't seem much better, but Kate also knew not to mess with a man on a mission.

"Hang on," Matt said, skittering around a hairpin turn. "It gets a little rough right here."

Kate's gasp was involuntary, and she wasn't real thrilled about the grin that appeared on Matt's face in response as she fought the urge to brace her feet against the dashboard. "Very Indiana Jones of you," she said. "I should have brought my bullwhip."

Matt's eyebrows raised a half inch. "Do you have a bullwhip?"

Kate smiled sweetly. Ms. Mysterious.

"Kinky," Matt said, "but I can deal."

He swerved around an unusually deep rut, barely missing a tree. They made a hard right turn onto a narrow ribbon of a drive. All that marked it as more than a trail was a huge, sour-faced plastic owl on a post.

"Horned Owl issue number two," Matt said. "If you've got a customer ambitious enough to come back here, get a sign. Don't scare them off with a weird fake owl."

Now that they were traveling at normal speed, Kate took a look around. She imagined that the woods were lush and green in the summer. On this crisp autumn day, though, the maples were turning crimson and yellow, with the oaks not far behind. Only the scrubby jack pines still held much green.

"The scenery's a good prize for making it back this far," she said. "It's gorgeous."

The woods had thinned, and a meadow lay ahead. At the far end sat an unassuming

double-wide home. To the right of that by a
hundred yards was the most amazing barn Kate
had ever seen. It might have been painted a
traditional red, but the structure's hexagonal
shape and the white cupola topping it were show-
stoppers. Someone had also added expanses of
windows and a pergola-shaded terrace that an-
gled off one of the back sides.

Kate blew out a whistle. "Definitely not issue
number three."

"Except for the location, it's perfect." He
parked next to a silver car that Kate had seen
almost every day in Depot Brewing's lot. "Ready
to go in?"

Kate climbed out of the truck. "First, let me
play tourist."

She dug her phone from her purse and backed
up until she found the perfect spot to take a picture of the barn. She liked that Matt was in the
shot, too.

"Smile," she said. And even though he was
laughing, she kept the picture. "This is turning
into a pretty nice day."

"Hold that thought."

They walked up a stepping stone path to the
microbrewery's entrance.

Inside, a taproom of sorts had been partitioned
from the work area by low walls made of silvery
barn wood. Above the dividers, Kate spotted a
couple of tall stainless-steel tanks back in a cor-

ner, much like the ones she'd seen at Depot
Brewing. The beer-making end of the business
remained a mystery to Kate. Bart Fenner, Depot's
brewmaster, was notoriously protective of his
portion of the domain. For all that Kate knew,
fairies and elves made the beer.

Matt scanned the room. "Travis? You guys
back there?"

"Yeah, hang on."

Travis emerged, and Horned Owl's issue number three was obvious. Kate doubted that Travis
meant to be scary, but the nose and eyebrow
piercings and a squinty-eyed stare did the job.
The full-sleeve tattoo on his right arm actually
served as a happy distraction. He appeared to
be younger than Matt, but that didn't mean he
wasn't old enough to have done some hard time.

"Travis, this is Kate, my newest employee.
Kate, this is Travis Holby, owner of Horned Owl
Brewing."

Travis fixed his stare on Kate. "What's Culhane got on you that you ended up working for
him?"

Kate laughed. "It's more what I have on him."

Travis smiled, and the tough guy aura disappeared. Kate noticed for the first time that once
you looked past the piercings, he had a true baby
face, complete with pudgy cheeks.

"This is a beautiful place you have here," she
said.

"Thanks. I've busted my a—, uh, back, putting it together. Why don't you have a seat?" Travis gestured to one of the three rustic-looking tables with low stools that served as seating in the taproom. "Hungry? Thirsty? Can I get you anything?"

Kate took the offered seat, but turned down food and drink.

"Hey, Bart," Matt called. "Why don't you come out here for a minute, too?"

Bart entered the taproom, and Kate thought there was no way she'd ever seen him at Depot Brewing. He wasn't the sort of guy a woman forgot. In fact, he nearly gave Culhane a run for the money in the looks department. But where Culhane was a rugged kind of hot, Bart had the exotic thing going. Looking at him was like taking a sexy trip to the South Pacific. He was tall and seriously muscled, with dark skin, soulful brown eyes, and black hair.

"I heard you sing last night," Bart said. "You're really good."

"Thanks," she said. "It had been a long time since I sang in public like that."

Matt smiled at her and her heart skipped a beat. The smile was intimate, as though they were the only ones in the room. She couldn't help fantasizing just a little about what she might do to enhance the moment if it wasn't for Bart and Travis's presence.

Bart sat down next to Travis but turned his body toward Kate. "I hear you have some issues with beer."

"It's more like beer has issues with me."

"When was the last time you tried it?"

"When I was in college."

Bart smiled, showing even white teeth. "So it's safe to say that it's been a couple of years?"

"Absolutely."

"What kind of beer?"

Kate shrugged. "I don't know. What kind do they typically serve in fraternity basements out of red plastic cups?" *Why was this beginning to feel like she was being set up?* "I try not to think of that night. But even though the details are fuzzy, the lasting impression is that it wasn't good."

Travis shook his head. "You know, you seem like the open-minded type. You put up with Culhane, you've stopped staring at my piercings, and yet you're judging all beer based on one bad, unfortunate game of beer pong."

"Believe me, I'd do the same with a rattlesnake, too."

Bart laughed. "It can't have been that bad."

"Okay, no, because I'm still alive." Kate glanced at each of them. "This is some sort of non-beer-drinker intervention, isn't it?"

Nobody answered, but the light of hope continued to shine in their eyes.

"Come on, Kate, what you drank was goat

pi—, uh, urine, compared to what we make," Travis said. "This is craft beer, the nectar of the gods."

"Nectar?"

"Try my peach beer," he said.

The hair on her arms rose. "I'm not so sure about that."

"No peach, then, but at least try something while you're here."

She was, to some degree, a captive audience. And not wholly unwilling, either. It *had* been a lot of years, and there remained the remote possibility that the whole beer incident had grown in her mind. Maybe it hadn't been that truly awful.

"And consider this," Matt said. "I can't move you to the front of the house until you've learned to speak beer. So unless you and Hobart really do want to establish an exclusive relationship, you should give this a shot."

Kate had come to see the downside to dishwashing. Running Hobart meant standing at Hobart. To be a good secret spy, she needed more mobility.

"Okay. Let's do this thing." She looked across the table at Matt's co-conspirators. "I'm assuming you already have this arranged."

"It's going to be an experience to be savored," Bart said as Travis left the table.

Kate looked doubtful. "On my planet, that

would be lounging in a Jacuzzi with a glass of wine and a good book." She could feel Culhane go still next to her, and she thought she should probably stop mentioning anything even remotely involving nakedness. Her imagination had already tossed the book and substituted her boss stripping down and making the tub blissfully crowded.

Matt gently touched Kate's hand. "All beer is made of four basic ingredients."

She drew on her last memory of beer. "Is skunk spray one of them, because that would explain the smell."

"Not even close. We're talking water, barley, hops, and yeast."

Travis returned to the table with a cooler bearing the Depot Brewing steam locomotive logo and a plastic cup. He set the cup in front of Kate and then got busy in the cooler.

"Those are hops," Bart said.

She squinted into the cup. "It looks like rabbit food."

"Check out the scent."

Kate took a whiff and immediately regretted it. The hops smelled like a mix of cheap perfume, soggy dog, and grass blades. She wanted to sneeze, and possibly gag, but could do neither with any measure of diplomacy. Instead, she rubbed the tip of her nose and tried to blink back the extra moisture in her eyes.

Matt fought back a grin. "I get the feeling you're not fond of hops."

Travis lined up three smaller cups. Each was filled with the same grain, but of varying shades. "This is all barley," he said.

"Barley is good. My grandmother made soup from barley."

Matt smiled at her, and she began to relax again.

"Note the lighter and darker colors," Bart said. "Different degrees of roasting will add varying aspects to the beer. When we boil up the wort—"

"The what?" she asked.

"The wort."

"That sounds a little creepy," Kate said. "Like something on a witch's nose."

Culhane laughed. "That's what the boiled mix of barley, hops, and water is called. Brewers make wort. After that's done, the yeast will make the beer."

That, too, brought images to Kate's mind she would have been happy to skip. "Before I get too much scary input, how about if we move along to the tasting?"

Bart reached into the cooler, brought out a bottle of beer, and set a small glass in front of Kate. It was taller and bigger than a shot glass, but not by much. If this was all she had to drink, she just might survive.

Bart handed her the bottle. "This is Dog Day

Afternoon. It was one of Matt's first beers and is still one of the brewery's most popular."

Kate smiled at the label's black pen-and-ink drawing of a goofy hound who was trying to look fierce. "That's the same dog in the mosaic out front of the brewery."

"Chuck's our mascot, even though Matt doesn't bring him around much. He's also Matt's longest lasting relationship . . . so far."

Both Bart and Travis were giving Kate suggestive grins as Travis took the bottle from her and poured for her. Kate focused on the tabletop.

"This is a summer brew," Matt said. "Technically, it's a Kölsch style beer, which you'll need to know when you're on the floor. But really, just think about a beach day when you're ready for some shade and a cool drink."

Kate lifted the glass and tentatively sniffed its contents. She steeled herself. One sip from a Barbie-sized glass couldn't do all that much damage, could it?

"Come on, you can do it," Travis said.

She took a sip, expecting to hate it, but she didn't. In fact, she went for a slightly bolder sip.

"Not half bad," she said. "It's bubbly like soda but not icky sweet."

Matt grinned, obviously proud but trying to keep it under wraps. "It's a good starting point. Low in hops and lower in alcohol than some of the others you'll be trying. Ready to move on?"

"Almost." Kate drained the sample glass. "An unpretentious beer, lightly floral, and of earthy peasant stock."

"You joke, but beer tastings are a big part of how our business has grown," Matt said. "A little less attitude than some wine events, but we have food pairings and tasting notes, too."

"Really?"

"It makes sense if you think about it," Matt said. "What was your first impulse when Travis poured you that sample?"

"To smell it."

"Exactly," Bart said. "Let's try an IPA on her for bouquet."

"IPA?" Kate echoed.

Bart handed her another bottle. This one's label was nearly psychedelic and read Goa for the Gusto.

"India Pale Ale," Bart said. "So called because when the British Empire was at its peak, British ale had to travel a long way to get to Britons. Lots of hops were added to each barrel as a preservative, and the product ended up way different than it started out. It became part of beer history."

Kate handed the bottle back to Travis, who poured her a sample. She lifted her mini-glass and smelled the ale.

"Wow! It smells almost like a sauvignon

blanc . . . all citrus." She drew in deeper. "Like grapefruit, and maybe a little lemon?"

Matt nodded his approval. "Exactly. Like all IPAs."

Emboldened by the so-not-beer aroma, Kate downed half the sample in one swallow, then had to fight not to gag it back up.

"Issues?" Travis asked.

Kate took several deep breaths. "Totally not my style. It tastes nothing like it smells."

She really could have used a food pairing. Something smothered in hot sauce to wipe out the flavors lingering in her mouth would have been dandy.

"For a lot of people, an IPA is an acquired taste," Matt said.

Travis rose and grabbed an empty pitcher from behind his pouring counter.

"Dump," he said.

Kate tipped out the last bit of beer in her glass. "Thank you."

"Technically, hops add both dryness and bitterness," Matt said.

"The bitterness I got. How about a little Dog Day to cleanse my palate?"

Travis gave her a refill. She downed it, then shuddered as the last memory of the Goa left her body.

Matt grabbed another sampling glass and set

another bottle on the table. "Dragonfly Amber Ale. Time to move one step darker in the ales."

"So long as you leave the Chuck beer in easy reaching distance, I'm game," Kate said.

"Dragonfly Amber is the first of my beers to place in judging at the Great American Beerfest," Matt said.

"What's Beerfest?" Kate asked.

Travis's face was heavy with awe. "It's like the Olympics," he said.

Matt poured Kate a sample. "Caramel malted barley, smooth finish, and dry hopped to eliminate bitterness while keeping the dryness in place."

Kate tried a sip and found she had no problem at all with the Dragonfly. "Okay, now *this is* the nectar of the gods," she said.

Travis pumped his fist. "Another beer hater bites the dust."

They moved on to stouts and porters, and Kate loved them all. Clearly, she had misremembered her earlier beer encounter.

Once the guys had finished up with the tasting, they started discussing Travis's recipes. Kate tried to follow the conversation, except she didn't have the background to know whether his autumn pumpkin ale was "cutting edge," as Travis claimed, or "too out there to turn a profit," as Matt contended.

"Is it getting warm in here?" Kate asked.

The men paused in their conversation.

"Not that I've noticed," Matt said.

"Okay. Carry on."

Kate wandered over to the small tasting bar and began leafing through Travis's beer notes and advertising materials. The editor in her quickly returned.

"Does anyone have a pen?" she asked.

All she received in response were blank stares. They had moved on to addressing the level of nutmeg in Travis's brew. No big deal. Her purse, which always held a fistful of pens, was in the truck.

When she returned, she asked the guys, "Mind if I grab another Dog Day?"

"Go for it," Matt said. "We shouldn't be that much longer, though."

She pulled a beer from the cooler and went back to flyspecking Travis's notes. She'd finished her first mini-glass and was pouring her second when Matt joined her at the bar.

"Sorry this is taking so long," he said. "I need to take advantage of the time I can be up here. Travis isn't hot on listening to Bart, so I have to be the enforcer."

"No problem." She slid Travis's brochures closer to Matt. "I've been keeping myself busy. I cleaned up the copy and kicked up the language."

Matt gave her a funny look. "Your face is kind of red. Are you okay?"

"Yes."

Or at least she thought she was. Kate touched a hand to her cheek. She *was* hot. Like a core-temperature-reaching-lethal-range kind of hot.

"I think I'll step outside for a second," she said.

Whatever Matt had to say in return was left in the dust as she bolted toward the door. Once outside, she climbed into Matt's truck and flipped open the passenger's vanity mirror.

"Oh, man!"

The whole beer issue was coming back to her now. That youthful flirtation had ended not because she'd drunk too much and made herself sick, but because beer was her Kryptonite, something akin to severe lactose intolerance.

She wasn't red. She was Chet-colored.

Kate sat back and fanned her face. She knew what was coming next. Her internal temperature would kick up even higher, her stomach would begin to ache, and finally she'd emit a rumbling last heard at Mount St. Helens. She had an hour and more in the truck with Matt on the way back to Keene's Harbor. No way could she pretend for that length of time that she had no idea where those noises might be coming from.

Damn.

Kate hopped from the truck to catch the October wind. If she could cut the heat, maybe she could kill the whole vicious cycle.

"Calm thoughts, cool thoughts," she coached herself as she headed upwind. "You can beat this."

Once she'd made the outer edge of Horned Owl's parking area, she pushed up her long sleeves and held out her arms for optimal wind exposure, slowly rotating like a deranged wind turbine. Still, she could feel sweat collecting between her breasts.

"I am so screwed."

She shot a look at the brewery's door. Thank heaven all was quiet and still. The guys could talk while she cooled. She returned to the truck and used the open passenger door as shield.

Kate pulled her arms from the sweater's sleeves. Inside the sweater's protection, she reached back and unhooked her bra. Those miserable years of middle school gym class had served a purpose, after all. She could still remove her underwear without showing a square inch of skin.

One hot-pink bra with black lace overlay was history in three seconds. Kate chucked it onto the truck's seat, then jammed her arms back through her sleeves.

"Please, please, please," she murmured. Just who outside of her own rebelling body Kate was begging, she didn't know.

Her digestive system emitted a groan that

silenced the chickadees up in the trees. Temptation grew. One polite burp that no one other than her feathered friends would hear might fix the whole issue. But then she flashed back to her last beer episode. She'd been sucked in by that whole "one burp" theory, and the aftermath hadn't been pretty.

She pulled on her sweater's neckline until she got some good air between herself and the knit fabric. Then she took the sweater's bottom, looped it up through the top, and drew it back down. The rig held, even though her posture made a gargoyle look good. She turned and just about smacked into Matt.

"How long have you been standing there?" she asked.

"Long enough," he said. "Do I even want to know?"

"Probably not."

"You've been gone awhile," he said. "Bart and Travis wanted me to come out and check on you."

Which was a lie. They were negotiating the terms of a winner-takes-all arm-wrestling match over the pumpkin brew recipe. A rabid fox dropped into the middle of the room wouldn't have distracted them.

"As you can see, I'm kind of having a problem."

"Either that or you're into some voodoo ritual. What's up with your face, though?"

"My face?" Kate's voice rose an octave in alarm. "What's wrong with my face?"

"You've gone from red to spotty. Is it possible that you have an allergy to something in beer?"

She clamped her hand over her mouth in what he would have said was an expression of shock, except for the way her chest and shoulders heaved.

"You're not going to hurl, are you?" he asked.

Hand still over mouth, she shook her head no.

In Matt's estimation, whatever else was about to happen appeared to be equally bad.

"Hang on," he said. "Let's get you back to town."

She nodded her head a frantic yes.

Matt returned to the barn, where Bart and Travis were going mano a mano.

"I upped the stakes," Bart said without turning his dead-eye glare from Travis. "If Travis loses, he's spending the next month of Wednesdays coming to Keene's Harbor for poker night and then he works for me on Thursdays."

"Sounds good," Matt said. Adding Travis to poker night would bring a new, if warped, dynamic. But Matt had more important stuff to deal with right now. "I've got to head out now. Bart, I'll catch up with you on Monday. Travis, you're not going to take him in any kind of match.

And even if you do, when it comes to your beer, he wins. Got it?"

"Dude, that is so not fair," Travis said.

"When you can pay me back, we'll talk about fair. Until then, it's all about leverage."

Bart slammed Travis's hand to the tabletop, winning the match and illustrating Matt's point.

"Just like that," he said.

Back outside, Matt found Kate waiting for him in the truck. As he climbed into his seat, a pink-and-black bra went flying into the back. He'd witnessed a bra toss before, but not in these circumstances.

"I think it's the hops," he said rather than comment on the projectile. "I've seen it happen to people before—the redness you started out with, at least—just not this bad."

Kate snorted, or maybe wheezed. "Great. Put it on my tombstone. Kate Appleton. Went to hell in a hops basket."

"So you're not feeling any better?"

"I'd give that a no."

He started the truck. "Let's get a move on, then."

"Gently, and unlock my window control, could you?"

They started down the road, Kate with her head out the window and hair rippling in the breeze. And Matt feeling really bad she was so sick but thinking how great she looked with her hair wild, blowing all around her face.

Kate never thought she'd be so grateful to work for a man who'd bought a kitschy, not to mention mostly dilapidated, motel.

"Are you doing okay in there?" Matt called through the bathroom door in the manager's tiny apartment.

Kate was still toweling her hair from the long and chilly shower she'd taken. "Better."

"I'm glad I had the utilities turned back on this week. Sorry there wasn't much hot water."

"It was perfect."

Actually, it had taken a while before she'd felt safe to go near the shower. First had come the belching with enough gusto to win a frat boys' contest. From her side of the bathroom door, she'd heard Matt saying that he'd be taking off for a while. Kate had figured he'd been engaging in chivalry or self-preservation. Either way, he'd missed the worst of the episode.

"I've brought you some stuff I thought you might be able to use," he called.

She opened the bathroom door enough to reach out her arm and grab a plastic sack. "Thanks. That was really nice of you."

Though, again, it still could have been self-preservation. Keene's Harbor remained over an hour away, and her stomach still sounded demonically possessed. Kate riffled through the bag. Antihistamines, as promised, plus antacids.

So much for Matt Culhane ever being tempted by her again, she thought. She was gross—inside and outside. Arms wrapped around her bloated midsection, she regarded her spotty reflection in the bathroom mirror. This was what she wanted, right? Not to have to worry about any hot and messy sexual entanglement that took place outside the privacy of her imagination. Now that she faced that reality, the answer came back an edgy maybe not.

"Can I bring you anything else?" Matt called.

"No, thanks."

After antacids, what was left?

Matt believed in choosing his moments and in letting others choose theirs. When Kate decided to stick on her bug glasses and pretend to sleep most of the way back to Keene's Harbor, he'd respected that choice.

"Hey," he said when she finally stirred.

"Hi."

"Feeling any better?"

"Yes."

"Are you up to having a conversation longer than one syllable?"

"No," Kate said.

"All the same, can I ask you something? Did

that happen to you the last time you drank beer?"

She didn't answer immediately. "Kind of, I think. I mean, I sort of recalled discomfort, but it wasn't this bad."

"In that case, I'm sorry. I never would have asked you to try it if I'd known this was what happened to you."

"My fault. Even with that vague memory, I shouldn't have risked it, except . . ."

"Except what?"

"Except I also did it because *I* wanted to, and because it seemed important to you. I mean, this is what you do. You've got great reason to be proud of all you've accomplished. Then, here I come and turn up my nose. I wanted to be . . . I don't know . . ."

"Nice?"

She sighed. "Yes, nice. You deserve that."

"So do you, Kate."

"I know, but it's been so long. It's like I can hardly recognize it. That long without nice in your life . . . and I don't mean that I was abused or anything . . . it was just the absence of nice. But, anyway, you forget how it feels."

He didn't know where she'd been, other than geographically, before she'd landed in Keene's Harbor. All he knew was that he liked it when she was happy.

"Okay," he said. "So, nice it is. And I'm

moving you to the taproom on Monday. I need to have you someplace where you can keep an eye on Jerry when I'm not there. You were right. He takes off, and I don't know what he's up to. And Laila's going to be out a minimum of this next week with her ankle sprain."

"I can do that," she said.

TEN

Early Monday morning, Kate pulled into Depot Brewing's parking lot. She was exactly on time for the training session Matt wanted to get in before the rest of the staff arrived. Matt, however, was not. With not a heck of a lot else to do, Kate exited her Jeep and meandered toward the building's front entry. She smiled down at the mosaic of Chuck and allowed herself a moment of yearning for Stella. She missed her dog every single day.

Pushing doggie thoughts from her mind, she glanced into the Depot's interior through the narrow window to the right of the front door. The large potted tree in the entry lay on its side. Kate moved closer and peered into the lobby. Opposite the tree, the low table that usually held brochures had been upended. She could have bought one tipped thing as an accident, but not both.

Running on sheer instinct, she pulled on the door's large bronze handle. The door swung outward. And because she was terminally curious, she stepped inside.

"Hello?" She paused to bring the tree upright. "Anyone here?"

Apparently not. She set the table on its feet, scooped up the brochures and replaced them. She also picked up a bit of string or something that the cleaning person must have missed. She tucked that into the front pocket of her khakis, along with a crumpled cocktail napkin. If she was going to tidy up, she might as well do it properly.

As she left the entry, Kate was greeted by a stale beer aroma she'd last smelled in Bagger's Tavern. Except unlike Bagger's, this place was all clean slate, wood, and ceramic tile. There was no obnoxiously absorbent carpet to be found.

Kate followed her nose to the taproom.

"This is *so* not good."

Every table and chair had been flipped. Beer was running, but with no pitcher or pilsner glass to catch the brew. She sprinted behind the bar and realized that not only had the taps been left running but every keg had been shot full of holes. A note had been spray painted on the mirror behind the bar in giant red letters: *You're Next.*

One foot hit where the rubber mats should

have been, but weren't. Momentum carried her forward. The wet floor brought her feet out from beneath her. And then she went down. Hard.

Kate wasn't the most predictable woman on Earth. Still, Matt felt pretty sure if her Jeep was in the lot, she couldn't be too far away.

"Kate?" he called before he unlocked the brewery's employee door.

No answer. Odd, he thought. She wasn't in her Jeep, she wasn't waiting at the door, and she hadn't answered his call. He was hit with a shot of protective male concern. He walked from the kitchen down the short hall, being drawn to a sound he'd caught plenty before, but never at this hour. A beer tap was spitting, then blowing. He hustled to the taproom and stopped dead at the bar's back side.

"What the—"

Kate sat propped on her elbows, feet splayed out in front of her.

She looked up at him. "It's a little swampy back here."

"Are you okay?" he asked.

"Everything but my tailbone and dignity. I was just working my way back to my feet."

"Let me help you."

Matt scooped her up and held her tight to his body. He reached around her with his free arm and pushed each of the eight beer taps back into their closed positions. The act was a formality, since all the barrels were now drained. No wonder Kate had gone down. The keg system's drains couldn't handle the volume, and that floor was damn slick.

"You're soaked," he said.

"Half of me, at least."

He grabbed a clean bar towel from the stack on the counter and began to mop her off. He was somewhere in the vicinity of her backside when she took the towel from him.

"I think I can handle it from here," she said.

"Sorry," he said, but not with a whole lot of repentance.

She smiled. "So I see. You might want to grab a towel for yourself now, too."

"I've smelled like beer before," he said, but wiped his hands just the same. After he tossed the towel back to the counter, he gestured at the floor. "Sorry about this."

Kate gestured toward the vandalized mirror. "The note is what's really freaked me out. Is this the first time the saboteur's ever targeted you personally?"

Matt shrugged. "Yeah. This is sort of new."

"Well, personally, I can't wait to have a chat with the jerk who did this," Kate said. "But right now, I'm wet and gross-smelling. I'd like to go home and change before we start my training."

"No training today," Matt said. "We'll start fresh tomorrow."

"I don't want to lose a day over a bruised butt. How about if I go home and get cleaned up? I'll come back at lunchtime and observe for the afternoon. It's not going to do me or you any good to have me sit home."

"True," he said. "Are you okay to drive?"

"Yes. I'll take some extra towels so I don't soak my seat."

Once he had Kate safely to her Jeep and on her way, Matt pulled out his cell phone and called in the law. Ten minutes later, just as he'd finished mopping the spilled beer, Lizzie arrived.

Lizzie surveyed the taproom. "Someone sure was busy."

She set her clipboard down and pulled a digital camera from her uniform pocket. "I'm going to take a few pics."

"No problem."

"So tell me what you know," she said between shots.

Matt looked at the messed-up room and felt his frustration surge.

"Kate and I were going to meet here at seventhirty. She got here first, found the front door unlocked, and the mess inside. Beer was freepouring in here. She went behind the bar to catch the taps and fell. The mats were still rolled from the floor mopping last night, and the back of the bar had standing beer."

Lizzie pocketed the camera and picked up her clipboard. "The front door is usually locked, right?"

"Yes, unless someone screws up in a major way."

"Who has keys?"

Matt righted a café table. "Jerry, Bart, Laila, and I. No one else that I'm aware of. I closed last night, and I know for sure I locked that door, which means someone else has a copy."

"Or Jerry, Bart, or Laila were here just a little while ago," she said as she jotted notes.

"Laila's down with an ankle sprain from Friday night, so she's out. You can check with Bart and Jerry, but neither of them had reason to be here. Though Jerry isn't exactly up for employee of the month at the moment."

"What's up with Jerry?"

Matt picked up a chair. "I've been told that he's been leaving work when I'm not around. It could mean something, or it could mean nothing at all."

"Told by who?" Lizzie asked.

"Kate. She'll be back here at lunchtime if you want to talk to her. She's pretty sharp. I trust her observations."

"Okay, but why didn't someone else on staff tell you about Jerry before this?"

Matt shrugged. "I don't know for sure, but

most everyone has been around for a long time. This place is family, and just like we did when we were kids, these guys tend to cover for one another. Which is why I don't want to believe that Jerry would sabotage the bar. We've been friends for too long."

"You don't have any real enemies, Matt," Lizzie said. "No matter who did this, it's going to be bad news, once we find out."

All the same, Matt wanted it done.

Lunch rush had arrived, and Kate was settled in at the taproom bar. She was one in a long line of females, most of whom were watching Matt pour beer as though he were making gold from lead.

Really, what was the big deal with beer pouring? And how had the jungle drums gotten word out so quickly that Matt was behind the bar? Kate figured they must have a calling tree or something.

"Just water for me, Matt, and a veggie quesadilla. Do you think you could make that with whole wheat tortillas and goat cheese?" asked a dark-haired female three women down.

"How about organic carrot juice?" asked the girl next to her. "Do you have any of that, Matt?"

He answered each of their questions in the negative, but with a style Kate envied. The next time around the rebirth wheel (if the reincarnationists were right), she hoped for a dollop of that charm. If she'd had to tell those women no, they'd be howling for the manager. Or Matt. Because he was all they wanted, anyway.

Kate took a sip of her iced tea and paged through the microbrewery's training manual. The chart of which glass to use with which beer was proving a little complex for her current attention span. She never would have thought that beer and a snifter could go together, but that weird combo was the least of her issues.

Kate's tailbone had begun to ache, and her pride still stung. Before she'd showered and returned to work, she'd retrieved the crumpled white cocktail napkin and the short bit of thin, braided string she'd picked up from the floor and stuck into her pocket. Those two items were the only clues she had. Until she was sure they wouldn't trigger some sort of *aha!* moment, they would rest in her dresser's top drawer.

"Kate, right?" said a voice from behind her.

Kate looked over her shoulder.

"I'm Liz Culhane, but everyone calls me Lizzie," the woman said. "I'm also Matt's sister."

Kate smiled. "Right. I saw you talking to Matt the night of the karaoke contest."

"I was a little more casually dressed then." Lizzie nodded to her police officer's uniform. "Mind if I join you?"

"Not at all."

Lizzie took the stool next to Kate. "It's nice to finally meet you."

"Finally?"

"My brother mentioned you the other night at dinner."

"Really?" Kate had tried to sound cool. She wasn't so sure she'd pulled it off.

"Yeah, in a Matt sort of way. Not with a whole lot of detail."

"Oh." Kate glanced at Matt. Though he was pouring a pitcher of beer, she could tell he was listening.

"And I also know you took a spill this morning," Lizzie said.

"I did, but I'm okay." Kate noted the other woman's clipboard. "I take it we're talking officially rather than personally?"

Lizzie smiled. "A little of both, I think."

Matt greeted his sister and set a glass of ice water on a coaster in front of her, then moved on to suggest items actually on the menu to the dark-haired woman, whose name was apparently Lana.

"On the official front, I'd like to ask you a couple of questions," Lizzie said to Kate.

"No problem."

"Matt said you got here before him. Was there anybody else around or leaving the Depot area when you arrived?"

"The last person I saw was Junior Greinwold walking down Keene Avenue with Harley Bagger. Otherwise, no one, which I'm coming to understand is pretty common this time of year."

Lizzie nodded. "It's quiet, which makes something like what's happened around here really stand out. And what frustrates me is that this building is like fingerprint soup. Even though it's the cleanest restaurant I've ever seen, it's still a public place. People are in and out all day long. Lifting prints would be pointless."

Kate nodded in agreement. "You know it's been more than the Dumpster fire and the vandalism, right?"

"Matt told me about some other events . . . flat tires, stolen supplies, and the open walk-in cooler."

"Plus the iffy Depot beer at Bagger's, though I have no idea if that was actually related. It's how I landed here, though. Harley fired me, and Matt hired me."

"Really? I thought he'd hired you because you two are involved."

A redhead one seat down from Lizzie aimed a surprised look Kate's way. Kate ignored it and focused on Matt's multitasking skills.

"How does he do that?" Kate asked Lizzie.

"ADD," she replied. "Mom always said Matt was either going to spend his life with a million tasks half done or learn to run the world." Her smile, so similar to her brother's, held a ton of pride. "It looks like he's taken the world-running route."

And he looked damn fine while doing it, too.

"Okay," Lizzie said. "One last official ques-

tion for you. I know it's unlikely, since you
haven't been back in Keene's Harbor very long,
but is there anyone here who could have a grudge
against you? Is it possible that yesterday's incident wasn't aimed at Matt at all?"

"From what Matt has told me, no one other
than Jerry knew that Matt and I were going to
be in early. I'm not tops on Jerry's list, but he
wouldn't endanger his job to get rid of me. Beyond that, I've kind of been on the fringes of
things since I came to town. Nobody much knows
me. I don't think I've even had the opportunity to
tick anyone off besides Deena Bowen, and I get
the sense that it's not personal in her case. She's
angry at the world."

"You've got that one half right. She might be
ticked off at the world, but she saves a lot of her
ammo for Matt. I think after Friday night, you
could have moved into target range."

"Do you mean by singing in the karaoke competition? That doesn't make sense."

"It does. I saw the way Matt was looking at
you while you sang," Lizzie said. "And if I saw it
from the side of the stage, guaranteed Deena
saw it from backstage."

Kate glanced down the bar, where Lana was
stroking the bar's laminated surface while talking to Matt.

She rolled her eyes at Lizzie. "Paging Captain
Oblivious."

Lizzie followed Kate's line of vision. "It's always been like that for him. The less he pays attention, the more blatant they become. Growing up with him in the house and the high school versions of Lana at the door was weirdly entertaining. If nothing else, it gave me a good perspective on how I didn't want to be around boys."

"No doubt."

"Hey," Lizzie said. "This is kind of spur of the moment, but would you like to come have dinner at my parents' with me tomorrow? It's Spaghetti Tuesday, which means it's a family tradition that we drag along friends. My mom makes a salad and a huge pot of spaghetti. If it all gets eaten, great. If not, my sisters and I have leftovers to take home."

"What about Matt?" Kate asked, and just as she did, he came to stand in front of them.

"Matt's our backwoods recluse when he's not at work. He never comes to Spaghetti Tuesday."

Matt looked at Kate. "Contrary to what my sister says, I'm not a hermit. I'd actually been planning on spaghetti night. How about if I pick you up?"

Kate put her hand on the smooth bar surface and quickly pulled it back. "Sure."

"Great. I'll be there at six."

"See?" Lizzie said to him. "You're dating!"

A gasp rose along the girls' all-star admiration line, then all eyes turned to scrutinize Kate. In the space of thirty seconds, she'd gone from being unknown to notorious. But for spaghetti, family, and time with Matt Culhane, she'd deal. And happily, too.

Just before five that evening, Kate walked into the post office. She smiled at the sweeping stairway to nowhere, created when the building's second floor had been roped off due to declining town population. Despite the passage of time, the interior of the ornate sandstone and yellow brick building was like a trip back to the early 1900s. Or maybe just to high school, considering the way Deena Bowen was giving Kate the stinkeye as she approached.

Deena stepped away from the wall of brass and glass-fronted post office boxes.

"Hey," she said.

Kate had never heard that one syllable delivered with more crankiness.

"I hear you're going out with Matt," Deena said.

Kate wasn't going to get into the technical aspects of whether a family spaghetti dinner qualified as a date. She worked up what she hoped was a noncommittal shrug and moved on to her mailbox.

"He'll dump you. Just wait and see," Deena called after her.

Kate didn't plan to get to the dating point, let alone the dumping point. She let the comment roll off and turned her attention to the accumulation of mail in The Nutshell's box.

"Junk, bill . . . more junk," she said as she pulled items from the tight space. "And . . . trouble."

Her mother's custom periwinkle linen stationery was unmistakable, as was her perfect cursive script—written with a black ink fountain pen, of course. So long as the letter wasn't directed to her, Kate found it cool that her mom kept up the dying art of handwritten correspondence. But when *Ms. Katherine Appleton* appeared on the address line, the envelope was often stuffed with ego-crushers. Not that Kate thought her mom meant to do that, but the end result remained the same.

Kate closed the box and took her load to the counter behind her for sorting. She dropped the catalogues filled with goods she couldn't afford into the recycling bin, tucked the electric bill into her purse, and opened her mom's letter. In the past, many of Mom's messages were like bikini waxes: best finished quickly.

The first few lines were about the weather and her mother's golf game. Then Mom offered a little chitchat about Kate's brother and sister and their respective brilliant toddler offspring, which led into the true purpose of the letter.

As I dream of Ivy League educations for my grandchildren, her mother wrote, *I can't help but feel a moment's sorrow that you didn't follow a more financially secure path. A business degree would have allowed for far more stability than a degree in the arts. It's a different world than when I was your age, Kate.*

"Doing what? Accounting?" Kate said to herself. She was fine with basic addition and subtracting, especially if she had a calculator. Start placing numbers in labeled columns, though, and she was a lost cause.

Kate had chosen the small liberal arts college her mom had attended, and it had been a good fit. She figured the love of history and art was something in her genes, something that she had inherited from her mother, but her mother might be right about changing times. Kate admitted to herself that she was struggling career-wise.

Ella joined Kate at the counter. "I've come to offer you safe passage." She hitched her thumb at Deena. "She seems to be lurking."

"No biggie. I'm getting pretty good with the end run when it comes to Deena, but I'm still not so good with this stuff."

Ella smiled and tapped the letter, which lay on the counter, just begging to be read to the very end. "Pretty handwriting, but I'm guessing it's not from a great-aunt leaving you a fortune?"

"It's from my mother, offering her perspective

on where I went wrong. It seems I should have gotten a business degree in college."

Ella shook her head. "But you hate numbers."

"You know that, and I know that, but Mom considers it a trifle in the Appleton scheme for world domination."

"And yet you read on."

"Yes. Because my mom is probably right."

Ella pulled the letter from the counter.

Kate made a grab for it. "Hey!"

Ella held the letter in the air above Kate's shorter grasp.

"Seriously," Ella said. "I'm taking custody of this. I've known you since we were kids. That means I also know how good you are at beating yourself up whenever your mother makes a comment, no matter how well intended. What constructive thing would come from finishing this letter right now?"

"I could learn something."

Ella handed her the letter. "Learn something later. Put off reading the rest of the letter and come with me for loaded nachos at Bagger's. It'll be just like the old days. We can pig out, then go home and sleep."

Kate stuck the letter in her purse. "So long as I get extra sour cream and guacamole, it's a deal," Kate said.

ELEVEN

MATT WASN'T WHOLLY ANTI-TRADITION. FOR EXAMPLE, he got a real kick out of Christmas, especially now that Maura had given him twin nieces to spoil and had another baby on the way. Thanksgiving was a winner, too, since his dad and he had a turkey hunting contest each year. Spaghetti Tuesdays, however, had to die.

The rite had started in junior high, and he'd always been on the losing side. Even when he was backed up by half the football team, they were no match for his sharp-witted sisters. Over the years, Matt had developed empathy for those poor, wild Thanksgiving birds looking down the barrel of a shotgun. It had been a while since he'd attended Spaghetti Tuesday, but he had no delusions. His sisters would cut him no slack. And heaven help Kate if she wasn't on her toes. His sisters weren't mean, but they were mercilessly honest.

"Let me know the second you start feeling tired, and I'll get you out of here," he said to Kate as they approached the house.

"I appreciate the sentiment, but we're not even inside yet."

"The offer still stands."

She laughed. "Come on, Matt. How bad can it be?"

"It all depends on whether you're the diner or the main course."

They reached the porch, and Matt held the door open for Kate. The sounds of laughter and conversation rolled from the back of the house, along with the scents of garlic and spices from his mom's amazing spaghetti sauce.

Kate ran a hand over the oak banister that had been scratched and worn by generations of tough Culhane kids. "This house is awesome," Kate said.

"It is." Matt ushered her past the entry, through the living room and into the dining room, where everyone always tended to gather.

All eyes turned their way. Matt could feel Kate hesitate. He didn't blame her. His sisters were quite the crew.

"Everyone, this is Kate. Kate, this is . . . everyone."

His mother laughed and approached them. "Matthew. Have you lost all your manners?"

Matt gave his mom a hug. "I just didn't want Kate to feel like there's a quiz at the end of the introductions."

Matt's mom smelled of the rich, flowery perfume she'd worn for as long as he could remember. She looked great, too. Her silver-threaded dark hair had been twisted into a knot, and while her khakis and blue sweater were standard mom-clothes, she wore them with flair.

She held out a hand to Kate. "I'm Matt's mother, Mary, and you're Kate Appleton. I remember you as a youngster. You were such a cute little thing with all those blond ringlets!"

Kate shook his mom's hand. "It's a pleasure to meet you, Mrs. Culhane."

"Please, call me Mary."

"Okay." Kate handed Matt's mom the shiny gift bag she'd been tightly gripping. "I brought a little something. It's not much, but my mother taught me never to arrive with empty hands."

His mom pulled a bottle of Chianti from the bag and laughed. "This is exactly what Barb would have brought, too."

Kate's eyes widened. "You know my mother?"

"Of course. It's been years since we've had the opportunity to spend any real time together, though. Back before we all got too busy with children and life, there was a group of us that would get together at Bagger's now and then during the summer." She smiled. "In fact, I recall one night when your mother and I had a contest to see who could get the most tips while dancing on table-tops."

Kate was dumbfounded. "My mom? At Bagger's?"

Matt's mom nodded. "Harley's place was very different in those days. It was the trendy spot to go, like Matt's is today." She gave Matt's arm a little pat.

Matt liked that his mom was proud of him. He was proud of her, too. "Are you thirsty, Kate?" he asked.

His mom eased into hostess mode. "We have water, milk, soft drinks, coffee, tea, wine—and Patrick, my husband—he's out back with the men—mixes a mean dirty martini."

"Thanks for the offer, but a soft drink would be perfect."

"I'll be right back. Matt, introduce your sisters before the other guests arrive and it gets too con-fusing." Matt's mom gave Kate a sunny smile. "You know, I'm so happy Matt decided to bring a girl along. It's been forever!"

He just hadn't had the right incentive, Matt thought. For Kate, though, he'd be willing to do a year of Spaghetti Tuesdays. And that was just for starters.

*   *   *

Matt turned to the family table, where a hugely pregnant woman—and Kate thought that in the very kindest of ways—sat with a woman identical to her, except for the burgeoning belly. Opposite them sat Lizzie and a twentysomething woman with wildly curly light brown hair.

"Kate, you know Lizzie," Matt said. "Next to her is Rachel, and across from them are my sisters Anne and Maura. Maura's the—"

"Don't you dare say I'm fat," Maura cut in, then winced. "Sorry, rogue hormones. I know I'm only having one this time, but I swear I feel like it could be three. Especially today. Just call me Supercrank."

"I was going to say that you're the oldest among us, but I'm guessing that wouldn't have scored me any points, either," Matt said.

Maura smiled. "Not a one."

"Maura and Anne are twins. I was born next, Lizzie eleven months after me, and then Rachel last."

"We surrounded him," Anne said.

Kate had no doubt that they had . . . and still did to this day.

"Where are Todd and Jack?" Matt asked.

"Outside," Lizzie said. "Hiding, I think." She focused on Kate. "Todd and Jack are Maura and Anne's husbands, respectively. They have coming to Spaghetti Tuesday but never really making it into the house down to an art."

Kate sat in the open chair in front of her.

"If you want to go hang outside with the guys, that's fine," she said to Matt.

"No way. I don't trust anyone at this table not to fill you with lies about my youth."

Rachel leaned forward, smiling conspiratorily at Kate. "Lies? Why would we have to bother with that when the truth is so entertaining?"

Matt smiled. "See what I mean? I'm going to go grab a beer." He shot Rachel a mock stern look. "Try not to do too much damage while I'm gone."

"So," Anne said as soon as Matt had moved off. "Word at the market is that you and Matt went away for the weekend."

Kate wondered if she was going to have to post a notice on the market bulletin board disclosing the truth of her nonrelationship with Matt.

"We were up in Traverse City for a day, but it was just business," she said.

"Business?" Maura asked. "What business does Matt have in Traverse City?"

Yikes! She'd screwed up already. But in her defense, she never would have thought that his family didn't know what he was doing.

"Well, sort of business. There were a couple of brewpubs he wanted to check out . . . a little comparison shopping, you know? Anyway, he asked me to go along. It was just a day trip."

"I don't know," Rachel said. "It sounds like a date to me."

Kate shook her head. "Trust me, it wasn't. I'm not dating right now, anyway."

"Why?" Maura asked.

"Maura! It's none of our business," Anne said. "But don't let that stop you if you feel like answering, Kate."

Kate laughed. She liked these women. In just minutes, she'd grown more comfortable with them than she was with her own sister, Bunny. Of course, Kate wasn't in the position of constantly being held up for comparison to the Culhane sisters, as she was to Bunny. And despite the goofy name her sister chose to go by in lieu of Barbara, Bunny was one fierce competitor: top of her class, rainmaker in her law firm, and very strategically married. Kate had never measured up especially well.

And Mary Culhane's story of Kate's periwinkle-stationery-loving mother dancing on a tabletop had been a mindblower. Her family had been all about proper manners and proper clothing and proper country clubs and schools back in Grosse Pointe. The idea of Barb Appleton table dancing was as improbable as Kate becoming an astronaut.

Right now, Kate might as well have been on Mars. No, not Mars. This place was warmer and a whole lot more hospitable, but still just as foreign.

"I got divorced about a year ago. After that, I

decided until I get the rest of my life in order, dating can wait. Plus, I tend to make some pretty atrocious decisions when it comes to men. I've got a whole lot of stupid to figure out."

"Matt's not an atrocious decision," Lizzie said.

Kate gave a little involuntary smile. Lizzie was right. "Well, anyway, my life definitely isn't in order."

Matt returned from the kitchen with his beer and a tall glass of cola for Kate, then rounded the table to take the open chair at its head. "That's my motto: Matt Culhane—he's not atrocious."

Lizzie laughed. "So just how much of our conversation did you catch?"

"Enough." He took a swallow of his beer. "And to save Kate further embarrassment—and you guys a whole lot of extra snooping around—I do have a few business things going on in Traverse City. Remember that Tropicana Motor Inn that Mom and Dad would take us to?"

"Yes," all the sisters chimed.

"I just wrapped up a purchase and renovation deal on it."

Anne raised her eyebrows in amazement. "You bought the motel with the hokey flamingos painted on it? Now, *that* is an atrocious decision."

Maura scowled. "I like those flamingos!"

"So do I," Matt said. "The place was sitting vacant, so I picked it up. And I'm just sharing this with you so you'll get off Kate's case about the two of us dating. And no more commentary about my flamingos or my dating choices, or I'll start dredging up your old dates."

Everyone was silent. No one wanted to discuss their dating history. It was Lizzie who changed the subject.

"Hey, isn't that annual beer festival thing in Royal Oak coming up in a couple of weeks? You should take Kate along."

Kate's somewhat homesick heart jumped. "Royal Oak? Really? I used to live there."

Matt nodded. "I remember you mentioning that."

He turned to Lizzie. "I'm going, but I have my usual road crew coming along."

"The groupies?" Lizzie asked.

"They're not groupies," Matt said, then gazed at his beer's label. Kate supposed he was just admiring his dog's smiling likeness.

"They follow you from event to event on their own money for the privilege of pouring your beer and hanging your banner. If that doesn't make them groupies, I don't know what does."

"There is the sexual connotation," Rachel said. "I don't think that applies." She paused, then added, "My university is teaching a class on the Grateful Dead as part of its cultural anthropology curriculum. Groupies would be an interesting topic, too."

"Rachel is working on her master's degree," Anne said to Kate.

Matt looked just a little annoyed. "All the same, they're not groupies. The thought of Harley and Junior as groupies could mess up a perfectly normal guy for life."

"I could pour your beer and hang your banner," Kate said.

"Actually, you can't pour his beer off-site since you work for him," Lizzie said before Matt could speak. "It's against state law for microbrewers."

Rachel pointed her finger at Lizzie. "Exactly. Which is why Matt has the groupies. Or sometimes one of us goes along, but with Maura due any second now, we're not up for a road trip."

"Other than Harley and Junior, who are your roadies, if I'm not allowed to call them groupies?" Lizzie asked.

"Mayor Mortensen and a couple of others have mentioned they'll be there, though they plan to catch a Pistons game, too, so I'm not sure how much actual pouring help they'll be."

"I could at least hang your banner," Kate said.

Anne smiled. "That definitely sounded suggestive."

"Okay, here's another thought," Kate said. "I could sell Depot Brewing merchandise."

"I don't bring merchandise," Matt said.

"You should," Kate told him. "If you sold

hats and tees downstate, you could really get your name out there."

He nodded. "I'm betting you're right."

"Where in Royal Oak is the event?" she asked.

"In the Farmers' Market building, downtown."

"I used to work a few blocks east of there, on Washington Avenue."

"One street away from most of the restaurants and bars, right?" Matt asked.

"Exactly."

"They've mixed it up some this year with a private charity party thrown in on Friday night. Great for them, but I lose my whole day on Friday now, since I have to be set up earlier."

"So an extra set of hands would be good. I could help."

Kate wanted this so much, and not just to see Royal Oak, either. Kate wanted to be with Matt.

"I'd like that," Matt said, and their eyes held for a long moment.

"But really, guys. They're not dating. Not even a little bit," Lizzie said in a deadpan voice. "Can't you tell?"

Maura made an odd sound. "Okay, and I'm about to be not pregnant. Not even a little bit."

"What do you mean?" Lizzie asked.

Maura settled a hand on her belly. "I've been trying to be cool about it, but all of a sudden my contractions are getting pretty aggressive."

Matt stood up. "Contractions, as in labor?"

"Bingo. I thought it was just Braxton Hicks lead-up stuff, or we would have stayed home. After all, who wants to disrupt a perfectly good Spaghetti Tuesday?" She closed her eyes for a moment and blew out a slow breath. "Guess I was wrong. If this is anything like last time, it's going to be fast. Lizzie, could you go outside and round up Todd?"

"Sure," Lizzie replied, then headed out through the kitchen doorway.

"You can still take the girls for the night as we'd planned, right, Anne? They're upstairs playing in my old room."

Anne pushed back in her chair. "No problem. Let me get Jack and we'll go take care of things at your house."

Lizzie reappeared with a tall, dark, and semi-worried-looking guy Kate knew had to be Maura's husband.

He rounded the table and took Maura by the hand. "I told you those contractions were the real deal, babe. Your suitcase is in the trunk, right?"

"Todd, this is Kate. Kate, this is Todd," Maura said.

Kate had to give Maura major props for having good manners during childbirth. She doubted she'd be able to show the same grace.

"Nice to meet you," Todd said to Kate, but his eyes never left his wife.

Kate gazed at the empty doorway after Todd and Maura left the room, smiling at each other, holding hands, and Kate realized she'd wanted that love and connection when she'd fallen for her ex. She might not have gotten it quite right back then, but she recognized a solid relationship when she saw one.

When she glanced away, she caught Matt watching her, and the warmth in his eyes had her heart skipping beats.

Matt's mom leaned her head out of the kitchen, ending the moment before Kate was quite ready to have it over. "Matt, could you and Kate take care of putting away dinner before you come over to the hospital?"

And then, suddenly the house was empty of Culhanes, except for Matt.

They moved into the kitchen, and Matt began putting plates away. "This is a new twist on Spaghetti Tuesday."

Kate helped him with the plates. There was something intimate about the two of them being alone in the house, she thought. A little exciting, too.

"Silverware goes in the drawer second down from the end," Matt said.

They worked in silence for a minute or so, then he asked, "So you've seen my crew. What's yours like?"

"Smaller. Different."

"Any sisters?" Matt asked while digging through the contents of a lower cupboard.

"One sister and one brother. Bunny and Chip."

"Seriously, those are their names?"

"Well, actually Barb and Larry, just like my mom and dad. Everyone calls them Bunny and Chip to save confusion." She pointed to a harvest gold–colored plastic bowl filled with salad greens. "Do you know where the top to this is?"

He rummaged through the bottom drawer, then paused to look up at her. "So among you summer people, when do adults become too old for names like that?"

"Never. The same holds true in the townie set. Witness Junior Greinwold."

Matt laughed. "Point taken."

He handed her the bowl's lid. "So how'd you luck out and end up without a nickname?"

Kate returned the salad to the fridge. "It was a near miss. Since mom and dad had already used up their own names, they could have moved on to the family parakeet's."

"Which was?"

"Spike."

Matt smiled. "I kind of like it. I think there might be some Spike in you. Remember, I saw you take down the fire chief," Matt said. "That was definitely a Spike moment."

Kate squelched a groan. "What should I do with the garlic bread?"

He handed her a box of aluminum foil. "How about if we take the bread and spaghetti to the hospital crew? I know Maura thinks this is going be fast, but I remember what it was like in that waiting room last time." He smiled. "All the same, it's totally worth the wait."

Kate hesitated in her wrapping.

"What?" he asked. "Maybe just the spaghetti should go?"

"No, definitely the garlic bread. But how about if I just help you get things packaged up? I'd feel a little intrusive being there. I mean, Maura and I just met."

Kate loved what she had seen of the Culhanes, but whatever she and Matt had going on between them didn't make her family.

"Huh. I guess I wasn't looking at it that way," Matt said. "I was thinking more about how I'd like you to be there."

"You would?"

He came closer and tipped up her chin so that their eyes met. "I like being with you. I like having you next to me. Haven't you figured that out yet?" Matt lowered his mouth to hers and brushed a light kiss across her lips.

TWELVE

KATE HAD BECOME A HUMAN BATTLEFIELD. TEN DAYS OF excitement over heading home to Royal Oak warred with ten nights' worth of nervous insomnia produced by the same trip. She'd been tempted to go with Matt to the hospital or his bedroom or wherever their kiss might lead, but in the end, she had him drop her off at her house before he went to find Maura and the rest of his family. The sun hadn't completely risen when Matt pulled up The Nutshell's drive. Kate, however, had been packed and ready for a good couple of hours. Preloaded with caffeine, she was waiting by the front door with her suitcase in hand. Matt exited the truck, took the suitcase, and stuck it in the backseat.

Matt opened the passenger door. "Do you want to lock up the house?"

"I can't lock it. I don't think we've had keys since my parents bought the place. All I can do is dead-bolt it from the inside. Let's just go."

"I don't want to be an alarmist, but since I just changed the locks at the brewery and hired a night guard, I'm tuned in to security issues. Keene's Harbor's a great place, but we have our share of crazies, too."

"All under control. *Avanti*."

Matt glanced at Kate. She was really ready. Almost too ready. "Is everything okay?"

Kate fidgeted in her seat. "Everything is perfectly under control."

The front door burst open and two or three workmen in hazmat jumpsuits ran out the door waving their arms frantically, screaming jibberish. Matt watched as they ran to the back of Kate's house and jumped into the lake.

Matt got out of his car and walked up to Kate's front door. There was a faint buzzing coming from inside her house.

He peeked inside the window. The entire living room was completely stripped of drywall, down to its studs. An angry swarm of bees filled a section of the exposed wall.

Matt walked back to the car and started up the engine. "Umm, Kate?"

"My house is completely filled with bees, isn't it?"

Matt nodded. "Maybe not completely filled.

Some of the space is taken up with honey. I'm sure it will all be gone by the time we get back. Do you know what all this is costing? Are you sure you don't . . ."

"I know exactly what I'm doing. Just drive."

As Matt started down the road, Kate ran a mental tabulation of the damage and its cost. Two thousand to fix the leaky plumbing. Two thousand to fix the bathroom tile. Three thousand for the mold cleanup and another five thousand to replace the drywall and damaged floor. She wasn't sure how much bee removal cost. And she owed Matt at least $9,000 on the mortgage. If she didn't get the house fixed by Christmas, her parents were turning it over to Matt, and if she didn't get Matt paid by Thanksgiving, he was going to foreclose.

Matt sensed her thoughts and patted her leg with one hand. "Remember. Just one foot after the other."

Good advice, she thought. Panic was counterproductive.

"Run me through what we need to get done once we're in Royal Oak," Kate said. "I've already double-checked the boxes of merchandise and found one of those old-fashioned thingies to run credit card slips through. You don't want to lose the credit sales. And I really think we should have brought the hoodies along with the tees. It's autumn, after all."

Matt said nothing, but handed her a travel mug filled with coffee.

What's next?" Kate asked.

"You tell me," Matt said. "You're my snoop. Anything new on that front?"

"Not a thing. Taproom work is harder than I thought. Servers are too busy to be good snoops. I did notice something about your menu, though. Who put it together?"

Matt lifted his mug from its holder. "I worked with a friend who used to be a regional manager for an upper-end chain."

"A woman?"

He took a swallow of coffee. "Yes, why?"

"Did you date her and dump her?"

Matt's eyebrows went up a fraction of an inch. "No."

"You must have ticked her off, at least. You have no fresh vegetables anywhere on your menu, aside from your iceberg wedge smothered in blue cheese dressing. Oh, and the mango poppy seed coleslaw, but don't get me started on that."

"No one else has complained."

"The customers who care the most are women—not your standard breed of beer lovers. And those women would eat fish bait if it gave them a chance at contact with you."

"What are you talking about?"

"Your lunchtime fan club. They know your

schedule better than you do. Haven't you noticed the daily lineup?"

"I see them. They're nice people, but I'm not
interested. And it's no big deal. Don't you see
the way men look at you?"

Kate laughed. "No. I'm pretty pragmatic about
my looks."

"And they are?"

"I don't know. . . . Kind of cute, I guess."

Matt glanced over at her.

"You're beautiful. And if you've missed men
checking you out, I'll start letting you know
when it happens. Like now. The more we're together, the harder it is for me to keep my hands
off you."

Desire rushed through Kate's belly and she
admitted to herself that she didn't want Matt to
keep his hands off her. She took a beat to steady
her voice. "Getting back to the vegetables. Do
you have something against them?"

"No, in fact I like vegetables. Especially French
fries."

She let that sit for a couple of miles and moved
on to another topic. "You can never go home
again. . . . Any idea who said that?" Kate asked.

"Nope."

"Well, I'm thinking it's true. You can't."

"Maybe for that unnamed person," Matt said.
"But I do it every day. In fact, except for a short
break long ago, I haven't left."

"Exactly. But I did, and now I'm returning. Today."

"And?"

"The magazine I used to work for will be there," she said. "The places I used to go will be there, and life will have rolled on without me. I'm going to be like a ghost."

"You look real to me."

Kate smiled. "But not to them."

Matt shook his head. "Kate, you've been in Keene's Harbor, not Brigadoon or whatever. You've made friends, found a job, even brewed up a little trouble, so it seems to me, you're doing great."

"The guy who took my job, he's got my office. And then there's Shayla the Homewrecker."

"Who?"

Kate gave a dismissive wave of her hand. "The woman my ex ran off with. She has my old bed, my ex, and even my dog. They all have lives, and I've been in a holding pattern. I don't have a clue what to do next."

He cut his eyes to her. "I'd suggest switching to decaf."

Kate realized she'd been jiggling her left foot at close to the speed of light.

"Kate, seriously, it's all going to be fine."

"But how can you say that? How do you know?"

"Experience, for one. And two, you're not the

kind of woman to let opportunity pass you by.
But that doesn't mean you need to dwell on
things. How about you look at your time in
Keene's Harbor as a gift? How about you slow
down and appreciate the present? The best I can
figure, the future takes care of itself."

"Nice philosophy, but I've seen how hard you
work."

"I'm not saying I don't."

"I need a plan," she said.

He looked her way again. "Eventually you do,
but not right now. There are no rules. There aren't
any Plan Police waiting to nab you. Give yourself
a break."

"Hmm," Kate said, liking the thought. No
plan. She could live with that. And truth was,
she didn't miss her old bed or her old job or her
ex, but there was a hole in her heart for her dog.
She desperately missed her dog.

Matt stepped back and took a look at the Depot
Brewing Company booth. It was, as it should be,
perfect. He and the road crew had set it up enough
times in the past. It had taken some adjusting—
and another table—to create Kate's merchandise
area, but Matt considered it effort well spent. He
should have started doing this sooner.

He also wished at least a couple of his sisters
could be here, but understood why they weren't.
The choice between a new nephew to pamper

and working a beer festival was a no-brainer. He'd put in his share of time admiring baby Todd, too.

Harley stood beside Matt, checking out the booth. "Thirty minutes before the doors open," he said. "You've done good, son."

Matt smiled at his friend, who had as big a heart as he did a skinny body. When Matt had been a kid, he'd always mixed up Harley with the Scarecrow from *The Wizard of Oz*.

"I couldn't do it without you. Any of it." And Matt meant it. After Matt's dad had booted him from the hardware store for an admittedly bad attitude, Harley had given him a job. He had also given Matt loans and advice when he'd opened the microbrewery. Matt had been mad at his dad at the time, but now he realized his dad had done it to help him spread his wings.

"Glad to help." Harley stuck two fingers in his mouth and whistled for Junior, who was flirting it up with a pair of pretty hot-looking beer pourers a couple of booths down.

Junior gave Harley a wave.

"Now if you don't mind, I'm gonna go grab Junior," Harley said. "We need to check out that spread of fancy finger foods before we're trapped behind the booth. I think I saw shrimp."

Matt could have pointed out that the food was intended for the party guests, and not Harley and Junior, but his friend was among the ranks of old dogs who refused to be retrained.

After they'd taken off, Matt headed toward Kate, who was putting her finishing touches on the merchandise table. Just outside of Keene's Harbor she'd lapsed into silence. He'd understood . . . or thought he had. She had a lot on her mind, and she was going to process it in whatever way worked best for her. It was nice to feel comfortable and relaxed with a woman, even in a mostly silent four-hour car ride. He'd just turned on the music and moved into his zone.

He looked down at Kate's table. "How's it going over here?"

"Almost done." She was concentrating on adjusting a pile of T-shirts. "I'm using the 'stack 'em high and watch them fly' approach."

"It's your turf. Arrange it however you want. We should be getting our first takers in about half an hour." He held out his hand. "Come on, let's take a look around before the place opens for business."

Kate surveyed the booths lining one of the two long aisles that had been set up in the cavernous building. "I had no idea there were so many microbrewers."

"More every day," Matt said. "But it's like any other business. Right now, it's surfing a high, but it will level out again in a couple of years. Only the best will be commercial concerns, and the others will go back to home brewing, if they really have a passion for it, or just move on to the next fad."

The walk was a slow one. He'd been in the business long enough that he knew most of the exhibitors.

Between booths, Kate asked, "What are you, some kind of cult hero? I don't think there's a single person here who doesn't know you or want to know you."

"It's not that big a deal. We don't land under the same roof all that often, so when we do, we talk."

Matt stared into the crowd of people in front of him and saw that Chet Orowski was heading his way. Matt already knew through the grapevine that Chet hadn't been able to find any other investors.

Orowski stopped a couple feet in front of Matt, and Matt extended his hand in greeting, thinking this was as good a time as any to re-establish a cordial relationship. "Chet, it's good to see you."

Chet slapped Matt's hand away and poked him in the chest. "Culhane, you're a crook and a liar."

Matt stood his ground, waiting for Chet to finish. "Do you really want to do this here?"

Chet's face was flushed and his hands were fisted. "You bet I do." His pupils danced around his eyes like Mexican jumping beans and his voice got louder. "If I'm going to go down, it's going to be in a friggin' blaze of glory. I'm gonna stand behind my booth and tell everyone who will listen what a bastard you are."

Matt glanced out of the corner of his eye at the booths to his left. Yup, spectators were already lining up.

"And this is why you drove all the way from Traverse City and rented a booth in Royal Oak?"

If the guy was going to slander him, he could have done it in a much more cost-effective fashion, Matt thought. Chet really wasn't much of a businessman.

"Yes. No. I also did it to look for a partner. Someone honest. Someone who follows through." He glared at Kate. "Someone who doesn't waste all his time chasing after tail."

Kate stuffed her hands onto her hips, narrowed her eyes, and leaned into Chet's personal space. "Excuse me?"

Matt clamped his hand on Chet's shoulder. To everyone but Chet it would look like a friendly gesture. Only Chet needed to know that this was a subtle warning of what could follow if he didn't tone it down.

"Now, Chet," Matt said. "We're all friends in this place, right?"

Chet went silent.

Matt made his warning marginally less subtle. "Right?"

Chet squirmed but Matt's grip on him stayed firm.

"Right," Chet gasped.

"And when we're among friends, we want everyone to have a good time, don't you think?"

Chet nodded enthusiastically, though Matt was pretty sure he'd spotted sweat popping out on the guy's forehead.

"Kate, here, is one of my friends, which would make her one of your friends by extension. You don't want to talk about a friend the way you just did about Kate, right?"

"Right."

"So how about you apologize to Kate—and to me, if you feel like it—and then we all get on with what's going to be a very good beer festival? After all, do good things and they come back to you."

"I—" Chet cleared his throat. "I'm sorry."

The words had been delivered without a helluva lot of sincerity, but Matt had no interest in pushing this scene a second longer than he had to. He released Chet's shoulder, then held out his right hand again.

This time, Chet did as he should have to begin with. He shook Matt's hand.

"No hard feelings," Matt said. At least not on his side. He wasn't going to speculate on Chet's.

Kate had been called a lot of things in her life: stubborn, nosy, and even some less nice stuff by her ex. But never had she been called *tail*.

She glared over her shoulder at Chet as Matt led her away. In a perfect world, where she was all-powerful and could smite the bad guys at will, she'd still be back there giving Chet a new perspective on life.

Matt took her hand and gave it a friendly squeeze. "Don't let him tick you off. He's not worth it. Or if it would make you feel better, how about if later I lure him to the parking lot and you can give him a fat lip?"

Kate smiled in spite of herself. "I just might take you up on that."

He laughed. "I guess I should consider my audience when I'm joking around."

"I promise I won't hold you to your offer," she said. But she did hold his hand almost all the way back to the Depot booth, where she moved on to finish up her merchandise fluffing. And just in time, too.

Kate could time down to the second when cocktail hour was starting in Royal Oak's bars by the flood of private tasting guests into Farmers' Market. She saw plenty of familiar faces in the crowd. Back when she'd been at *Detroit Monthly,* she'd always gone out with coworkers for cocktails. Richard had worked late every Friday. Or so he'd claimed.

As people streamed by, she exchanged waves and greetings with casual friends. It felt good to see them, and that scared emptiness she'd been anticipating never materialized. She was no ghost; she was a new and improved version of Kate.

She looked past the guys checking out the De-pot baseball caps and locomotive bottle openers and on to Matt, who was giving one awesome beer spiel. He was smart and funny, and his crowd was eating it up. Except one person. The guy was busy playing with his BlackBerry in exactly the same way that had made her insane from the day he'd bought the thing.

Richard.

Her ex's black hair was absurdly long, but his perpetual slight frown, English tweed jacket, kha-kis, and ever-so-retro loafers were just the same.

Kate felt trapped. Fight-or-flight instinct kicked in, and flight didn't look to be a viable op-tion. Running out of the building wouldn't be very subtle, and she'd have to slip past him un-noticed to pull it off, anyway. Maybe Richard would drift off without seeing her.

She automatically made change for a guy who'd decided to buy ten bottle openers to give as family Christmas gifts. Somehow she didn't think Grandma was going to plotz with grati-tude, but Kate wasn't about to stop the dude. After he was gone, she ducked under the table to grab more stock. She briefly considered hiding, except the space was a little tight and dark for her taste. And no doubt Matt would come look-ing for her. She'd rather not explain the whole ex thing to him.

Kate rose, and Richard spotted her. She wished

she'd gone for full makeup instead of her usual mascara and lip gloss. It never hurt to look fabulous when seeing the ex for the first time since moving out of the marital home. But what she lacked in cosmetics, she could make up for in attitude. If Matt could talk nicely to Chet, she could do it with Richard.

Maybe.

Kate rounded the merchandise table and extended her hand. "Richard."

"Kate." His handshake was on the limp side, but at least he'd given it a shot.

"I'm surprised to see you here," she said. "You're not a beer drinker."

"This is a charity function that a client supports. I have to make a showing. But I'll say, you can't be nearly as surprised as I am. I'd heard you'd lost your job and had to move in with your parents."

"I have a job," she said.

"So I see. And Larry and Barb are well?"

"They're fine, I'm sure. They're at the Naples house until May, and I'm staying at The Nutshell."

"Really? The Nutshell? That must be interesting."

To anyone else, his comment would have sounded positive and sincere. Kate, however, knew how much he'd disliked both The Nutshell and Keene's Harbor. And she felt very protective of both.

Kate smiled. "It's wonderful."

"Really? Living in your parents' cottage and working in a brewery?" He glanced at his phone. "That's a far cry from what you used to do."

Kate wondered if Shayla was texting him, just as she had when Kate had been his wife. Water under the bridge, Kate thought. Shayla could text him all she wanted now. Kate had loved Richard, but his affair had taught her something. She couldn't be the person she was meant to be when she was with someone she couldn't trust. If she ever decided to marry another man, it would definitely be someone like Matt—someone who made her feel more herself than she did alone.

"I like it in Keene's Harbor. I always did," she said. "I'm happy there."

"How nice."

Funny thing, but he didn't look very happy about her being happy.

"So can I tell you a little about our beer?" she asked, knowing this would roust snobby anti-brew Richard.

"No thanks," he said. "I should move along."

Not quickly enough, she thought as he stepped off.

Then he turned back. "Oh, I forgot to mention . . . We had to give Stella away."

THIRTEEN

KATE FELT AS THOUGH SOME VITAL CONNECTION IN HER brain had just snapped. "Would you mind repeating that?"

A faint little smile was forming on Richard's usually passive face. "We had to give Stella away."

Stella had been their baby. They'd spoiled her like mad. When they'd separated, leaving her had been wretched for Kate, far more painful than leaving Richard. Stella had been faithful.

"What do you mean, *had* to?" Kate asked.

"Stella didn't take to Shayla. We couldn't have her biting all the time."

"Who, Shayla or Stella?"

"Very funny. Really, Kate, it's great that you still have your sense of humor to keep you going."

"And so you gave her away instead of sending her to me?"

"I didn't know where you were."

"My cell number hasn't changed."

Richard flipped his bangs out of his eyes like a pop star. "Don't be difficult. It's not as though you cared enough to take her in the first place."

"Don't even start with that stuff. I was ordered by the court to surrender her to you, and you know it. You had the fenced backyard. I had the loft apartment and no dog park in walking distance. I didn't even get visitation rights, thanks to your high-priced, evil divorce lawyer. So tell me, who has her now?"

Her ex hesitated, and Kate knew this was going to be *no bueno*.

He looked down at his feet and Kate knew that for all his posturing, he felt bad. Richard had truly loved Stella, but Richard was a weak person. Richard was no match for Shayla.

"I'm not sure," he said. "Shayla handled it."

"Stella was ours before Shayla became part of the picture, and you let *her* handle it—whatever that means? How could you allow any of this to happen?"

He kicked the ground with his right shoe, then looked back up at Kate. "I'm engaged. Shayla wouldn't agree to marry me unless Stella went. She knows how busy I've been at work, so she just took care it. I'm sure she found Stella a good home. You should just move on, Kate."

Move on?

Stella had probably been dumped at the city shelter, where her chances would have been slim. Everyone wanted cute puppies, not seven-year-old ginger-colored miniature poodles who had just a bit of a bad attitude. But Kate wanted her with all her heart. She also wanted to shake Richard until his teeth rattled, or boot him one in the rear, or . . .

She wrapped her hand around the closest open beer from the pouring table. She didn't have a firm plan, but if Richard's ridiculous hair ended up looking like stringy black seaweed, that wouldn't be so tragic. Before she could do anything, though, two muscled arms gently wrapped around her from behind.

"Steady," Matt said low into her ear, drawing her closer. "Take a breath, sweetheart."

Kate's eyes were focused on Richard. "I want Stella *now*."

Richard's gaze darted from the beer bottle to Kate. "I told you, I don't know where she is."

Matt tightened his hold on Kate. "Why don't you set down the bottle?"

"He gave away my dog."

"I take it you know him," Matt said.

"This is my ex, Dick." Which he hated being called.

Richard turned to Matt and offered the same limp hand he had to Kate. "And you are?"

"Matt Culhane, Kate's boss."

"I should press assault charges against your employee."

Kate rolled her eyes. "For what? I didn't even touch you."

"Harassment. Intimidation," Richard said.

Kate's throat tightened. She was going to cry, but damn it, she wasn't going to do it in front of her idiot, rotten-to-the-core ex.

She pushed at Matt's arms. "I need to go outside."

Matt slid his arms away, and Kate hustled for the door. She walked blindly down the parking lot's first aisle, looking for some privacy and Matt's truck. It didn't take long to find something that big and red. She tugged at the passenger-door handle, but the vehicle was locked.

"Hang on," Matt said from behind her.

Kate turned and flung herself at him. "He gave away my dog to some stranger, Matt. I never should have let him have her."

Matt rubbed her back and gave her a chance to settle down. After a moment, she stepped back and wished for a tissue.

"I'm sorry." She wiped her eyes. "I feel awful. I should have never trusted him with my dog, but honestly, I didn't have a choice."

Matt unlocked the truck and opened the door

for her. "Why don't you take a couple of minutes in some quiet? Harley and Junior have it
covered inside."

Kate nodded and climbed in.

"I'll be back to check on you in a minute. I
just have to . . ." He gestured back at the market
building. Kate figured that could mean anything
from "use the facilities" to "hide from the weepy
woman." Either way, he'd been there when she'd
needed him, and in her book, he was already a
hero for that.

Matt had to sprint the forty like a high school
kid to catch up with Kate's ex, but he did it.
Richard was standing next to a black BMW, getting ready to leave.

Matt walked slowly up to Richard, trying his
best at friendly. "That was pretty weird stuff in
there."

Richard's mouth turned down. "It's always
weird with Kate. Fire her now while you have
cause."

"Thanks, but I'll handle my own employment
decisions."

"Then keep her around, but you can't say I
didn't warn you. She's a soul-eater."

Total bull, but Matt had the feeling this guy
dished a lot of that. Matt got down to business.
"So, Richard, I couldn't help overhearing you

and Kate, and I've gotta say I think you know where her poodle is."

Richard took a half step closer to his car. "Why would I lie?"

"Good question, since you're pretty bad at it. You were obviously scrambling when you talked to Kate, and now can't meet my eyes. So what's up with the poodle? Susie? Sniffy? Whatever the mutt's name is?" Matt asked, figuring a little goading might work.

The color started to rise in Richard's face. "Her name is Stella."

"See? You care about the dog. It's obvious. I'm a dog guy, too, and have been for a lot of years. I get the relationship between man and canine. But I'm also a big fan of Kate's, so if there's something I can do to help her get her poodle back, I'm going to do it."

"Is that a threat?"

It was kind of funny that this professor-looking dude was ready to rumble, but Matt wasn't a rumbler anymore. He didn't have to be.

"If you're asking whether I'm going to beat you up over a poodle, the answer is no. If you're asking whether I'm going to put time and effort into getting to the bottom of this, the answer is yes. And when it comes to Kate, I have all the time in the world."

"Don't bother. Stella's fine."

"Really? And you claimed you don't know where she went. Want to tell me the real story?"

Richard hesitated, but finally made a sound of capitulation. "I found her in the city shelter where my fiancée, Shayla, had dropped her. I had some friends adopt her. I visit her all the time."

So he was cheating on his fiancée with a poodle. Matt couldn't say he'd encountered that before or wanted to again. Mostly, though, he wanted to ask how the guy could want to marry a woman who'd done what this Shayla had. But he already knew Richard's judgment sucked. After all, he'd let Kate go.

"Kate would be with the dog full-time," Matt said. "She loves Stella."

"I want Stella by me."

"She'd be better off with Kate." Matt paused. "And I think you know that."

After some sour-faced deliberation, Richard pulled a slim notepad and a gold pen from his breast pocket. He scribbled something on a piece of paper, tore it out, and handed it to Matt.

"Give me five minutes before calling," Richard said. "I'll need to talk to them first."

"You're doing the right thing," Matt said. He pocketed the paper and hoped this was the very last time he'd see Dognapper Dick.

Fifteen minutes later, after a call comprised of some detailed poodle negotiations, Matt stepped back into the party. Kate was at the merchandise table. She gave him a smile, but it wasn't up to her usual wattage. Mayor Mortensen and his wife, Missy, stood behind the beer table with Harley and Junior. Missy was as thin and cheery as Torvald Mortensen was rotund and generally glum. After saying hello to Torvald, Matt turned to Missy.

"Kate and I need to go take care of a few things," he said.

"I do?" Kate asked.

"You do."

Kate looked confused. "Okay, then."

"Do you think you could cover the merchandise table?" Matt asked Missy. "The party wraps up at eight."

"Absolutely. I'd love to help," Missy said. "Just let me get with Kate and learn the ropes."

While Kate and Missy talked, Matt made sure the rest of his troops knew what to do: all spare beer in the bins below the table, merchandise boxed and stowed, and everything wiped down and ready to roll when they opened again tomorrow at eleven.

"Come on," he said to Kate when Missy and she had finished. "We're going to sneak out on the boss."

Her smile was a little brighter. "That should be a challenge, especially for you."

"I'm pretty good at it."

Now if he could just pull off the rest of his plan.

After giving Kate some lame excuse about picking up supplies, Matt headed his truck out of downtown Royal Oak and south on Woodward Avenue. When they merged onto the freeway heading west, Kate started getting suspicious.

"What kind of supplies are we getting? They must be pretty exotic if you couldn't have picked them up someplace in Royal Oak."

"They're one of a kind," he said.

"Gotta be," Kate said before lapsing into silence.

Matt exited the freeway and, a few minutes later, turned into the subdivision he'd been told to look for. Two blocks down, first house on the left, he pulled into a driveway and parked.

"Friends of yours?" Kate asked.

"Not exactly."

She looked at the unassuming beige brick colonial with its perfectly clipped shrubs. "Okay, this is weird. I feel like I've been here before."

"It's possible," he said. "These are friends of Richard's."

"And you know this, how?"

"Your ex-husband and I had a talk. The usual guy stuff. We shared, we laughed, we bonded."

"No, really," Kate said.

"And he told me where your poodle is."

"Stella? *Here?*" She opened the truck door.

He settled a hand on her arm. "Before you go all Rambo, here's the deal. These people have had your poodle for almost six months. They love her and think of her as their own. They've even renamed her Bitsy."

"*Bitsy?* Granted, living here is better than what I'd imagined for her, but Bitsy? They probably have her in a pink ruffled collar and clipped with a little ball at the end of her tail. I need to go get her."

Matt held his palms toward her, trying to slow her down a little. "In a second, but first you have to listen. The only way they're going to let her leave with you is if she does it of her own free will."

He didn't add that if the poodle picked Kate, he'd be buying the couple a replacement dog. That was his bargain and his responsibility.

"You mean I have to sweet talk my own dog back to me when we haven't seen each other for over a year?"

He nodded. "That's the deal."

"It's insane."

"I know, but it was the best I could do." And that had taken some major persuading.

She drew in a deep breath, then slowly let it out. "Okay. I can do this."

They walked to the front porch, and Kate's

finger hovered over the doorbell as she asked, "How am I going to handle it if she doesn't choose me?"

Matt spoke from the heart. "How could she not?"

As Kate stood waiting for the door to open, she finally recalled who would be on the other side—Myrna and Ed Savage. They were a nice couple about twenty years older than she. Ed was an accountant and one of Richard's clients. Kate had been to a dinner here once, years ago. She'd reciprocated, and that had been the end of any couples' socializing. She thought maybe Richard and Ed still golfed together, though.

The door swung open, and Myrna greeted them. She looked no happier to see Kate than Kate felt about this entire mess. But since this wasn't the Savages' fault, Kate took care to be super polite.

Myrna ushered them into the living room, where Ed stood waiting with a dog's travel crate at his feet. Kate caught a glimpse of Stella's ginger coat and her heart began to drum. She wouldn't be able to breathe properly until this was done and she had her poodle back.

"If you don't mind, I'd like to propose a few guidelines," she said to the couple. "How about if you're on one side of the room, and I'm on the other? Matt can put Stella—"

Myrna stood her ground. "Bitsy."

"The poodle," Matt suggested.

Kate pressed her lips together. "Matt can put *the poodle* in the middle of the room. Whoever she goes to first, keeps her."

"How do I know you're not cheating?" Myrna said, suspiciously sniffing Kate. "You smell like bacon."

Kate emptied her pockets onto the table. No bacon. Myrna sniffed again. "I think you still smell like bacon."

Matt picked up a can of Febreze from beside the couch. He generously sprayed both the women and stepped back. "Okay, then. Let's do it," Kate said, wiping her sweaty palms on her pants legs.

Matt retrieved the travel crate from Ed while Myrna moved to her husband's side.

Matt placed himself in the middle of the room. "Everybody ready?"

"Yes."

Matt opened the crate and withdrew Stella, who emerged with an obvious show of stubbornness. She didn't care that she weighed five pounds. She was mistress of her own domain.

Stella looked healthy, though she probably felt a little embarrassed by the hokey haircut—a pom on the end of her tail and balls on each hip, just as Kate had suspected.

Stella looked around, her brown eyes bright with curiosity, and Kate focused on her poodle, willing her to look her way. *Please, baby. Please remember me.*

Matt set Stella down.

Myrna clapped her hands and made some kissy noises. "Bitsy-kins. Come to Mommy."

Stella looked Myrna's way once, then took a casual sniff at Matt's shoe before turning away from him, too. Kate smiled. Who wouldn't love a poodle that played hard to get?

"Come on, Bitsy. . . . Be a good precious babykins," Myrna cooed.

Kate figured that even in the time Stella and she had been apart, her dog couldn't have had a personality transplant. And that being the case, Kate knew just what to do. She plopped herself down on the beige carpet, her back to the beige wall, and feigned total disinterest.

Stella grew a tad miffed at Kate's nonchalance. She took one step, then another toward Kate, just as Kate had hoped. Now was the time for a little girl talk, Stella-style.

"Hey, Stella," Kate said. "You're looking pretty good. How have you been doing? Scare any Dobermans lately?"

Stella's ears perked up, and she ran to Kate and settled in her lap.

Kate nestled her cheek against Stella's soft fur. "You're the Best Dog Ever. I missed you so much."

And Matt was the Best Man Ever, Kate thought. He'd brought her back together with her Stella.

FOURTEEN

STELLA MUST HAVE BEEN ROYALTY IN A PRIOR LIFE. KATE could find no other reason for the dog to be so unimpressed with the hotel Matt had chosen. Kate, on the other hand, was wowed by the Townley Inn. Her room looked like something out of an English country manor—all dark woods, plush carpets, and rich upholstery. And her bed was a fantasy-worthy, feather-down dream made for lovers. At the moment, though, she shared it with a cranky poodle.

Kate sat alongside the dog at the end of the mattress. Matt sat opposite them in a desk chair he'd pulled up to their white-linen-covered room service cart. "They must have been feeding her from the table," Kate said. "Look at the way she's turning up her nose at the food I bought her. It's going to be tough getting her back on regular dog food."

Stella was eyeing the final bite of tenderloin on Matt's plate. He speared the meat with his fork, and the poodle huffed out a sigh as her last shot at prime beef disappeared down Matt's throat.

Chicken breast with roasted autumn vegetables demolished, Kate set her fork aside. "Have I thanked you for Stella in the last ten minutes?"

Matt's expression was a cross between amusement and resignation. "I just did what any other guy would have."

"Not Richard."

"No, not Richard."

There were a lot of things about her ex she could have shared with Matt, but none of them really mattered.

"Luckily, he's not my problem anymore," she said.

Matt smiled at her, his eyes softened, and the room grew warmer as those big bed fantasies charged to the front of Kate's mind.

"I'll clear the cart to the hall," Matt said.

Kate watched him push the cart out the door. This was it, she thought. Here they were in a romantic hotel room. Just the two of them . . . and Stella. Perfect, right? Wrong. Not perfect. For starters, she was wearing a T-shirt that advertised beer. Plus, she suspected her lipstick had

gotten gnawed off at Myrna's, and her hair was
a wreck. He, on the other hand, was hot. His
T-shirt molded suggestively to his gorgeous body.
His butt looked great in his jeans. His hair was
tousled just enough to be sexy, and he had a
manly five o'clock shadow going.

Okay, don't panic, she told herself. Get a grip.
Should she stand? Should she sit? Should she
lounge back onto the bed? Should she get un-
dressed? No, definitely no undressing. She wasn't
ready for undressing.

Matt returned to the room, closed the door,
and Kate jumped up from the bed.

"Well?" Kate said.

Their eyes met and held for a moment, and
Matt glanced over his shoulder at the door.

Either he was checking to make sure it was
locked, or else he was planning on leaving, Kate
thought. Best not to take any chances on him
leaving, she decided. It was now or never, so she
moved in and kissed him. Definitely not her best
work, but then in her defense, she was a little
rusty.

He tilted his head and looked at her. "What
was that?"

She stepped back while finding some way to
hedge her poor move. "A good-night kiss between friends?"

"Really?"

"More or less."

He looked at her with the same hot intensity he'd shown the night she'd sung in the karaoke contest. But this time she wasn't scared. At least not much.

"I thought we were closer friends than that."

"How close of friends?" she asked.

Matt didn't answer with words. Instead, he kissed her deeply. Intimately. Kate could swear she heard herself moan as his hand moved to the small of her back. She'd been starving for this.

For him.

There was no point in fighting it. Her will-power was shot. He was too sexy. Too near. Too perfect. She wanted his body heat and the feel of him taking her to that place she'd missed so much.

"Hang on, sweetheart," he said.

No problem, because she'd already wrapped her arms around his neck.

He scooped her up and settled her on the bed. He switched off the bedside lamp, and Kate reached for him. His weight settled over her, pushing her deep into the heavenly soft comforter.

She let her fingers flex into the muscles on the back of his shoulders as he claimed her mouth with his once again.

A low growl sounded. Kate was pretty sure it hadn't come from Matt, and she was almost certain it hadn't come from her. She nudged the pillow that Stella had to be occupying and got an angry grunt in response.

Matt moved on to kiss Kate's throat. She arched her neck and asked for more while she tried to work his shirt free of his jeans. She wanted to touch skin. *Now.*

Matt knelt above her and pulled off his shirt. Kate wished she had the patience to focus on his body's details but she was too far gone. She pulled him back down.

"We've got all night," he said.

"Not good enough."

"Trust me, it's gonna be good," he said in a low voice that made Kate's body hum in excitement.

Kate fumbled with his belt, thinking the damn thing was like some sort of Mensa brain challenge.

Stella let loose a series of high-pitched yips. Someone in the next room added a couple of firm raps against the wall.

Kate gave up on the belt. Her dog was going to ruin everything. "Stella, no!"

The poodle brought it down to a whine.

"Ignore Stella," Matt said, his lips skimming along Kate's neck, her ear. "Focus on me. Would it help if I howled?"

Stella went back to barking. The neighbor slammed on the wall, and the poodle amped it up to the point that Kate's ears rang.

Matt lifted his head and gave Stella a glare. "Stop!"

The poodle curled her lip, but obeyed.

"Now where were we?" Matt asked as he opened the top four buttons on Kate's chambray Depot shirt, his last word ending on a sharp breath of pleasure as he settled his mouth between her breasts. Kate murmured encouragement and Matt cruised on, making quick work of the rest of Kate's buttons.

"Gotta admire a man who's talented with his hands," she managed to say.

When Kate's shirt went flying, Stella let loose a snarl that sounded like it came from a Rottweiler.

Matt paused in his body exploration. "That wasn't a good sound."

Kate's poodle stared at them from one pillow over. The dog's eyes glowed in the dim light. And it wasn't an *I'm a happy dog* kind of glow, either.

"Settle down," she told Stella, but the poodle was focused on Matt.

"I'm sensing a turf war," Matt said.

Kate kissed him and popped the top button on his jeans. "No way."

Rrrrrrrrrrrrrrf! Grrf. GRRF!

"No doubt about it. Your dog doesn't want me touching you," Matt said.

"She doesn't get a vote. Give me a second."

Kate unwrapped herself from Matt, corralled

Stella, and tucked her into her travel crate, which sat beside the brocade love seat.

"Be good," she said to Stella.

Yip, yip, yip, yip, YIP!

Matt yanked a burgundy-colored throw from the love seat and dropped it over the crate.

Aroooh, roooh, roooh. Arooooooh!

The guy in the next room pounded the wall as though he planned to hammer his way through.

"Sorry," Kate called. "We're trying to get her to stop."

But Stella kept on in howl mode.

"I'm calling the front desk," the guy shouted through the wall.

Kate had a vision of security at the door. With the police. And the ASPCA. And just like her last legal run-in, she'd be only half-dressed.

Matt rolled to his feet. "This isn't going to work."

"I'm sorry. She's really a great dog."

"No problem. I understand where she's coming from. I feel exactly the same way about you as she does." He gave Kate a quick kiss over Stella's warning growl. "Lesson learned. Beware the overly protective poodle."

Saturday morning, Matt did his best to put Friday night behind him. He'd never seen a dog smirk, but damned if the poodle hadn't been doing just that as he'd left Kate's room. During a mind-clearing, wake-up run, he'd decided on a plan to win Stella over and clear the way for him to Kate's heart. Plus, he was far better off than Harley and Junior, who'd shown up for breakfast visibly and brutally hungover. Junior had turned gray at the sight of Kate's wheatgrass-and-mango smoothie, and had left the hotel dining room without ordering.

While Matt could stomach the idea of a wheatgrass smoothie, he couldn't deal with Kate's total silence now that they were on the road and headed for the beer fest. Stella was stowed in her crate, on the backseat, but probably still shooting him death rays.

"You're mighty quiet," Matt said.

"What would you like to talk about?"

"Last night."

"I didn't think guys talked about stuff like that."

"It's true. It's rule number five in the Code of Manliness handbook. I'm making a one-time exception."

Kate sighed. "Okay, so here goes. I'm kind of glad for the poodle alarm last night. I made myself a promise not to get involved with anyone until I figured out my life. For the first time, I feel like I might actually be making progress with that."

He had to give Kate credit. Not only did she

have an impressive amount of willpower, she was also tenacious, passionate, and forthright. It was all he could do not to pull the car over and kiss her. But patience and planning had helped him succeed in business, and it would help him succeed with Kate. First things first. Win over the dog.

"I understand completely."

"You do?"

"Sure. I was lucky to be able to find my calling in a hobby I loved, but it was hard work figuring out how to build and run a business. It took all the energy I had. Right now, your business is your life. There's no reason to rush things between us."

Kate's body relaxed, and when she smiled up at him, Matt once again had to fight not to pull over to the side of the road. Sooner or later, Kate would come around, but how he'd help her get there was a more complicated proposition than charming the poodle. All he needed for Stella was a lamb chop in each pocket. Kate would take finesse.

They pulled into the parking lot at the Farmers' Market a few minutes later and noticed a police cruiser was parked in front of the main entry door.

"What do you suppose that's about?" Kate asked, looking at the cruiser.

"I suppose it's just life in the big city."

They entered the building and made their way back toward the Depot Brewing booth, stopping in the middle of the aisle, grimly gaping at the Depot Brewing Company banner hanging in tatters.

Harley, Junior, and Torvald Mortensen stood in front of Matt's booth with two police officers. A scarecrow manned the booth, dressed in a Depot Brewery T-shirt and hat. A huge jagged hunting knife was stuck in its belly and a corkscrew protruded from its right eye.

"The leftover beer from last night is gone," Junior said. "We set up the tables again, though. They were all wrecked."

Matt clapped his friend on the shoulder. "Thanks, pal. I appreciate the help."

Matt, Harley, Junior, and Torvald answered the officers' questions while Kate sat on the floor, sorting through upended boxes. Matt was handing one of the officers his card when Kate joined them.

She held out a vintage lighter decorated with a black-and-white enamel eagle. "Sorry to interrupt, but I found this with the merchandise. I thought maybe it was Harley's?"

Harley barely glanced at it. "Nope."

"Are you sure?" Kate asked. "It looks like one from your collection."

"Sure, that's yours," Junior said. "I got it for you last Christmas."

Harley absently patted his pants pocket. "Huh. I must be worse off from last night than I thought. It's mine, all right. It must have fallen out of my pocket a coupla minutes ago when I was moving that stuff near the table. Thanks for finding it."

She handed it to him and turned her attention to Junior.

Junior clutched his blue cooler, searching for something to say. "I heard you've got bees in your house. You should be careful, because bees can be very dangerous."

Kate opened her mouth, thought better of telling Junior what she'd like to do with her bees, and snapped her mouth shut.

Matt asked the police what they knew so far, and it was nothing helpful. The building manager had opened the place at five to let in the cleaning crew. They'd done their job and left. The manager had stayed in his office. He'd also admitted to dozing off. Anyone could have slipped in at any point. Matt thanked the police and asked to be sent a copy of their report. Beyond that, he doubted that he'd hear from them again.

"Let's get to it," he said to his crew.

Harley volunteered to get the rest of the beer from Matt's truck while Torvald and Junior bought ice. It would be a shorter pouring day, but not a total wipeout. Kate got her hands on a ladder and roll of duct tape and began piecing the banner together from behind.

"Looks like you're going to need more tape," Matt said.

Kate leaned precariously from the top step of the ladder, trying to fix a torn piece. "I've got just enough. It's not going to be perfect, but it will do."

Harley rounded the table wheeling a dolly stacked with cases of bottled beer. His labored breathing made it clear that he was too hungover and out-of-shape to be a beer hauler.

"You're handling this situation like a champ," Harley said to Matt.

"I didn't know I had a choice."

"Most guys would be bitchin' and moanin'."

Matt smiled. "I've discovered it doesn't make much of a difference whether I do or don't, so I'm opting for don't."

Chet Orowski strolled up. "Looks like what goes round, comes round, huh, Culhane? I heard what happened to you." He looked at the scarecrow. "Looks to me like you screwed the wrong guy. You oughta be more careful."

"It's no big deal," Matt said. "We've still got some beer, the banner's okay, I'm thinking of using the scarecrow so I can ride in carpool lanes, and we're going to have fun. Because that's what we're in the business for, right?"

Chet threw up his hands, looking around the room, hoping for an audience. "Yeah, yeah, yeah. Great PR spin, but we both know the truth.

Someone here hates you. I guess you're not the big star you thought you were."

"I've never thought of myself as a big star," Matt said. "I brew beer, and that's it."

Chet snorted. "Sure thing. You've got your pride the same as all of us, and now your nose is getting rubbed in it. It couldn't happen to a nicer guy."

Kate finished taping the sign and started down the ladder. The ladder rocked left and Kate leaned right, trying to keep from falling. For a long moment, both Kate and the ladder seemed to hover in the air before they both came crashing down. Straight onto Chet. And as they lay there in a heap, Kate was as grateful for Chet's bulk as she was for her small stature. Between the combination of the two, she didn't actually kill him.

"Chet didn't do it, you know," Matt said to Kate that night as they headed west through Detroit's endless string of suburbs.

She peeked into the backseat to check on Stella in her travel crate. "How can you be so sure?"

"Because he's a lot like your ex-husband. Lots of bluster and no action."

Kate looked out the window. "You don't know the half of it."

"All I'm saying is that Chet couldn't get out of his own way to pull off this stuff. And even if he did trash the booth—which he didn't—he doesn't have the right contacts in Keene's Harbor. Yeah, spare brewery keys could have been floating around, but how would Chet have gotten his hands on one?"

Kate sighed. "Okay, good point, but we're right back to where we started. *More vandalism and too many suspects.* We'll put Jerry on the back burner, since he wasn't around. That leaves us with the Mortensens, Junior, and Harley. Do we know where the Mortensens were last night?"

"In bed by nine, probably. They're a pretty low-key couple."

"We'll put them aside for now." She paused. "I did pick up Harley's lighter, though."

"He said he dropped it while straightening the booth. Did you find it someplace where that couldn't be possible?"

"No, it was on top of a box of coasters."

"Not exactly enough to convict the guy," Matt said. "Besides, Junior and Harley have each other for alibis. They were at a sports bar until the Pistons game ended, then back at the hotel bar until last call. Judging by the way they looked today, I'm sure they can prove it."

Kate sighed again. "I'm sure they can."

Stella whimpered from the backseat.

"Do you mind if I get her out?" Kate asked.

"No problem."

Matt kept his eyes on the road as Kate violated a couple of traffic laws while freeing her poodle.

"I can't believe how tired I am," Kate said once she and the dog were safely in front. "I think I'll just close my eyes and . . ." She yawned, and Matt filled in the rest of her words for himself.

Somewhere just east of Lansing, a slight whistling sound drew Matt's attention from the road. Kate was curled up with Stella. Both woman and dog were out cold. A louder whistling came his way. The dog was snoring.

FIFTEEN

On Thursday morning Kate woke to a poodle nestled next to her head. And, as had been true every morning since the workweek had started, her phone was ringing. Kate's. Not Stella's. Kate had spoiled her baby with long beach walks, but the dog would not be getting a phone.

"Hello?" Kate said, feeling rested and ridiculously content.

"Let me guess," Matt said. "You overslept."

Kate sat upright, and Stella grunted her disapproval of the change in her sleeping arrangements.

"No way. Again? I set my alarm. Really."

She couldn't stop smiling, though. Several nights in a row of more than eight consecutive hours of sleep. She might not have any walls or a master bathroom or a living room floor, but at least the mold and most of the bees were gone. She felt human again.

"If you could amble on in here before I take any more guff about giving you special treatment, I just might forgive you," Matt said.

He sounded amused, and Kate's smile grew into a grin.

"Let me take a shower and give Stella her morning walk, and then I'll be right there."

Matt laughed. "So, like noon, right?"

"No later than ten, I promise."

"Hey, and find Bart when you get here, okay? Laila's ready to come back, so you're going to be assistant to the assistant brewers."

"Sounds filled with responsibility," Kate said. But really, she didn't care what Matt had her doing so long as she was earning and snooping . . . and getting to see him. She had fallen for him, and the ginger poodle had sealed the deal.

At precisely ten o'clock, Kate found Bart the brewmaster by a large wipe-off board where he was scribbling dates and other random things. Floyd, his assistant, stood to his right. The older man possessed a rather impressively sized beer belly. Kate had to appreciate a guy who showed that much love for his chosen career.

Next to Floyd was Nan O'Brien, assistant brewer number two. Nan was an Amazon of a woman, at least six feet tall, and fit. A hunter, triathlete, and seasoned sailor, Nan could whip any television survival show dude with one arm tied behind her back.

"Hey, Bart," Kate said. "Sorry I'm late."

"Let's talk before we get started," he said. He waved off his assistants, telling them they'd finish later.

Kate joined him at the whiteboard. "So tell me what you're going to be doing back here today."

"I'm going to be getting another batch of Dog Day ready to boil, which means that *you* are going to be cleaning the brewhouse for me."

She looked around. "The whole place?"

He laughed. "It looks like you're in need of a little more training, eh?"

Bart led her across the room and patted a big, almost bullet-shaped, tank that stood seven or so feet tall. "This is the brewhouse. A thirty-barrel brewhouse, to be exact. And those other tanks attached to it are the fermenters. After the boil, the wort is sent through the pipes to its left, and into those fermenters, where the yeast is added."

Really, the brewhouse was kind of pretty, all copper and stainless and shiny. And it looked very clean already, which she pointed out to Bart.

"It's not the same picture on the inside, and that's what you're going to be concerned with," he said.

"Hang on. You mean I have to get in there?"

"Yes. And believe me, it's a much easier fit for someone your size than it is for me or Nan or Floyd." He hitched his thumb toward the two assistant brewers who were now in conversation by the door to the large keg cooler room.

Great, Kate thought. She'd panicked in the walk-in a few weeks ago, and that room had nothing on this bomb-like capsule.

"I'm not a huge fan of dark, enclosed spaces," she told Bart.

"Who is, other than bats and mushrooms? You'll have a flashlight. And you won't be in there long. It's just a matter of doing a wipe-down to get rid of any leftover debris from the last batch before we quick-flush the system."

"Right, then," she said over the scared slamming of her heart.

"You'll be fine. I promise. I've got to get a couple of things lined up for a meeting with Matt, but Floyd and Nan will get you set up and keep a good eye on you."

He called them over, and Kate began to reconcile herself to this process. All the same, she was no longer impressed by the brewhouse's shiny rivets and copper accents. And its pressure gauges, valves, and pipes freaked her out.

"It's not as bad as it looks," Nan said. "We'll help you get in through that hatch at the top and then hand the supplies to you."

"How about I just watch you this time and I do it the next?" she asked Nan.

The other woman grinned. "Let me think about it. *No.*"

It had been worth a shot.

"I'll be right back with water, towels, and a flashlight," Nan said. "Floyd, why don't you grab the ladder?"

Floyd returned with the ladder, set it up, and climbed a couple of steps until he could reach the hatch at the top of the brewhouse. Once it was open, he scrambled back down.

"I've got it secured. Your turn now," he said.

"Okay . . ."

Nan returned and handed her the flashlight. Kate jammed it into the back of her jeans, for lack of another secure location that would also keep her hands free.

"You're a big, strong dog who can jump high," she said to herself.

"What?" Nan asked.

"It works on my dog when she's scared, so I thought I'd give it a try on me," Kate said as she climbed the ladder. But the affirmation hadn't helped. She peered into the darkness and then back at the assistant brewers. "So I just . . ."

"Climb in," Nan said.

Kate took a deep breath and tried to maneuver her body down the hole. Coordination and grace were not going to be part of the equation.

She slid through the hatch in the top of the brew-house, dropping herself into the darkness.

Once there, she sat and assessed the situation. Except for the lingering, evil smell of hops, it could have been worse. Light shone in through the open hatch like a big, fat ray of hope, and the confines weren't as tight as she'd thought they would be. She pulled the flashlight from the back of her jeans and switched it on. Nothing happened.

"Hey, the flashlight batteries are dead," she called to Nan.

Nan's face appeared in the hatchway. "I could look for more, but by the time I find them, you'll be done." She threw a roll of paper towels down to Kate, quickly followed by a spray bottle.

"Nan, Floyd, come on into my office. It's time to meet with Matt," Kate heard Bart saying.

Nan stuck her head in the hatch again. "Sounds like I have to take off."

"Couldn't you hang on a minute?" Kate asked. She liked knowing there was a lifeline outside her copper kettle.

"Don't worry about it. You're going to do great," Nan said. "Be sure to pay attention to all the seams and outlets. That's where the grunge sticks. Just throw the used paper towels out the top."

"Okay," Kate said. There was no answer. Nan had disappeared.

And the sooner Kate finished, the sooner she could stop being brave. She ripped a couple of paper towels off the roll and reached for the spray bottle. Taking a top-down approach, she began to wipe the tank's interior and hum a little vintage Eric Carmen, which she knew courtesy of her parents' ancient stereo. When she reached the chorus, she burst into full song.

"*All by myyyyy-self . . .*"

The tank's hatch fell shut with a clang.

"Hey, I wasn't even off-key," she said.

And then reality hit her. She was trapped. Sweat popped out on her palms and, she was pretty sure, the soles of her feet.

"You're a big, strong dog who can jump high," she said.

Kate braced herself on the sides of the tank and pushed at the hatch. It didn't give. She might be a big, strong dog, but she couldn't sit alone in a metal coffin.

"Come on! Open the hatch!" she shouted.

The only answer was the rattle of the ladder being removed. And then water began flowing into the tank. It crept its way up her ankles and to her calves, and panic set in, big-time.

"Someone, *anyone,* come get me!"

Kate kicked at the side of the tank. She knew what was going to happen next. Wort was boiled. She was about to be boiled alive.

* * *

Matt paused in his discussions with his brewing staff.

"Did you hear something?" he asked Bart.

"Just you being too damn stubborn about the winter ale recipe," Bart said.

"No, from out there."

Nan shook her head. "I don't hear any—"

Matt raised his hand to silence her. A dull thud sounded again. "That!"

Matt shot from Bart's office and back into the brewery. The ladder to the brewhouse lay on its side, the hatch was closed, and Kate was nowhere to be seen. He caught the sound of running water and a muffled shout.

Matt grabbed the ladder and was at the top hatch in an instant. Someone had locked the unit, and the only ones who could do that had been with him. He flung open the metal door.

Kate stood down in the darkness.

"Are you okay?" Matt called to her.

"I think I need a raise."

Matt reached in an arm. "Can you make it up here?"

She grabbed his hand, scrambled out, and pinned herself against his body. She was soaked from the waist down.

Kate was gasping so much she could barely get her words out. "That sucked. That really, really sucked. I know you're supposed to face your fears, but seriously, never again."

Whoever did this to her would pay, Matt thought. He'd find them and then it would get ugly.

"Come on, let's get you dried off," he said.

By the time they'd reached the ground, Bart had dragged over a chair and Floyd had shut down the brewhouse.

Matt led Kate to the chair. "Bart, could you call the police?"

Bart looked shaken. "Sure thing."

Kate settled into Bart's chair, bent over, and untied her soggy sneakers. "Why would someone do that to me?"

Matt had his guesses, and they had to do with what—and who—he held of value.

"I don't know," he said. Now wasn't the time to point out the obvious.

She pulled off her shoes and socks. Matt noted that one sock was light blue and the other gray with little yellow ducks on it. Despite his tension, he smiled at the mismatch.

"Do you have any other clothes here?" he asked.

"No."

He did a mental inventory of his office, then said, "Hang on."

"Believe me, I'm not going anywhere."

And he didn't want her to, either. But for her own safety, she would be. After today, Matt was going to make sure Kate was far from Depot Brewing Company.

Maybe boyfriend jeans were in style, but boss-or-whatever-more-he-was-to-her sweatpants weren't. Kate rolled the waist over as many times as possible and still she swam in the fabric. She paired the sweatpants with a T-shirt from the brewery store and did a small grimace. Okay, she thought, so she looked like a goofus, but at least she was a dry goofus.

Matt was waiting for her by the brewhouse with Chief Erikson.

"Do you feel up to answering some questions, Kate?" the police chief asked.

"Sure."

Matt glanced toward the latest in a stream of sympathetic Depot employees who'd been checking on Kate since her big swim. "How about in my office?" Matt suggested.

Clete closed the office door behind them. "Kate, did you see your attacker?"

"I was at the bottom of a tank, Chief Erikson. It was just me and a whole lot of dark."

The chief scribbled some notes, then turned to Matt, who'd taken a seat behind his desk. "You were close enough to be the first to Kate, Matt. Did you see anything unusual?"

"No. Bart, Floyd, Nan, and I were in Bart's

office. We'd been having a pretty intense discussion, so I didn't hear or see anything at first." He picked up a pen and started jotting on a legal pad. When he was done, he tore off a piece and slid it across his desk to Clete. "These are the names of the people who were here this morning at ten. The taproom was still closed, so there were no customers in the house."

"Not paying, at least," Clete said. "But could an outsider have gotten into the brewery?"

"It's possible, I suppose," Matt said. "Except it's unlikely an outsider would have known that someone was in the tank."

"Not so true," Kate said. "I was singing 'All By Myself.' Kind of loudly, too."

Clete smiled. "Good song. Other than the brewers, does anyone else touch the brewing tank?"

"No," Matt replied. "The only exception would be if Bart has given any private tours. You'll have to ask him about that."

Clete nodded. "Matt, I don't know what you had planned for that unit today, but I need to call in my fingerprint team. We'll need to fingerprint your staff and you, Matt, though I suppose we already have your prints on file."

Matt showed a flash of a smile at that. "Yeah, I suppose you do from way back when. The file might be a little dusty."

The police chief rose from his chair. "Remember, no one near the brewhouse."

Clete left, and Matt's face grew somber.

"Kate, we have to talk," he said.

She knew what that meant. She'd last heard those words from Harley Bagger. Would she never hold a job in this town for longer than a month?

"You're kidding, right?" she asked. "You can't possibly be about to fire me."

Matt looked shocked. "I'm sorry."

"I don't want sorry. I just want my job."

"Kate, I have to do this," he said. "Yes, you survived this just wet and scared, but you said it earlier—this attack was aimed straight at you. I can't keep placing you in harm's way."

"I know all that, but you're forgetting one crucial thing. I can't eat, repair The Nutshell, or begin to plan for the future without money. And I need the bonus to stop the villain who plans to take my house if I can't get current on my mortgage by Thanksgiving."

"How about if I keep paying you? You can have the bonus money, the whole thing."

She shook her head. "I'm not going to let you pay me for doing nothing."

"Why not?" Matt asked. "Apparently, I do it for Jerry all the time."

"With you or without you, I need to find out

who did this, or I'm never going to be able to put what happened in the brewhouse behind me. And what about you? You need this thing solved as much as I do. We must be getting closer if the creep's pushed it this far."

Matt started to speak a couple of times, but cut himself off. She waited.

"Okay. Work here," he finally said. "But understand that means you're going to be with me twenty-four/seven."

She smiled. "I think they have employment laws against those sorts of hours."

He gave her another frustrated look. "You know what I'm saying, and you know why. Someone is after you, and that person isn't messing around. So when we're here, you're with me, and when we're not, you're in my house."

She wanted to say he was exaggerating the situation, except that she'd just been treated like a beer additive.

"And at the risk of sounding even more like I'm trying to run your life, did you get the locks changed out at your place this week, Kate?"

"Actually, no." She'd been in a haze of poodle contentment and had forgotten Matt's suggestion.

"So anyone can walk in and hide until they're ready to come out. Does that sound about right?"

"Yes," Kate admitted.

"And do you have any walls or floors or a bathroom?"

"Jeesh. I have some walls and floors. And the bees are practically all gone."

"You like living with 'some' bees in a gutted house with no locks on an isolated stretch of the lake with a psycho after you?"

Kate kicked at the floor and looked at her shoe. "It's not gutted, it's decorator-ready. And, besides, every house has 'some' bees."

Matt rolled his eyes. "Then it's settled. I'll come with you while you pack. You and your poodle will stay with me until an arrest is made and your house is renovated and one hundred percent bee free."

"That could be a very long time."

Matt shrugged. "True."

He'd sounded almost happy, and secretly, Kate was, too.

"And you know that we'll probably end up wanting to kill each other," she said.

He smiled. "Old news."

"And that people are going to talk."

"They always do."

But what was gossip mere seconds ago now would be true. She, Matt Culhane, a fussy poodle, and a three-legged dog were going to be shacking up. The circus had just come to town.

SIXTEEN

MATT THOUGHT HIS HOUSE WAS PRETTY COOL. HE'D PUT A good couple of years into harvesting the timber from his property and then building the place. Because it had been designed to suit his needs, he'd never thought too much about how others might view it. Until now.

Kate climbed out of her Jeep, then scooped up Stella, who'd hopped into the driver's seat as soon as it had been vacated. That was close to their actual dog/woman relationship. To be totally accurate, Stella should have been driving the car.

Kate checked out his house. "I take it you had a thing for Lincoln Logs when you were a kid. This is one very impressive adult version thereof."

"You know what they say . . . The bigger the boys, the bigger—"

"We'll probably do better if we don't talk about the size of anything, especially your toys," she said, lingering by her vehicle. "This seemed a lot more sensible in the abstract than in reality. You . . . me . . . under one roof . . ."

He smiled. "I like it. A lot."

"That's what I'm worried about."

Okay, and she was worried that she'd like it a lot. She was worried she'd like it way too much.

"Come on in and have a look around," he said.

They climbed the cut flagstone steps to his front porch. He opened the door for Kate and the pooch.

She hesitated again. "Is Chuck in there?"

"Yes, but don't worry about him. I'll lock him in my bedroom until you and Stella get settled."

Kate stepped across the threshold. "Wow. This is gorgeous. There's a lot more light than I expected."

Matt had designed the house so that the back of the main living space had an expanse of windows overlooking the pond and woods beyond.

"It's a good-sized place, but there aren't that many actual rooms," he said. "I've put you in the only other fully enclosed bedroom, right next to mine, since I didn't think you'd want to deal with the loft." He pointed to the ladder that led to the house's half-floor. "The space up there is good, but the climbs up and down might be tough on the poodle."

She set her dog down. "A Stella-accessible room would be nice."

If this were Chuck, he'd be cruising and sniffing around. Not Stella. She checked out one floor tile and put her nose in the air. Matt guessed she wasn't much for the scent of hound. And she clearly wasn't into him.

After stowing Chuck away, Matt led Kate to the guest room. Stella stuck to her side.

"It's pretty basic." He gestured at the queen-sized log bed he'd built from wood they hadn't been able to use in the house. "You have your own bathroom through there."

"Works for me."

She sat on the edge of the bed, and Matt watched as she leaned back on her palms like she was testing the mattress for play. His favorite kind of play . . . Matt couldn't look away. In his mind, he'd already joined her. They were both wearing a helluva lot less, and Stella was napping elsewhere.

"Nice," he said.

Kate flopped back, arms spread, luxuriating on the patchwork quilt he'd swiped from his mother. "It is. It's wonderful."

Matt hadn't been talking about the bed. He'd been thinking out loud, congratulating himself for maneuvering Kate into his house and his life. He moved closer to Kate and the wonderful bed, and a low growl sounded from somewhere very close to his left ankle. He looked down to see Kate's dog baring piranha-sharp teeth.

"Stella, stop that," Kate said. "You're going to have to get over it. We're guests here."

The dog's lip curled upward even more and Matt knew he had to make a tactical retreat until he stocked up on treats. He was going to lose this battle, but the war wasn't over.

Matt backed off. "What do you say we move on to the kitchen?"

The galley-style kitchen wasn't large, but Matt had built it to last, with granite countertops and quality appliances. Not that he used much of anything but the microwave.

"We haven't talked about cooking," he said.

"And we should probably keep it that way, too," she said. "My cooking would scare you. How about I'll fend for me and you fend for you?"

"Sure. But if I decide to actually cook a meal, I'm going to cook for you, too."

"Thank you," she said, smiling. She moved closer to the fridge, where he kept various niece— and now nephew—photos and scraps of kid art on the door.

Kate pointed to the hospital baby shot of Maura and Todd's latest. "There's TJ."

Matt nodded. "Yup, that's the bruiser. How did you know they were calling him TJ?"

"From the birth announcement."

"You got a birth announcement?"

"Of course," she said. "And I'm going to the pamper mom party that Lizzie is throwing next week."

"Party? I didn't know about a party."

"It's for women only. Lizzie probably wouldn't think of mentioning it to you."

Apparently, Kate was more looped into the Culhane clan than Matt had known. This was yet another sign that his sisters had a full underground social machine in place. A slightly ominous thought, but since it also meant Kate was both watched over and building friendships that might make her feel more at home in the town, he'd learn to deal.

"Anything else you'd like to share?" he asked.

"Not a thing."

After six days with Kate under his roof, Matt was having a hard time imagining her not being there. Unfortunately, the man-and-poodle relationship remained nothing to brag about.

"Are you sure you're okay with me being here on card night?" Kate called from the kitchen. "I could always meet up with Ella for a girls' night out."

"You're cool here," Matt said as he stowed beer by the poker table set up in his living room. "Chuck likes having you around."

Plus, Matt didn't want Kate too far out of sight. He remained spooked by last Thursday's near miss, and he flat-out enjoyed her company.

Kate came into the room with her dog trotting after her. She handed Matt a bowl of potato chips, and he stuck them on the table.

"I'm glad *Chuck's* fond of me," she said. "Probably best that I stay in tonight, anyway. After all the fries I chowed at work today, if I ate any more bar food, I'd never fit in these jeans again."

"Couldn't have that," Matt said, eyeing both the jeans and the hot curves that filled them. For two days, Matt had fought hard not to give in to temptation and touch her. He was done fighting.

Matt took a step toward her. Stella growled. He glared at the poodle.

Kate couldn't help a little smile. "I'll go grab that sandwich tray."

She cruised into the kitchen, but Stella kept eyeballing Matt.

Figuring it couldn't hurt, he tossed the dog a potato chip. The poodle crunched through it in three chomps. She wagged her tail at Matt, clearly seeking more. Just to see if the chip-eating had been a fluke, he gave her another. It disappeared immediately.

Matt smiled. "I think this is the beginning of a beautiful friendship."

A knock sounded at the front door, and Bart

and Travis came in. After they dumped their jackets on the sofa, Bart handed out cigars.

Kate popped out of the kitchen with the sandwich tray. While she said hello to Travis and Bart, Matt put the tray up high enough that Chuck, who was faking a nap by the fireplace, couldn't grab it.

Kate spotted the cigars and wrinkled her nose. "Do you guys really smoke those things?"

"Sure," Matt said, though his usually just smoldered in the ashtray.

"Gross."

Travis cut his eyes to her. "Ever tried one? You should before dissing them."

Kate laughed. "Thanks, but I'm still recovering from the beer tasting. I'll just mosey on into the kitchen and think healthy thoughts while I eat my salad. Come on, Stella, let's go."

Stella stared at her owner, but didn't move from Matt's side.

Kate motioned to her. "Come on, girl." When Stella stayed put, she said to Matt, "It looks like you two are getting along better."

"We're working on it," Matt said. *One chip at a time.* "Don't worry about her. She can hang with us for a while."

Kate gave the poodle one last, speculative look and headed back into the kitchen alone. Five minutes later, Matt's brother-in-law Jack arrived with a bottle of Irish whiskey in hand.

"Let's get rolling," Matt said. "Todd called this afternoon. He can't make it. TJ has him too sleep-deprived to function."

"Which is why he should be here," Jack said. "We could use a donkey."

Bart poured everyone a shot. "We still have you." For a second, Jack looked as sharp-edged as his red brush cut, but then he joined in on the laughter. After that, the ceremonial opening whiskey was downed, some bull was shot, and stacks of quarters were lined up.

Matt slid the dealer button in front of himself on the table and shuffled the deck.

"Texas Hold 'Em," he announced to the players.

Kate wandered back into the room. "Is Stella still here?"

Matt grinned. "Right next to me. Jealous?"

"Possibly."

Matt chose to take that as a sign that she wanted his company, and not the poodle's.

"Have you ever played poker?"

She paused. "Once." Maybe no one else in the room could read her, but Matt knew she was messing with the truth. Kate's tell was a subtle widening of her eyes.

"So, Kate, want to join in?" Jack asked in a casual voice.

"I guess I could. I mean, if it wouldn't slow you guys down too much?"

"Never!" Jack said.

He clearly thought he'd landed his donkey, but Matt bet Jack was going to keep the tail and big ears.

"Sure, then," Kate said. "I'd love to."

Matt gave Kate his chair and half his quarters. After he'd brought another chair from the kitchen and settled in next to her, a low growl sounded from beneath the table. Matt grabbed a couple of chips. He popped one into his mouth and subtly let the other one drop to an overly possessive poodle.

"Since we have a new player, how about we go with a little straight poker, aces high, sevens wild? And I'll sit out on the first couple of hands and help Kate get started," Matt said.

The table agreed, and Matt dealt.

Once Kate had her hand, he moved his chair closer to coach her. Stella wasn't square with the new arrangement and let everyone know by barking.

Matt edged the potato chip bowl closer. He was going to need it.

A couple more chips and many hands later, everyone was played out. Jack, Travis, and Bart had rounded up their remaining change, razzed Kate about her big win, and headed home.

Kate now sat at the kitchen table as Matt worked his way through the last of the night's mess. Stella was flopped at her owner's feet, zoned out on carbs.

"So how many times have you really played poker?" Matt asked, hoping to keep Kate's attention from the chip-enriched poodle.

"Lots," Kate said.

Matt smiled. "As I thought."

He finished packing away the guys' unsmoked cigars. While they'd played, he'd silently nixed any attempt to light one. Matt had wanted Kate next to him too much to risk her leaving the game over a stogie.

She rose and reached for the nearly empty potato chip bag. "I started playing a while back. Casino night fund-raisers were a fad downstate a couple of years ago. Any time one of Richard's clients' pet charities had one, we'd go." Kate moved on to put glasses into the dishwasher, and Stella followed. "Anyway, after a couple of events, Richard stopped playing at my table," Kate said. "It irked him to see me kick butt. It was luck, mostly."

"Luck and being able to read others," Matt said.

He was done hiding what he wanted from Kate. It was time to be read, loud and clear. He tucked a couple of chips into his right hand while she was closing the dishwasher.

"I liked having you next to me tonight," he

said. "And Stella didn't seem to mind us being close."

She held so still that Matt wondered for an instant whether she was going to bolt from the kitchen. But he knew she wanted him, too.

"In fact, I'll bet my winnings we could get even closer," Matt said.

As he moved in to kiss her, he dropped a chip for Stella. Then he wished like hell that dogs chewed with their mouths closed.

Kate glanced down. "Did you just give her a treat?"

Matt kept it short and sweet. "Yes."

"Now I know why you two are making friends. Smart move. But I didn't see you get anything from the treat jar. The last thing I saw you near was that bag of potato chips. Did you give her a chip?"

"No."

She stepped back, looked him up and down, and smiled. "You are the worst bluffer, *ever*."

Which was bull. Except when it came to Kate.

"Open your hand," she said.

Matt shifted his feet, stalling. "Which one?"

She wrapped her fingers around his right hand and squeezed. Matt's lone chip died an ugly death.

"Now open it," she said.

Matt did as directed. A few crumbs slipped from his hand, and Stella dove for them.

"Stella, no!" Kate said.

Too late. Stella snapped up the bits before they hit the floor.

Kate gave Matt a stern look. "You know I don't feed her from the table."

Matt dumped the remaining crumbs into the wastebasket. "We aren't at the table. We're in the kitchen."

Stella trotted up to Matt and braced her front feet on his shin as she begged for more.

Kate sighed. "You've created a monster. Down, Stella."

The dog grudgingly obeyed, but stayed close to Matt.

SEVENTEEN

FOR ABOUT THE TENTH TIME SINCE WEDNESDAY POKER night, Kate tripped over a pair of Matt's shoes . . . and it was only Friday. Why would a guy think it was smart to drop his shoes exactly where he'd taken them off? He had big feet, too. And many, many pairs of shoes.

Kate picked up the latest pair and chucked them just to the left of his closed bedroom door, where they joined a bunch of their kin.

"If you want to develop a shoe-eating habit, I promise I won't say a word," she told Stella. "It would be a good payback for Matt getting you hooked on potato chips."

The dog was now a serious chip junkie. Even though she'd gotten sick on them, she still sat longingly in front of the pantry cabinet, where Matt always kept his stash.

Kate's poodle had food issues on another front, too. Stella had been raised with an open supply of food. Kate would put kibble in her bowl in the morning and the poodle would graze at will. But now, the second Kate filled Stella's bowl, glutton Chuck appeared, excited as if Thanksgiving had come around yet again. The instant Kate looked away, the chow was gone in one gulp. Chuck did not believe in chewing.

As though he knew Kate was thinking about him, a bark rolled into the hallway from the living room. And then another. These weren't excited sounds, more expository statements.

"*Woof.*"

Kate joined Chuck in front of the fireplace.

"*Woof.*"

He had barely lifted his head from his napping position.

"What?" she asked him.

"*Woof.*"

Kate looked at Stella, who had followed in her tracks. "You speak dog. Tell him to stop."

But Stella couldn't be persuaded to negotiate, and Chuck had no intention of stopping.

"Okay, Lassie. Did Timmy fall down the well again?"

"*Woof.*"

"Am I the prettiest princess in the land?"

"*Woof.*"

Kate could have played her game awhile longer, but Chuck's hound bark was beginning to make her teeth rattle. She walked through the kitchen and on to the basement door, which was by the house's back entry. Stella stood at the back door and stared expectantly at her.

"Okay, you first, then I'll deal with the big dog." She stuck Stella on the outdoor lead that had been brought over from The Nutshell, and headed back inside.

"Matt?" she called.

He was downstairs working out, a daily event. She heard the whine of a treadmill going at warp speed, but no word from Matt.

"Hey, Culhane!" she yelled, cupping her hands to either side of her mouth.

"What?"

"Your dog needs you."

The treadmill's hum lowered as he brought its speed down, then stopped entirely.

"*Woof.*"

"See? Like that," she said as he climbed the steps.

When he made the top, Kate was transfixed. He used his right hand to wipe sweat from a six-pack of abs so hard she wanted to trace each ridge with her tongue. Twice.

His smile was slow and knowing. "You probably should let me by."

Or not, she thought.

"*Woof.*"

"He's just lying there, barking," she said.

Matt moved past her, close enough that she could catch the heat rolling off his body . . . though it just might have been hers.

Kate followed him to Chuck.

"What's up, buddy?" he asked the dog.

"*Woof.*"

"What's he barking at?" Kate asked.

"He's barking *at* nothing. That's his water bark. He has specific barks for specific things."

"You've got to be kidding."

"You think? Come with me to the kitchen."

Kate trailed after him. "Amazing," she said as she watched him claim the empty water bowl and refill it.

And really, she wasn't just talking about the dog. When it came to Matt, the view from the rear was almost as impressive as that from the front. She catalogued each of these moments to tide her over in her lonely, dog-guarded bed.

"So Stella the Wonderpoodle doesn't have different barks?" he asked.

"No, but she can now identify an unopened potato chip bag by sight."

Matt laughed. "A lot of dogs have different

barks for different needs. Stella's pretty smart. Maybe you just don't know her signs anymore."

"Maybe, but for now, let's talk about shoes."

"Isn't that the kind of thing that would go over better with Ella and my sisters?"

"Doubtful, Imelda," she said. "I'm betting if I stacked all of my shoes against yours, you'd win."

He looked almost wounded. "I don't have that many."

"This way, please." She beckoned him away from the kitchen and to the bedroom hallway in tour guide fashion. "And here we have Mount Culhane, an active volcano, altitude six pairs and growing daily."

He regarded the pile suspiciously. "How did they all end up here?"

"I've been moving them every day."

"From where?"

"Exactly where you take them off, it appears. It was becoming a minefield out there."

He was still staring at the shoes. "I'd wondered where they all went."

"What? They're right by your door. Don't you look at the ground?"

"No need," he said. "I could walk this house blindfolded."

"Then next time, I'll trip you up and take them all the way into your bedroom."

A slow smile spread across his face. "Would you?"

Kate realized she had just committed a tactical error and morphed into his maid.

He leaned down and kissed her. "Thanks, sweetheart."

Okay, make that two tactical errors, because she didn't stop him. And now three, because she was kissing him back.

It had been tough work forgetting just what it felt like to be kissed by Matt Culhane. And it had been tougher yet to block the thought that she was one wall away from him every night. She knew that he sometimes talked in his sleep. She knew that he woke and showered at six. And she knew that right now she'd be beyond blissed-out should they make love.

Telling herself she was ten kinds of crazy, Kate deepened the kiss and touched the wall of muscle on his chest. And while they kissed some more, she ran her fingers down to the waistband of his shorts.

She didn't know for sure what he'd look like totally naked, but she could give it a good guess based on the size of his shoes. He brought her tighter against his body. She drew in a surprised breath. She had underestimated.

"Aren't you going to do that magical thing where I'm suddenly on a bed?" she asked. Because she really, really wanted him to.

He made some space between the two of them. "I don't know. I haven't made my mind up yet."

"What could possibly involve our minds?"

She'd been joking, but he looked serious.

"One question," he said. "If we do this . . . if I make love to you . . . what happens next?"

"We go unconscious?"

"No, after that. Does it mean that you're going to move from your room and into mine?"

"Well, no. But it does mean we'll both be less tense."

He shook his head. "That's not good enough for me, Kate."

"But back at the hotel you would have . . ."

"You're right. But I've been thinking about this since we were out of town, and it turns out that I'm not a fling sort of guy. Actually, once I considered it, I realized I never have been."

Something wasn't computing. "What about your Keene's Harbor's reputation as the resident Don Juan?"

He shrugged. "I've dated my share of women, but none of those women have anything to do with you," Matt said. "You and I are in a different place. We're friends—the kind of friends I don't want to give up unless we become something more. So if you and I go there, it has to be with the full commitment to be my lover, because no way am I going to risk our friendship for less."

"You're scaring me a little."

"I probably should be scaring you a lot. Because I mean it, Kate. Once I'm in, I'm *all* in."

So unless she was ready for commitment, she had struck out?

"And what about The Nutshell?" she asked.

"It has nothing to do with us. It's all business."

Kate crossed her arms. "You wouldn't say that if it was your house or your brewery."

"Kate, I paid the bank $200,000 for that mortgage. I gave you until Thanksgiving to make a go of it. But I can't afford to wait any longer than that. I need the money, either from you or from the restaurant I plan to open next summer."

"I'm sorry," she said. "I'm just not ready for this."

And while it was tougher than any trek she'd ever taken, Kate retreated to reclaim her poodle. She might be ten kinds of stupid, but for now, she'd managed to avoid adding an eleventh.

The next morning, Matt walked into his office—or what had been his office before he'd made Kate his personal assistant. Now ownership was questionable.

"Ginger just called," Kate said.

"What did she want?" Until he had a signal from Kate otherwise, he planned to keep it all business.

"She'd like to know your Traverse City schedule. We're working on coordinating your calendar so that someone other than you has a clue where you'll be at any given time."

"Nobody but me really needs to know."

"Nice try, but untrue. We also talked about getting bids from subcontractors on the Tropicana, since you've decided to be the general contractor. I know you wanted to keep the bids local, but it's a motel, Matt. You need to take advantage of that. We think you should widen your net some, since you can offer up rooms in exchange for lower price quotes."

Matt smiled. "You look comfortable there."

She looked around. "Where?"

"Behind my desk. With your papers everywhere." There was a certain order to his pile filing system, and he hoped she hadn't messed with it.

"Where else would I work? I mean, I suppose I could go use the phone at the servers' stand, but I figure folks should have to work a little harder for their gossip than just lurking behind me."

"How about we switch off and at least I get the spot behind my desk for a while?" he asked. "I need to get to the computer."

She rose. "Do you want me out of here?"

And that was the thing of it. Even though they had a long way to go on a personal basis, and it made him a little crazy to have her close, he wanted her nearby.

"You can stick around," he said. "I'm just placing a yeast order. We're coming to the last generation we can use to brew."

Kate had just moved to the visitor's side of

the desk when a knock sounded at the door and Lizzie poked her head into the office.

"So, business or pleasure?" Matt asked.

"Business, definitely." Lizzie sat down. "Chief Erikson asked me to stop by and give you an update on the incident with Kate in the brewhouse."

"I'm guessing that it's more of a no-news update, or Clete would be here himself," he said.

Lizzie nodded. "You've got his act down. The bottom line is that the brewhouse is as clean of evidence as the arson event. There were no prints that couldn't be accounted for. I can rule someone out, though."

"Really? Who?" Matt asked.

"Jerry. It seems that he took on a second job when his wife got laid off from the bank. He was there when Kate took her swim."

"Good to know. Sort of," Matt said.

"He thought he could pull off a second job without rocking the boat, but it's been a scheduling mess," Lizzie said. "He's going to come talk to you."

Matt nodded. He wished his manager had done that earlier, but he knew all about overconfidence sending a guy out to the end of a branch about to break. Matt had done it both literally and figuratively. He could forgive Jerry for doing the same.

"It's a start, but not much of one," Lizzie said. "For now, let's keep things status quo. I know you've got the guard service, but we'll continue with the extra drive-bys, too. And Kate, you keep staying at Matt's."

Matt looked down at his desk to hide his reaction to this mixed blessing. Then he started reading the papers Kate had left there. He picked one up.

"Kate, what's this about?"

"It's a booking contract."

"I see that. And I see that Depot Brewing Company is contracting with someone named Dr. Love."

"A blues band. I need you to sign the contract first, of course."

"Nice of you to recall that detail," he said.

"I know where I am on the org chart."

"I don't have an org chart."

Kate pointed at a file folder at the top edge of the desk. "You do, now. I was going to post it by the time clock."

"This is a microbrewery, not a multinational corporation," Matt said. "With the possible exception of you, everyone knows who's in charge here."

Lizzie stood. "I'm all done here. I'll just leave you to do . . . whatever it is you're doing."

"Witnessing a pretty impressive attempted coup, I think," Matt said.

"Okay, then." Lizzie gave Kate a wave. "Coup away!"

Matt turned to Kate as soon as Lizzie left the room. "What is the brewery going to do with a blues band?"

"Start a summer music series out on the terrace when the weather allows and in the taproom when it doesn't?"

At least she'd made her statement sound more like a question.

"Look, I'm not saying that the idea is bad, because actually it's great," he said. "I just don't have the time to deal with it. I've got too much going on up north."

"That's the best part. I can do all the grunt work," Kate said. "You don't give me enough to do, so if I have this on my plate, there's a good chance I won't be nosing into everything else."

"How good of a chance?" About all she had left to do was alphabetize the pantry and tick off the cooks.

"Very good. And I really think this could work, Matt. You have a lot of summer people who will drive all the way to Traverse City for live music. Keep them in town, and your business will jump."

Matt just shook his head. She was right. "Write me up a proposal."

Kate came around the desk and stood close to him. She riffled through some papers, then held up a neatly bound document. "Already done."

He opened the report and paged through a

market study, cost analysis, and financial projections, complete with pie charts.

"You're good, Kate. *Very* good."

Kate smiled wickedly. "You don't know the half of it."

But he wanted to.

EIGHTEEN

KATE DIDN'T WANT TO JINX THINGS, BUT SHE WAS ON A roll. Over a week had passed since Matt had given her permission to schedule music events, and she'd gotten next summer booked. And because she was in overachiever mode, she'd also finished all the promo materials. Okay, maybe she wasn't so much in overachiever mode as fill-every-waking-hour-so-she-couldn't-think-of-Matt mode, but no matter. The results were the same. Kate rose and double-checked the events calendar she'd hung on the office wall.

Even better, her house was nearly repaired. The contractor had been very cooperative. He said he needed the work, so she could pay after the holidays. All it needed was some fresh paint, some new furniture, and a head-to-toe cleaning.

She stood hands on hip, pleased. "You're golden," she told herself.

Matt had scheduled a mandatory 10:30 staff meeting this morning. For no reason other than pride, she'd wanted to be done with these projects before then.

Kate's cell phone rang. She went back to the desk, picked it up, and did a double take at the name on the caller ID: Barb Appleton. She and her mom didn't talk frequently. It wasn't that her mom didn't love her, or that she didn't love her mom. They were just in different places in life. But today, Kate felt happy that her mom was calling.

"Hey, Mom."

"Hello, Kate. You're a tough one to reach."

"I answered on the third ring," she said.

"I didn't mean now, dear. I've been leaving messages on the phone at The Nutshell for days. Where have you been?"

Kate searched for an explanation. Her mom liked her kids in one piece.

"I . . . I've been having some work done out there and staying with friends until it's complete," Kate said.

"What sort of work?"

"I've been getting the exterior doors re-keyed," she replied. Which wasn't a total lie, because she still planned to. Eventually.

"Why would you do that? We've owned that

cottage for decades and kept it unlocked for just
as long. There's no place safer than Keene's Harbor."

Kate withheld comment.

"How is the house looking?"

"Just fine. Why?"

"Your father and I are feeling a little nostal-
gic. I know we usually stay in Naples October
through May, but we were thinking that popping
up to Keene's Harbor for a family Thanksgiving
would be wonderful. Just like the old days."

"But we always had Thanksgiving at the country club," Kate said. "You know, the Thanksgiving Day Parade in Detroit, then turkey with your
choice of stuffing and sides, overlooking the putting green."

"We must have had it at The Nutshell once,"
Mom said.

"No. Never."

"Then it's definitely time. Your father and I
aren't getting any younger, you know, Kate."

Man, she hated it when her mother played the
aging card.

"Neither am I, Mom."

"True. So this year, let's get you, Chip, Bunny,
and all the family up to the cottage for an old-
fashioned meal."

A couple weeks ago, Kate might have been
horrified. The insecurity and jealousy that had
infected her marriage to Richard had just sort of

bled all over her other relationships, including the one with her family. But the truth was that, before Richard, holidays like Thanksgiving had always been a really big deal to her.

Suddenly, Kate realized that she missed her mom. She missed her dad. She missed her brother and sister. They were her family and they loved her and she loved them. She might as well get on the turkey train. "That sounds fun. Can't wait."

"Good, dear. Now see if you can find a chef to cook for us. I just want to relax with the family. If you can't, we might have to come up with another option. Perhaps a restaurant up that way?"

"I'll start looking."

"Keep me abreast of the plans."

"Sure thing. Give my love to Dad."

Kate hung up and went facedown on the desk. She'd forgotten about Matt. How was she going to explain that they were living together to her parents? Matt entered the room and settled into a guest chair. "What's up?"

Little wrinkle lines were forming on Kate's forehead. "My whole family is coming to The Nutshell for Thanksgiving."

"And?"

Kate bit her lower lip. "I've got two problems. One is of the big variety. The other could be huge."

"Lay it on me."

Kate sighed. "You know how Charlie Brown

had a Thanksgiving party for Peppermint Patty, except that he could only make popcorn and toast?"

Matt laughed. "Yeah."

"Well, I can only make toast."

Matt got out of his chair and hugged her close. It was nice—friendly and loving. Like she had known him all her life. "No worries. I'll help. It'll be fun. Was that the big or huge problem?"

In Matt's arms, her problems seemed small. "My parents are a little . . ." She paused. "Conservative."

Matt smiled. "No problem. We can bond over our shared opposition to the hippie menace."

"If they find out I'm living with a guy, they'll be horrified. They won't understand that cosmic forces are to blame."

Matt shook his head. "Isn't this Barb the table dancer we're talking about?"

"Barb, the *married* table dancer," Kate pointed out. "It's like the 1960s in my family. It's all about the order of events. You don't skip past the entrée straight to dessert and you don't shack up. The only thing that could make it worse is announcing at Thanksgiving that you're my baby daddy."

Matt's eyebrows perked up. He held her tighter. "That can be arranged, too. And, on the plus side, no one will care about only having toast for Thanksgiving."

"I'm serious."

Matt brushed her hair away from her face. "So we have a minor inconvenience to deal with."

Kate looked at him for a long while. "And it's Thanksgiving. And if I can't find your saboteur by then, my house belongs to you. So it really isn't a 'we' problem. It's my problem."

"I see."

Kate felt bad. The truth was, she wanted it to be their problem. And, in her heart, she'd said something very different to Matt. But her hasty words had just sort of popped out and hung in the air like a bad smell. Kate decided to change the subject. She'd try to make it right with Matt later, after work.

"The first thing I need to do is get a locksmith, then move back and get The Nutshell ready for them," she said.

"Thanksgiving is still over a week off. What's the rush?"

"I just think it's time. It's been pretty quiet the past few weeks. Maybe the jerk has gotten bored with the whole thing and moved on. Anyway, I'm feeling safer now."

She hesitated and looked at Matt with wide, hopeful eyes. "And you can get your life back."

"For the record, I'm okay with my life the way it is. But all the same, even though I don't like it or fully understand it, I'm not going to stop you from moving back out there," Matt said.

"Thanks."

It was what she'd asked for, but it wasn't what she'd wanted. She wanted to add that she knew she was being weird. That this was what dealing with her parents did to her, and she just couldn't stop herself.

"Chuck has kind of grown to like having Stella around," Matt said.

She knew what he was saying, and it had nothing to do with dogs. But maybe she was more traditional than she wanted to believe.

"Maybe I can bring Stella over to visit every now and then?"

"Chuck would like that," Matt said. He hitched his thumb toward the door. "Do you think you could head out to the taproom? I need a couple of minutes to get my notes together."

She needed a couple of minutes to pull herself together, too. This had hurt way more than she'd thought it would.

After Kate left, Matt sat at his desk. He had no notes. All he had was a numb sensation he'd last felt when he'd fallen off his roof and nearly knocked himself out.

Matt couldn't nail the exact moment, but at some point reality and he had parted ways. Having Kate in his house and in his life had felt real to him, not just an arrangement. But even though they'd had breakfast together, gone to work together, and flipped a coin over whether to watch football or movies at night, it hadn't been real.

If he'd been rational, he'd have known it had been all the illusion and none of the substance of being a couple. But he wasn't rational. He was in love.

Still, no matter how crappy he might be feeling, he had a roomful of people waiting for him out there. So he'd move on and deal with his feelings for Kate later. Matt joined his crew in the taproom, and when he looked at his gang, he felt better, if not perfect.

"Thanks to those of you who weren't scheduled for coming in, and the rest of you for being here early," he said. "I don't have a lot of big-picture updates about what's going on here at Depot Brewing, except to officially announce the start of a music series next summer that Kate's been putting together, and I'm sure most of you have heard about it, anyway. I think we're going to see a big jump in business on formerly slow nights, and I want to put on more part-time staff. If you know of anyone good, send them my way."

Steve, the server, raised his hand. "I've heard that Bagger's is cutting staff down to one server a shift. You might pick up someone there."

"Thanks," Matt said.

He'd known that traffic had been down for Harley, but he hadn't known it was that bad. If it was time to give Harley a hand, Matt was glad to do it.

"And now on to other news," Matt said. "I

know that a lot of you have had questions about where I go when I'm not around the brewery. To make a long answer short, I've been spending a lot of time in Traverse City, and that time investment is starting to pay off. By next summer, I'll be looking for staff for a microbrewery up there, plus for a new motel and restaurant. I'm also opening a new restaurant in Keene's Harbor. It's a couple miles out of town on the lake. If any of you are interested in making the move, you'll get first shot at the openings. Think it over and let me know. No rush, okay? And now I'm going to turn the meeting over to Jerry to update you on front of the house matters."

His manager had just started talking when Matt motioned Kate over. They walked into the hallway by his office.

"Why don't you take the rest of the day off? Get your locksmith and whatever else you need done lined up so that you can move back to The Nutshell," he said.

"And what's the point?" She felt anger rising in her voice. "New locks on a great old house you're just going to bulldoze. I never had a chance. I wouldn't be surprised if you put Junior up to the mess he caused me just to seal the deal."

She knew she'd gone too far, but he'd caught her by surprise with his announcement, and it had all come gushing out.

* * *

Four days later, Kate stood in The Nutshell's living room steeling herself for her parents' impending arrival. She was pretty sure she had her act together, since she'd prepared as she would for any natural disaster. Kate had stocked up on Manhattan mixings and maraschino cherries for her dad and champagne and crossword puzzles for her mom. She'd also hidden a handful of candy bars and three bags of potato chips in her bedroom in case she needed to take shelter for an extended period of time.

It was nearly six, and a pot of beef stew simmered in the kitchen. Kate had thrown in a jar of cocktail onions and some red wine, hoping she could fake her mom into thinking it was a classic *boeuf bourguignon*. Mom had always been all about dinner being a sit-down meal, even if the house had been falling down around them. When she was a kid, it sometimes seemed inconvenient. Now, she realized it was one of the best parts of her childhood—a constant in her adolescent life that made her feel safe and protected.

Kate smoothed her hands over the black pencil skirt, which she'd last worn when working at *Detroit Monthly*. Mom didn't believe in jeans, paper napkins, or ketchup at the dinner table. As a teen, Kate had tried to assure her mother that all those things were perfectly real and even kind of cool. Mom had never bought in.

Tonight, Kate didn't mind being dressed up. If nothing else, the change in wardrobe kept it front and center in her mind that she'd been right not to expose Matt to this. Somehow, she couldn't picture him wearing a button-down shirt just to eat beef stew.

Stella's ears perked at the sound of a car in the drive. She trotted toward the front door and gave a welcoming yip.

Kate gave the dog a gentle pat. "Sure, it's all happiness and sunshine, now. But let's see what tune you're singing by turkey day." The truth was, she was excited, too.

Kate pulled on her jacket and went outside to greet her parents. Stella, who wasn't a fan of the icy wind off the lake, lurked indoors.

Though Kate had visited with her parents just a handful of months ago, she felt a surprising sense of nostalgia seeing them here, at The Nutshell. The years had treated her father well. With his Florida tan, silver hair, and aristocratic features, he still reminded Kate of a diplomat in the foreign service.

Mom was no slacker, either. Her hair might have tipped the scales from blond to gray, but otherwise, she looked much as she had when Kate was a teen. And she still stood a good four inches taller than Kate, too.

After hugs and greetings, Kate looked into the back of the SUV her dad had rented.

"That sure is a lot of luggage, Mom," Kate said.

Kate's mom removed a suiter from the back. "It might seem excessive, but you never know what events might pop up and how the weather might be."

"In this case, not many events and freezing would be good bets." Kate glanced at her mom's pale pink and very thin cardigan sweater. "Do you have a coat in one of those suitcases?"

"I have another sweater or two, but I left my mink in cold storage."

Kate was no fan of furs, but if her mom had to wear one, now would be the time. "You can borrow one of my jackets while you're here."

"That's all right. I'll ring up Bunny and ask her to bring something appropriate," Mom said. "In the meantime, your father and I can pretend we're snowbound and stay indoors. It could be very romantic."

Kate put her muscles to work, helping her dad haul the luggage. In the time it took them to get everything inside, Stella had fallen asleep on her mom's lap.

Kate's mother sat on the flowery sofa, stroking Stella. "Your dog's a charmer, Kate. What do you think I should get her for Christmas?"

"Anything in cashmere would probably do."

Her mother laughed. "Well, naturally. She is an Appleton female. And how about you?"

"I . . . uh . . . Let me get back to you on that one." Kate couldn't think of the last time her mother had gotten her anything other than a gift card. Of course, she also couldn't recall when she'd gotten her mother anything other than a silk scarf. "Why don't you two get settled in, and I'll get dinner on the table?"

Half an hour later, after her parents had their cocktails in hand, the family sat down to Kate's fake *boeuf bourguignon*. The onions tasted weird even to Kate, but no one mentioned them. In fact, her dad said that stew made the perfect meal when snowed in. Never mind that they weren't really snowed in, and that Kate had started the stew hours before their arrival.

Toward the end of the meal, Kate's dad stuck an old Johnny Mathis album on the stereo. "Katie, the house looks just great. Better than I remember. I really think you could make your plan to turn this place into a B&B work."

He turned to Kate's mom. "Remember seeing Johnny perform that winter in Lake Tahoe?"

The two of them shared a smile and clasped hands on the tabletop. Kate pushed around the onions in her stew, not wanting to break into their moment.

"Kate, if you'll excuse us, your mother and I need to have this dance. And don't worry about clearing the table. We'll do that . . . later."

"Sure," Kate said. "I'll just go take care of

some stuff in my room." She didn't feel like telling them right now about Matt and his plans to
turn the house into a restaurant.

She listened to her parents laugh through the
walls of her room. If this was to be a nightly
event while playing snowed-in, Kate was going to
need more chips and chocolate in her stash. For
crying out loud. These people were her parents.

According to Kate's clock, it was now ten at
night. It felt more like three in the morning. Kate
was bored out of her mind. The music downstairs was still going strong, though her parents
had moved on to Frank Sinatra.

For lack of anything else to do, Kate dumped
her purse onto the dresser and began to sort
through the bag's contents. A cleaning might
make it weigh less than a ton. Kate pulled out her
wallet, makeup bag, and the notepad she carried
to write "to do" lists that she could then ignore.
At the purse's bottom, in a nest of pennies and
market receipts, lay the letter from her mom that
she'd tucked away and never finished reading.

"Now's as good a time as any."

Kate settled on the bed. Because she'd already
heard a fresh update on all nieces and nephews
during dinner, she fast-forwarded past the opening chat and the bit where her mom wished that
Kate would have gotten a business degree.

But there's no remaking the past. Your road

won't be as easy as mine, her mother wrote. *Still, I know you're up to the challenge. Yes, you've been struggling, and it was obvious to both your father and me how much it upset you to ask us for help. But we were happy to give it, darling. And though it's not kind to say, neither your father nor I were especially fond of Richard. He tended to try to build himself up at your expense. You'll be a happier woman without him.*

"You've got that right," Kate said.

I think in many ways, I envy you, Kate. You have a spirit I didn't have at your age. Oh, I had my moments, but you have me beat. You also have the determination to weather the tough times. I'm not so sure I would have had your sort of grit. I am very proud of you. I need to tell you that more often, and you need to begin believing it. Then we'll rule the world.

Kate smiled. Maybe she could imagine her mother dancing on tabletops, after all. And maybe she had been wrong about her parents all these years. It wasn't that they thought she couldn't do anything, it was that they thought she could do everything.

A while before midnight, Matt sat alone at his closed bar nursing a tall glass of water. Since Kate had moved out, his universe had been totally jacked up. He'd even been feeling sorry for himself, which was a new and unpleasant sensation.

When the cuckoo clock over the bar struck twelve, Matt planned to get the hell over this. Somehow. And in the meantime, he'd watch the clock's minute hand move.

A sharp rapping sounded on the taproom window, pulling Matt's attention from the clock. Lizzie stood at the glass in her police officer's uniform, flashlight in hand.

Matt pointed her toward the front entrance.

"What are you doing here?"

"My promised late-night rounds," she said. "The bigger question is, what are you still doing here?"

"Waiting for midnight."

"Why? Are you going to turn into the guy version of Cinderella or something?" She grinned. "Kate mentioned your shoe fixation."

"More like I was hoping to turn back into myself."

"I didn't know you weren't yourself. I mean, you skipped last Friday's fund-raiser and everything," Lizzie said.

He rubbed the back of his neck. "Yeah, well, Kate moved out, and I wanted to enjoy my new peace and quiet, but Chuck really misses her."

"He's really stuck on Kate, huh?"

"This isn't the kind of stuff we talk about," he said. "It feels wrong."

She gave him a crooked smile. "It's just that

'Chuck' doesn't generally have relationship problems, and I don't generally have relationships."

"Good point," he said.

Lizzie sat down on a barstool next to Matt.
"So why did Kate move out?"

Matt was surprised by the question. Kate and
Lizzie had grown pretty close.

"You mean she hasn't talked to you?"

"Not in the past few days."

"She found out her parents were coming in for
Thanksgiving, and she kind of freaked out. Apparently, they don't believe in sleeping in a guy's
guest bedroom before you're married."

"Interesting," Lizzie said. "And in more ways
than one. Kate slept in the guest bedroom?"

"Don't let it get around. My false reputation
is at stake."

"As if I would. And no one would believe me,
anyway. But, really, so what if she moved home?
Things have been calm here, and she'll be safe."

"Well, I'm also about to foreclose on her
childhood home and destroy her dreams so I can
expand my evil empire."

"I know."

"You do?"

"Yeah. I'm a police officer and I'm a woman.
That makes me a big snoop. I also know you
made arrangements with Kate's contractor to secretly pay him yourself and have him reimburse

you once he gets the money from her. Does she really believe a contractor would ever wait for his money?"

Matt grinned sheepishly. He'd been caught. "Does anyone else know?"

"No. I don't think so. Why'd you do it? You have a lot of money invested in this project, don't you?"

Matt shrugged. "I love her."

Lizzie burst out laughing. "Look at you. You're a mess. Do you want my advice?"

"Give it your best shot, because I'm coming up blank."

"I love Kate. I think she's fabulous. I hope you two work it out and have a million kids, or whatever it is you're looking for. You're my big brother . . . heck, my *only* brother. I want to see you happy. My advice to you is—Suck it up."

Matt raised an eyebrow at his sister.

"Since when was Matt Culhane a quitter? You never gave up in football or hockey. You didn't give up in the eighth grade when Mary Lou Petty refused to go to junior prom with you. You certainly never gave up on Depot Brewing—even when a lot of people thought you should. If you love Kate that much, go get her!"

Lizzie was right. He'd go to Traverse City for a couple of days, giving Kate the space she needed and a chance to get reacquainted with her parents. When he returned, he was sure Kate would be ready to invite him to dinner, and if she wasn't, he'd invite himself. Desperate times called for desperate measures. After all, Chuck really missed her.

NINETEEN

IT WAS THE MONDAY EVENING BEFORE THANKSGIVING. Kate's mom and dad were still living out their snowbound fantasy, and Kate was beginning to lose her mind. Sinatra playing on the stereo twelve hours out of twenty-four was part of the issue. The rest was that her parents gave her little privacy.

In a house this size, how could they be everywhere at once? Kate was beginning to think cloning was involved. She was currently holed up in her bathroom for both prime cell phone reception and a little alone time.

The doorknob rattled. "Kate? Are you in there?"

"Yes, Mom," Kate said from her resting spot in the dry bathtub.

"You've been in there awhile."

"Yes, I have. I'm taking a bath."

"That's odd. I didn't hear the water run, and you know how the pipes in this place are."

Kate turned the page in her magazine and readjusted the pillow beneath her head. "Maybe Sinatra drowned it out."

"Maybe," her mother said. "Are you going to be out soon? I think Stella needs to go potty."

Kate felt a little guilty for having abandoned her poodle in the name of solitude, but Stella would get over it. Dad could feed the dog table scraps, since Kate wasn't out there to stop him.

"Her chain is at the kitchen door, Mom," Kate said. "Just put her on it, and she'll do the rest."

"You're sure you're okay in there?"

"Absolutely."

Her mother moved off, leaving Kate to her thoughts and a cell phone that didn't want to ring back. She knew from Ginger that Matt was going to be up in Traverse City on Tuesday and Wednesday. From Matt, she'd heard nothing directly. Not even so much as a hello since the staff meeting early last week. She missed him. She wanted to find a way back into his life. It was chilly here on the outside.

"Attempt number four," she announced, then pressed the speed dial number she'd assigned him. At this point, she didn't really expect an answer. It was more for the sport of hearing his voice mail message that she called. But this time, Matt answered.

"Hi, Kate."

Kate's hands started feeling a little sweaty. For the love of Mike! She hadn't felt this nervous since asking Scotty McDougall to the Sadie Hawkins dance in ninth grade. "I hear you're heading out of town for a couple of days."

"I'm on the road now."

"I was wondering if you'd like me to help take care of Chuck? I can check on him as many times a day as you think he'd need, and he knows who I am, so that would be nice for him." She was babbling and couldn't stop. "And, honestly, it's no big deal. You'd be doing me a favor by giving me an excuse to get away from here in the evening for a while, and—oh hell, I really miss you."

"I miss you, too."

Kate smiled with her entire body. She felt like the Grinch when his heart grew three sizes that day.

"How are you doing with your parents?" he asked.

"I'm hiding in the bathtub to make this call. No place is private anymore. If I go into my bedroom, my mother wants to have a girl-to-girl. She wants to know if I'm recovering from my divorce. She wants to tell me how to find a new man. I mean, I'm glad we're talking a whole lot more than we used to, but sometimes I just need a break from her advice."

He laughed. "That good, eh?"

"That 1960s outlook. I don't get it, but I guess I don't have to. Bottom line is that I love her and Dad."

"I think I'd like your parents," he said.

Kate smiled. "You probably would. And they'd like you, too."

They were silent, but it wasn't in the least uncomfortable.

"So I'd really be doing you a favor if I had you check on Chuck?"

Kate's smile had taken up permanent residence. "Definitely."

"Actually, that would be great," he said. "Lizzie has promised to stop by, but she has the next couple of days off. Before I enlisted her, she'd been talking about visiting a college friend downstate."

"I'd be happy to cover for her. Really."

"Well, thank you. I'm going to try to hustle it along, but I need to meet with my attorney and get things wrapped up with Chet before we get any closer to Thursday and family time."

"Thanksgiving . . . That's kind of a tough time of the year to be doing something like that. I never thought I'd say it, but I almost feel sorry for poor Chet."

She paused before continuing. "I want to tell you something, though. . . . I know Chet has been thinking about things. He's probably sitting in his bathtub right now, feeling a little selfish and hoping that he hasn't messed up a great friendship."

The bathroom door rattled again.

"Kate, is there someone in there with you?"

"No, Mom, I'm just talking to myself."

"I worry about you, Kate."

"I'm fine. Promise. Could you check on Stella? I think I hear her barking." Another lie, but she wanted to finish this call.

"Goodness!" her mother said. "That dog is worse than a toddler."

"I think she's gone, but I know she's going to be back," Kate said to Matt after listening to the sound of her mother's footsteps fade. "How often should I check on Chuck?"

"Lizzie's going to be there tonight, but if you could stop out tomorrow morning, then again in the evening, that should work. And Wednesday morning should be good. I'll be back in the afternoon. And I know he doesn't like it, but put him on his leash when you let him out. It's deer season."

"And you haven't painted him orange," she said, and smiled at the sound of his laughter.

"Chuck has enough dignity issues as it is," he said.

"So true."

Kate sat upright at the sound of her mother back at the door.

"I have to go. And thank you for letting me watch Chuck."

Her mother was back, rapping on the door. "Kate? It's almost dinnertime, and I can't find a single thing to light the candles."

After waiting an appropriate amount of time to theoretically dry off and get dressed, Kate cruised downstairs. As she'd expected, Dad was slipping Stella some of whatever Mom had served as an appetizer. At least he was keeping his double Manhattan, extra cherries, to himself.

He looked over at Kate. "Who'd have thought a dog would like kippered herring?"

She chose to take the question as rhetorical, since she couldn't say she knew many humans who liked the stuff. "Just do me a favor and don't feed her too much."

He raised his Manhattan and gave her a wink. "All things in moderation, Katie-bug."

Her mom popped into the room. She was a festival of color this evening. Her dress competed with the sofa for which held the most flowers. But her mom's dress was more in Monet watercolor shades than the sofa's warring hues.

"Are you positive you don't want to join us for

dinner, Kate? We'd love more time with you before the rest of the family arrives tomorrow."

"Thanks, but I'm not all that hungry."

Which wasn't quite accurate. She'd turned down dinner before she'd talked to Matt. Now that they'd talked, the knot in her stomach had disappeared and she was starved. But no way was she interrupting what looked to be another major romantic event. She'd just grab something from the kitchen and go read a book.

Kate's mom looped a lock of her silver-blond hair behind one ear. "Sorry to be a bother, but I still don't have the candles on the dining table lit. And they set the mood for love, after all."

Kate managed not to wince. "Let me go look in the kitchen." She was totally okay with the senior set having an active love life. It was just growing to be TMI as it pertained to her parents.

"Now that I think of it, that might not be necessary." Kate's mom gave her husband a teasing smile. "Larry, you must have a lighter with that box of cigars you think you're hiding from me."

Her father laughed. "It could be. Let me go check."

He rose and stopped long enough to kiss her mom's cheek. Kate smiled. Her parents made love and intimacy look easy. She could learn a thing or two from them.

* * *

Sunrise was approaching. Still, Kate couldn't sleep. Even her furry Stella comforter, who snored from the next pillow over, hadn't been enough. Kate reached for the nightstand lamp and switched it on. Her parents' talk of lighters and love had dug its way into her mind. Until she figured out why, she was back in insomnia land.

"Lighters and love," she said aloud, not that Stella woke to listen.

Kate opened the nightstand drawer. Maybe if she wrote down everything she'd been dwelling on, she could sleep. Before she could even reach for paper, though, an image of Laila lighting jack-o'-lanterns outside Depot Brewing popped into her head.

But why?

Kate flopped back against her pillow and focused on the details of that moment. It had been cold and windy, and Kate had been crushing on Matt. Nothing new there. . . .

Laila had used the same kind of lighter Harley carried. That would be no biggie, except it had been fancy, complete with crystals. Like a gift from a sweetheart. Maybe one who had a lighter collection, like Harley Bagger. Kate considered the concept of a Harley-Laila hookup. Both were single, so why not? The idea was kind of cute.

Or maybe not so cute, after all.

She'd finally made the connection. Between the two of them, they had every event of vandalism covered.

Kate bolted from bed and went to her dresser. She pulled out the stuff she'd found on the floor at Depot Brewing before she'd taken her beer Slip 'n Slide ride.

The white cocktail napkin meant nothing. It could be found in a hundred bars within a hundred miles of Keene's Harbor. But the string, that was another story. She twisted it, noting the slender red thread laced through it. This was no ordinary utility twine, and now she was pretty sure she knew what it was.

Taking care not to disturb her parents, Kate padded downstairs to the computer set up in the corner of the living room. She fed a couple of words into the images section of her favorite search engine.

"Bingo!" she said as she looked at the pictures on the screen.

The string in question was a replacement wick for a vintage windproof lighter. Laila had been laid up and couldn't have turned on the taps. But her lover could have. Kate had pegged at least one saboteur. His name was Harley Bagger.

Tuesday morning was still fresh with frost, and already Matt was running out of reasons to stay in Traverse City. A two-day trip had made sense when it had seemed easier to be far away from Kate than close enough to rush things and do something stupid. Now that they were talking, he was all for soon and stupid.

He'd met with his attorney over coffee at seven, and a suit would be filed to collect from Chet unless the brewer was willing to settle out of court. For both their sakes, he hoped Chet would.

A quick stop out to see Travis last night had been positive and productive. The guy had come up with a business plan and some ideas for a citrus summer beer to celebrate the opening of the Tropicana. All was well with the world.

Almost.

At just past nine, Matt walked out of his office and into Ginger's reception area. She looked up from the crossword puzzle she was doing.

"What's a four-letter word for idiot?" she asked.

"Matt."

"Really. Throw me a word."

"Dolt."

She frowned down at the puzzle, then smiled up at him. "That fits."

And it fit him, too. Since when had he not grabbed for what he wanted?

"Can you call and reschedule tomorrow's meetings until next week?" he asked.

"Sure. What's the matter?"

"Unfinished business back home."

Ginger snorted. "Right. Business. Blond unfinished business, maybe?"

"Yeah, another four-letter word, and it means happiness," Matt said.

He'd let Ginger guess on her own, because he wanted to get home and grab love.

Kate glared at her cell phone as she parked in front of Matt's place. It wasn't quite ten, and already she'd struck out on three separate calls.

First, she'd called Matt, but the call went straight to voice mail. Then she'd called the police station and come up empty. She'd sort of expected that, since she'd noticed the office was unattended a lot this time of year. Clete's voice on the answering machine had instructed her to hang up and call 911 if this was an emergency. Having a suspicion of who'd been sabotaging Matt didn't seem to fit the bill, so she'd left Clete a message, asking him to call her as soon as possible.

Because she was trying to be thorough, she'd done the same on Lizzie's voice mail, even though she knew Matt's sister was probably on her way downstate. She'd try all three again, once Chuck had been fed and loved.

Kate exited her Jeep. The air was crisp enough so that it felt sharp in her lungs. By the time evening fell, it was going to be nose-numbingly cold out here in the country. She'd be back at The Nutshell by then, and Chip and Bunny and their respective crews would be, too. All the more reason to cherish the quiet out here.

But as Kate walked toward the front door, a *"Buh-woof"* sounded from the back of the house.

She halted. Only one dog she'd ever met had a voice that could carry with such conviction.

"Chuck?"

"Buh-woof."

Kate rounded the side of the house, her shoes sweeping through the blanket of leaves underfoot. Chuck stood on the back deck, tail wagging.

"Dude, when did you become an escape artist?"

"Buh-woof."

He butted the back door with one broad shoulder, begging to get in. She supposed that Lizzie might have accidentally left him out when she'd departed last night. Kate pulled out her keys, opened the back door, and ushered Chuck in. He gazed up at her with worried hound eyes and let roll another round of *"Buh-woof."*

"I don't speak dog as fluently as your owner, so we're going to have to play a game of twenty questions. I know you don't need to go out, so what's the deal?"

"Buh-woof."

"Water? Do you need water?"

He wagged his tail. *"Buh-woof."*

Kate checked out Chuck's water bowl. Over half remained, but, hey, she appreciated the concept of not drinking one's own slobber. If he wanted fresh, fresh he'd get. She bent over to pick up the bowl and caught a faint whiff of something. Thought number one was that Chuck had passed gas, but the scent was more wood smoke than unpleasant.

"You're off the hook, buddy."

"Buh-woof."

"You're welcome." She rinsed his bowl at the kitchen sink, and the same scent grew strong enough to make her eyes burn. *Just like fire.*

Chuck's metal bowl clattered against the bottom of the aluminum sink as the thought sunk in. Kate turned off the water and followed the scent to the main living area. Flames flickered through a haze of suffocatingly thick smoke.

Okay, so *buh-woof* meant *The place is burning, you idiot human!*

Kate turned back to the kitchen, grabbed Chuck by his collar, and hauled him toward the back door. She needed him safe before she did anything else. He dug in his heels once they'd reached the back deck.

"Come on, buddy."

It seemed unsporting to shove a three-legged dog along, but it was for his own safety. Once they were on solid ground, Kate pulled her cell phone from her jeans pocket, dialed 911, and waited. When the operator came on the line, Kate said "fire" and gave Matt's address. Then she caught a glimpse of Chuck going back inside.

"Are you out of the house?" the operator asked. "Can you tell me what's going on, ma'am?"

"Chuck, no!"

But Chuck didn't seem to speak human any better than she spoke dog, because he kept going. It was her fault for leaving the door open, and she'd never be able to live with herself if she didn't make an effort to snag the hound. And she never, ever wanted to have to tell Matt how she'd screwed up.

"Just please get the trucks here," she said to the operator, then hung up and jammed the phone back into her pocket.

Kate climbed the deck's steps. "Chuck, come on out!" She could risk this. The fire had been limited to the front room, and while Chuck was crafty, speed wasn't part of his repertoire.

Kate stepped inside, and the smell of smoke assailed her. It now drifted in a thick haze at ceiling height.

Stupid dog.

"Chuck, treat! Side of beef! Whole turkey!"

Kate started coughing. She should have asked Matt what magic words brought his dog running.

But all she could do now was go inside. Of all the fire advice she'd ever learned, she discarded *get out* and focused on *stay low*.

Three more steps in and she heard a familiar voice behind her saying, "You never learn."

Kate turned and opened her mouth to ask what was going on. A sharp pain shot through her head. Then Kate could say nothing at all.

TWENTY

KATE AWAKENED SLOWLY. SHE WAS LYING ON A FREEZING cold, rotted plywood floor that was gritty with dirt. She touched her fingertips to the side of her head and they came away sticky with blood. Kate fought a wave of nausea.

Harley Bagger stood over her. "You're heavier than you look," he said.

She scoped out her surroundings. "And you're meaner than you look."

The shack smelled decayed, and its narrow doorway and window slits didn't let in much air. She'd bet she was in an old deer blind that had fallen to the ground. Not a helpful clue, since deer blinds dotted the woods for miles around.

"You made me do this," Harley said.

"Made you? How do you figure that?"

"You shouldn't have come back for the stupid dog. I coulda gotten away, except for you. I could have been in and out that window I jimmied." He glared at her. "You messed up my work."

Kate's heart turned over at the thought of poor, sweet Chuck. The dog had gone back in to fetch Harley and had probably paid with his life. But she couldn't think about that now, or she'd break down. She braced her hands against the floor and sat up.

Harley pointed a gun at her. "You stay right there."

"What are you doing, Harley? Do you really think that's going to help matters?"

He wiped the sweat off his forehead. "Not for you, maybe."

"What have I ever done to you?" She inched her hand toward her front right pocket and her cell phone.

"Don't bother. I threw the phone into the pond in back of his house. Do you think I'm stupid?"

Honesty wasn't always the best policy. Kate kept her mouth closed.

"It's Culhane. All Culhane. He's ruining me," Harley said.

She closed her eyes for a second, trying to push back the pain. "How?"

"He's got all the business in town."

"When you fired me, you'd let that keg of his beer go flat, hadn't you?"

Harley paced back and forth. "It wasn't about you. It was about messing with his reputation a little."

"And after that you started messing with Matt, too."

"Prove it," he said.

"Not that it matters at this point, but I can. The morning you left all the taps open at Matt's place, I found a replacement wick to one of your lighters on the floor. And I even know who gave you the keys to get in . . . Laila."

"Wh—what do you mean, Laila?"

"I know you two are an item. She was using one of your vintage lighters before Shay Van-Antwerp's party. From what I've learned cruising around on my computer, that crystal number is far too valuable to toss to a buddy."

"Well, it's none of your business. But just so you know, she had nothing to do with this. I copied her keys without her knowing."

"Do you love her?" If she softened him up, maybe he'd let her go.

Harley nodded. "We've been keepin' it quiet-like, since she's still collecting a pension from her last husband that'll go away if we get married. All we want are winters in Florida and good food, but I spent my savings when business dropped."

"That's not Matt's fault."

The gun shook in his hand. "The hell it's not. I'm the victim here, not him! All I wanted was

Depot Brewing down for a while so people would come back to my place. But that boy is like that battery rabbit on television. No matter what I do, he just keeps on going and going and going. And then he's got the nerve to ask *me* if I need a loan. I made him—not the other way around!"

Kate kept calm, figuring it was all she had left. "I'm sorry all of this has happened. But maybe it should all just stop now. Maybe we should just walk out of here."

"I can't. And don't you see? I had no choice in any of this. I'm getting too far along in years. Laila and I shoulda stayed away from the casinos. All we were looking for was some money for retirement."

She'd been nearly boiled and now kidnapped so Bonnie and Clyde could go to dog races and jai alai and eat grouper?

Hell, no!

Harley's hand had stopped shaking. He had made a decision. "I'm not gonna go to jail. No way!"

Kate didn't like the calm that had replaced his anger. "Serving even more time for murder doesn't make much sense. Think you could put that thing away?"

"At my age, murder and arson are both life sentences. Why should I go to jail for either when if I finish you off, there's no witness left?"

She wouldn't have thought until today that Harley had a murder in him, but then again, she also would have said that arson was out of his range, and he had already tried to drown her in the brewhouse. "Don't get carried away, Harley," she said. "Relax and let's decide what to do next. Why don't you sit down?"

"No! Shut up and let me think!"

Kate realized Harley had crossed the line into crazy land. She was going to have to find a way to run.

Matt had ten miles of tight road before he reached Keene's Harbor. That was ten miles too many with a slow-moving rusty red tractor in front of him. He needed to talk to Kate while he had all this love stuff straight in his head. It had taken him damn long enough to get it that way. He spotted a break, passed the farmer, and put his foot to the floor.

Another mile down the road, Matt's cell phone rang.

"Matt, it's Ella."

He smiled. He liked Ella. Hell, he loved her for being Kate's first friend in Keene's Harbor.

"Hey, how are you doing?"

"Are you in town?"

Something about her usually cheerful tone was off, he thought. "No, I'm just outside it, on my way back from T.C. Why?"

She paused. "I want you to pull to the side of the road, okay?"

This wasn't going to be good.

He put the truck in park and threw on his flashers. "What's up?"

"I've got some bad news. There was a fire in the main room at your house. Kate called it in, and we got it under control with as little damage as you could expect, all things considered."

Which was the least of his worries. "But what about Kate? Did she and Chuck get out okay?"

"That's why I asked Captain Norm if I could be the one to call you. Kate's car is out front, but there's no sign of her or your dog in the house."

"Did you check the outbuildings?"

"All we found was Harley Bagger's car parked behind your pole barn. The police, including your sister, are on the way, but I was kind of hoping you'd heard from Kate?"

"No."

"Okay," Ella said. "Well, let's not worry before we have to. It could be that everything's just fine."

Matt's gut was telling him otherwise.

Sunday, when he'd dropped in on Harley to offer him a loan, it had been a mess. Harley had been angry and insulted, and Matt had ended up feeling like a jerk. If Harley had come out to Matt's place just to talk to him, he wouldn't have parked behind the pole barn. And if he'd come to do something more, Kate might be in danger.

Again.

"Ella, I have to hang up now. I need you to find Clete and tell him I said that Harley is his man."

"I'll do that," she said.

The wind was pushing through the woods. And Harley had taken to muttering to himself. Kate was trying to be a big, strong dog who could jump high, but she was scared. Very scared.

She needed to focus on the positive. Someone had to be looking for her by now. Her car had been right in front of Matt's house. And she couldn't be all that far away, either. She would be no easy drag for a man in Harley's shape. Plus, with all her scrapes and aches, and all the grunge clinging to her, she had to have left a trail.

Harley sprang to attention, his voice shrill. "Did you hear that?"

She'd definitely liked it better when he'd been ignoring her. "Hear what?"

"That!"

Kate picked up the distant sound of under-brush crackling.

"It was a deer, maybe," she said, though she was hoping for something better armed than Bambi. Say, like the police.

Harley moved to the blind's doorway. He gripped his gun in two shaking hands and aimed. At what, she wasn't sure.

"He has a gun," Kate shouted.

Harley jumped, and a shot went off. Whatever was heading their way rolled on through the leaves.

"*Woof!*"

Kate laughed with relief. "It's Chuck!"

Harley didn't seem to have the same level of happiness. He lowered the gun and started muttering to himself again.

"*Woof!*"

Chuck clambered past Harley and went to Kate.

Kate wrapped her arms around the dog. "I'm so glad you're alive."

"*Woof!*"

Kate flinched. "I'm having sort of a headache issue. Could you keep it down?"

"*Woof!*"

Harley waved his gun at her. "Make that dog shut up!"

"If I could, I would," she said.

"*Woof!*"

"Do it, now!"

"*Woof! Woof!*"

Harley swung his arm violently, waving the gun. "Get out of here, mutt!"

"Hey! Do *not* threaten the dog." Kate got up on her knees and urged Chuck toward the doorway. "Just go on out there, dude. I'm right here, and pretty soon Matt will be here to take us to Stella."

"*Woof! Woof!*"

Harley gave him a boot to the rear, and Chuck yelped.

Something inside Kate snapped, the same way it had when her ex admitted he'd dumped Stella.

"Nice, Harley. Kicking a three-legged dog. This is your day for proving just how low you can go, isn't it?"

Chuck advanced on Harley. The dog's cheerful bark had been replaced by a vicious growl. His hair stood up along his spine, and he eyed Harley as though he were a Porterhouse steak.

"Back off!" Harley screamed at the dog. He aimed the gun at Chuck.

As a former sensible city girl, Kate had taken a self-defense course. "Use your strongest weapons against his weakest targets," her instructor had said. Kate's strongest weapon was surprise. Or anger. It didn't matter which, because Harley was about to get hammered by both.

Kate scrambled to her feet and went in low.

Cut him off at the knees, then go for the throat.

Together, they hit the cold earth outside the crumbling shack with a hard jolt. She heard the *swoosh!* of the wind being knocked from Harley. Out of the corner of her eye, she saw the gun go skittering. No way was he getting near it again. Still on top of him, she took the flats of her palms and slammed them hard onto his ears.

Harley howled.

"I was just warming up," she said. "Because you're going down."

Until Matt had to cover sixty acres of dense woods at a dead run, the privacy of a big property had always seemed like a good thing. If nothing else, it gave him a buffer from the semi-militia types living on the other side of the trees. He'd heard his share of strange sounds out here, but never anything quite like this. And he knew it wasn't coming from his arms-bearing neighbors. The howls he heard were Chuck exercising his right to free speech . . . plus something more. Matt picked up his pace.

"The deer blind's just ahead," he yelled to Clete and Lizzie, who were a stretch behind him.

He cleared a cluster of trees and high brush and stopped just short of Kate and Harley. Harley was thrashing around on the ground, and Kate was whacking the bejeezus out of him.

Matt hauled Kate off Harley and hugged her to him. Harley started to rise and Chuck chomped into Harley's pants leg. A beat later, Lizzie and Clete burst onto the scene.

Matt held Kate at arm's length and looked at her. "Are you okay?"

"Yes. Except for my head."

Matt took in the blood-caked blond hair and wondered if he could persuade Clete to let him take a shot at Harley.

Lizzie flipped Harley over and cuffed him. "Good dog," she said to Chuck, scratching him behind his ear.

Matt cuddled Kate back against him and gave her a gentle kiss. "What happened here?"

"He was going to kill Chuck. And I love Chuck."

"Chuck, huh?"

She nodded.

"Any chance you might love me, too?"

She nodded again.

"That's good," Matt said, "because I love you."

Kate looked up at him. "You do?"

"I told you, sweetheart. When I'm in, I'm *all* in."

And Matt was in. Forever.

Kate sat on the edge of the emergency room's triage cot. She could sum up her state as hurting and happy. She was going to have one heck of a headache, but she could handle it because she was in love. She'd tried to hold her heart safe from Matt, but it had opened anyway. Everything seemed brighter and better, though she supposed that could be from the pain meds, too.

"Are you ready to leave?" Matt asked her.

"Absolutely."

He took her elbow while she stood. She smiled up at him. It wasn't so bad, having a handsome guy's occasional help.

Matt motioned to an envelope that had been left near her purse. "Don't forget that."

Kate opened the envelope. It contained a cashier's check for twenty thousand dollars.

"You caught my stalker. You earned every penny," he said. "I suppose I'm going to have to look for another place to build my restaurant."

Kate felt herself starting to cry. "Maybe you'd rather be the part owner of a struggling B&B. I need a partner to help me, since I have a second job at this awesome brewery working with a guy I absolutely love."

"I love you, too."

"We should get me back to The Nutshell," Kate said. "I know my mom and dad must be wondering where I am."

Kate had called them from Matt's cell phone on the way to the hospital and said she'd been a little delayed, but would be home soon. She figured this sort of story was better delivered in person. That way, everyone could see she was still in one piece.

Matt looked toward a set of double doors. "I should warn you that a whole lot of people are out there waiting for you."

"Really? Why?"

He smiled. "It's Keene's Harbor. Word got out among the locals about what happened, and they want to be sure you're okay."

So this was what it felt like to belong. Kate

never wanted to lose the feeling, even if she did have a couple of tears threatening to roll.

Everyone was there. Ella and Lizzie, the whole Culhane clan, Marcie Landon, Junior Greinwold, a horde from the Depot, Mayor and Missy Mortensen.

Kate waved Miss America style. "I'm fine," she said.

Marcie made a clucking sound. "Not yet, you're not." She held out a brown paper bag. "No Keene's Harbor local comes out of the hospital without getting some of my chicken noodle soup."

Kate accepted the gift. "Thank you. That's really sweet of you, Marcie, but you didn't need to fuss."

"You're family, now. It's no fuss."

Kate sniffled. "Okay, now I'm going to cry. How uncool is that?" But, really, she thought this whole scene was cool, possibly the coolest thing ever.

Kate moved through her friends, accepting hugs and words of reassurance until she finally found herself face-to-face with Junior Greinwold.

Junior held out the blue cooler to Kate. "I feel really bad about the mess I made, what with all the bees and dooky. This is for you."

Kate opened up the cooler. It was filled with Snickers bars and wadded-up hundred dollar bills. Enough to cover the cost of Kate's repairs.

Junior leaned close to Kate so he could whisper in her ear. "Don't tell anyone. I won the lottery a bunch of years ago, but I like being a handyman."

Matt finally pulled her away from the crowd. "We'd better get you home." Which was exactly how Keene's Harbor now felt to her.

Twenty minutes later, Kate and Matt sat in his truck, the last in line behind three luxury cars in The Nutshell's driveway.

"So," Matt said, "are you going to be okay in there?"

"About that . . ."

"Yes?"

Kate had thought this was going to be hard, but everything felt so right. "I was wondering if you'd like to come in and meet my family?"

"You're not asking me just because you don't feel like explaining what happened, are you?"

She laughed. "And if I were?"

He smiled. "You know I'd do it."

"I'd love the help, but that's not why I asked. I want them to meet you. I want them to see why I've fallen in love." She unbuckled her seat belt and slid closer to Matt. "If I'm going to stay in Keene's Harbor and put down some roots, this is where I want to start." She leaned in until her lips met Matt's. "Right here."

And this time the kiss was perfect.

Read on for an excerpt from

THE HUSBAND LIST
by Janet Evanovich

Coming in January 2013 in hardcover from

St. Martin's Press

ONE

"CLOSE YOUR EYES AND THINK OF CHOCOLATE CAKE," Caroline Maxwell told herself. It was the only way she could get through this tedious dress fitting. Even in the advanced year of 1894, an American heiress had certain rules to follow, and allowing herself to be a pincushion for the House of Worth seemed to be one of them. What Caroline really wanted was adventure, independence, and to see the world. But she doubted her parents would ever come to their senses enough to set her free.

The seamstress, who had accompanied Caroline's new wardrobe from Worth's Paris dress shop across the Atlantic to the Maxwell family's Fifth Avenue residence, wielded another pin. Caroline winced in anticipation.

The angry-looking woman had already caught
skin twice. Maybe her aim was off due to the
lingering seasickness that had delayed yesterday's
fitting. Or perhaps she was intimidated by the
dozens of china figurines Mama had introduced
to Caroline's enormous sitting room. The sense
that one was being watched by countless beady
little eyes could be unsettling. Not to mention the
house itself . . . With sixty rooms, it, too, could
rattle a soul.

"Your measurements have changed," the
Frenchwoman accused.

And then there was that.

"Impossible," Caroline fibbed.

She glanced at her mother, who kept an eye on
affairs from her regal perch atop the massive red
velvet and gold-gilt settee that she'd also insisted
must be part of Caroline's quarters. Normally
her mother wouldn't tolerate such talk from a
servant, but Agnes was secretly intimidated by
the French, which was why they'd left Paris before the dresses were done. Mama brushed away
an imaginary crumb from the fabric of her conservative, high-necked dove-grey morning dress
and then fussed with the tiny bit of lace at each
cuff. Caroline knew she was on her own in the
battle of the pins.

The seamstress stepped back on the thick carpet to assess her work. Caroline caught her own
reflection in the cheval mirror that was positioned

so that Mama could see Caroline in profile. Mr. Worth's style sense was clearly incomparable.

The low-cut—almost risqué—ivory silk ball gown Caroline wore had been embellished with what felt like pounds of pearls and dark green crystals. Assuming she could bear up under the weight, it would complement her clear complexion and hair as dark as her mother's. Rumor had it that Mama's maternal great-grandmother had been a Cherokee princess, which Mama would not confirm.

Worth's skills had also made Caroline's slight surplus of curves an asset rather than a detriment. Come the season, she was doomed. She had no idea what she could do to top last year's anti-marriage efforts. All the same, she intended to escape this year's marriage market as she had 1893's: unwed, unpromised, and as independent as she could be. Which, in her opinion, was not saying much.

Caroline released her breath and unclenched clammy palms as another pin met only fabric. And in other sunny news, her mother's insecurity meant at least Caroline would not be facing French *ducs* on top of the English dukes Mama kept pushing her to marry.

"*Absolument*, you have gained since your last fitting," the seamstress said. "And more than a little."

Caroline answered with a vague smile. It would

never do to confess that she'd begun midnight kitchen forays to ease her tight nerves.

"Caroline, have you varied from our agreed-upon menu?" her mother asked. Alarm had made her dark brows arch closer to her perfectly coiffed hair with its beginning threads of silver.

There had been no agreement. There hadn't even been negotiations, just no outright objection from Caroline. She'd decided long ago that working around her mother was more diplomatic than upsetting her. Easier, too. And since her mother's eating edict made Caroline fifty percent a spectator at family meals, she felt she deserved a fat slice of chocolate cake whenever she wished. It wasn't noon yet, and her mouth watered at the thought of tonight's pilfered treat. Actually, not so very pilfered since Cook had caught on to the scheme and now left cake waiting for her.

Mama pursed her lips and scrutinized Caroline more closely. "You must have been straying. You're looking plumper in the face when Amelia and Helen are still as slim as can be."

At sixteen, her twin sisters didn't yet have the avoidance skills Caroline possessed at twenty-one. Or the same ability to hold their tongues under their mother's inquisition techniques. They *always* confessed.

Caroline kept her silence.

Mama narrowed her eyes.

(317)633-7020

(800)233-0020

(317)-633-7020

(800)233-0020

Celtic Thunder

Caroline widened hers.

Mama cleared her throat, giving warning of a lecture to come.

Caroline did her best to exude an aura of innocence as strong as her mother's favored gardenia perfume. It must have worked because Mama heaved a resigned sigh.

"Stand taller," she ordered. "Shoulders back and chin up."

Caroline complied, though the gown would be no looser around her waist for the effort. Tonight's cake would have to be her last for a while. It wasn't as though she could eat her way to freedom. American heiresses were as popular with unmarried and underfunded English noblemen as chocolate cake was with Caroline.

"If you are to wear a coronet, you must look as though you were born to it," Mama said. That, and "you are this family's crown jewel" were two of her mother's favorite things to say. Caroline found both statements as uncomfortable as the corset currently mashing her innards.

Mama had been about to issue another proclamation—probably about crown jewels—but was distracted by a one-person stampede down the mahogany parquet hallway.

Annie, Caroline's new personal maid, appeared. Breathless, she took an instant to compose herself. It was hopeless. During her dash, her red curls had sprung free from their tight bun and were now nearly at right angles from the white cap atop her head.

"Mrs. Maxwell, ma'am, O'Brien has asked me to tell you that Mrs. Longhorne is calling," Annie said.

She thrust out a calling card. She did not, however, have the silver tray that the butler used, so Caroline's mother pretended not to see it.

Annie waited for a response, then plowed on, either unaware or uncaring of her breach of decorum. "Ma'am, she's on her way up here now."

"Really, here?" Agnes asked, rising.

Annie was saved. Mrs. Longhorne venturing to private quarters without invitation was an even greater violation of Mama's rules than Annie's slip-up.

Mildred Longhorne rushed in, her hands fluttering on either side of her face like two of the finches that Mama kept caged in the conservatory. Her pointy nose was red at the tip and her usually nondescript grey eyes sparkled with excitement. She hadn't even changed out of the black riding habit she wore for a morning turn about the park, and the knot of early June pansies at one buttonhole looked ready to jump ship.

"Agnes, I have the most exciting news! Lord Bremerton is visiting with friends at Newport this season."

Caroline's mother sat. "Bremerton, the son of

Viscount Bellingham, grandson of the Duke of Endsleigh?"

"Yes."

"He's married," Mama said in a dismissive tone.

While Caroline was hardly in love with her mother's determination to marry her into English nobility, she had to give her credit for an impressive level of study.

"No, no . . . not that one. He's dead. There's a new Bremerton!"

"Dead?" Caroline's mother repeated. She'd sounded a little gleeful, too.

"Yes, a riding accident, I heard. The younger son has taken the title, and his father is rumored to be in poor health. You know what that means, don't you?"

Mama rose again. She walked a circle around Caroline and the seamstress. Apparently content with what she saw, she returned her attention to Mrs. Longhorne.

"He'll be a duke," she replied.

"Yes!" her friend cried. "And Caroline will be a duchess!"

Where was a slice of chocolate cake when a girl needed one?

At ten minutes until eight that evening, most of the family sat in the Oriental drawing room awaiting the call to dinner. All they lacked was

Caroline's brother, Edward, who at almost twenty-seven, lived down Fifth Avenue in the lesser mansion the family had left behind when this one had been completed.

"Any time Edward isn't where he's promised to be, he's off with that Jack Culhane," Mama was complaining to Caroline's father.

Caroline hid the smile that seemed to work its way across her face whenever she thought of her brother's best friend. She could guarantee that wherever they were, Eddie and Jack were having more fun than she was. From the time she'd been old enough to tag after them—well, mostly after Jack—she'd tried, but with little success. When she'd walk in on their tale-telling, she'd catch just enough to make her more determined to be part of their adventures.

They were all grown now, with Eddie working at Papa's side, and Jack buying up businesses almost as quickly as his father did. But Caroline's greatest adventure had been frightening off a handful of dukes last year, and that was before Mama had taken away most of her freedom. She hated to sound ungrateful because she knew how lucky she was. All the same, she'd trade a steamer trunk packed with Maxwell money for just a few days of living like Jack and Eddie.

"Edward said he'll be here at eight, and he will be," Papa replied. "He's a Maxwell man, which means he's a man of his word."

He turned his attention to Caroline, who had been doing her best to blend into the bold orange and green chrysanthemum-patterned brocade of the chair in which she sat—never an easy job when one was wearing a peacock blue dress.

"Maxwell women, too. Am I right, Pumpkin?" he asked. Pride shone from his craggy features, and his thick gray moustache—so startling when one considered his fading auburn hair—moved upward with his smile.

Caroline hesitated. His question was simple enough on its surface, but since just minutes ago her parents had been discussing Lord Bremerton's visit, she knew what Papa really meant. She searched for a comment positive enough to make her father happy, yet still not an outright promise to lure and marry some Englishman she'd never met. Not when she had someone oh-so-much better in mind.

"Really, Bernard, you must stop calling her that," Mama said, saving Caroline another diplomatic dance. "It was bad enough that it slipped out at the Astors' ball last year. Imagine if you said it in front of Bremerton?"

"There's no mistaking her for a gourd, Agnes," Papa said. "And you'll always be my Pumpkin, won't you, Caroline?"

"Of course I will." Even from across the sea.

Deep male talk and laughter sounded from outside the room. Jack was here with Eddie. This time Caroline couldn't stop her smile from appearing. They walked in more or less shoulder-to-shoulder, since Jack stood inches taller than Eddie, who was of average height. And where Eddie was on the wiry side, Jack looked as though he could take on Calcutta street thieves and win.

Jack's black frock coat sat well across his broad shoulders, and the white of his starched shirt and collar set off the sun-darkened color of his skin and deep brown hair. She liked that he was clean-shaven, too. Eddie's attempt at a moustache seemed a little scant, though she'd never say so to her brother.

"Six minutes to spare," Eddie said before kissing Mama on the cheek. "You were counting, weren't you?"

"I was doing no such thing," she said, but bright flags of pink on her face let Eddie know he had caught her.

Mama's gaze drifted past Eddie and on to Jack. While she didn't permit her disapproval to show in her expression, she still managed to convey it by stiffening her posture. Even Pomeroy, the little mop of a lap dog Mama had acquired so she could feel a bit like Queen Victoria, seemed to tighten up.

"Good evening, Mrs. Maxwell," Jack said, giving a slight bow.

"We were late getting back from Jack's new

business concern. I hope you don't mind if he joins us for dinner," Eddie added.

"No, really, I need to be on my way," Jack said. "I just wanted to say hello to the family."

His smile briefly settled on Amelia and Helen, who wore matching yellow satin dresses in appropriately girlish styles. And because Mama believed in playing the asset of their twin-hood to the fullest, their wavy auburn hair had been upswept in identical fashions, too. They smiled prettily and inclined their heads to Jack, but never met his eyes.

His attention moved on to Caroline, who had no qualms about meeting Jack Culhane head-on.

"Hello, Caroline. Are the social rounds treating you well?" he asked, a devilish light shining in his blue eyes.

How her girlfriends could not find him handsome was beyond Caroline. They used phrases like "too earthy" when they spoke of him. She thought the men they found attractive looked half-starved.

Jack was perfect.

Her heart beat faster at the sight of the two dimples that always appeared when he teased her. He knew how she felt about the endless gatherings that Mama insisted she attend. And Jack felt the same way, too. He might slip into a party, but he was always quickly gone.

"Very well," she said. "I've been having a wonderful time."

"Really, wonderful?"

"Bordering on delirious."

His smile became a full-out grin. "I'll bet."

"Stay for dinner," Eddie said to Jack. "Tell my father about the new brewery and your plans for expansion."

Caroline waited for his answer. She'd make a devil's bargain of her own and trade away tonight's final slice of cake if he would.

"Another brewery?" her father asked Jack in a tone that was disapproving and yet curious, too.

"Yes, sir," Jack replied.

"Don't you already have one in Pennsylvania?"

"And one in Boston, as well."

Papa frowned. "Then why buy any more?"

"For the same reasons your grandfather bought those regional railroads, sir. Consolidation of power and resources."

Papa flicked his hand as though shooing away a gnat. "Breweries aren't the same thing at all."

Caroline settled in to eavesdrop. She felt sheer joy at hearing a conversation of more import than whether it was appropriate to have the lettering on one's calling card embossed.

"With all due respect, sir, you're wrong," Jack said.

Papa rose from the ornate carved chair Mama claimed was Imperial Chinese. He joined Jack and Eddie in front of the cavernous fireplace, stepping on one of the two tiger skins on the floor while on his way. Caroline tried to avoid looking at the tigers. She'd been thirteen when Papa had brought them home from a hunting trip, and she'd cried well into the night upon seeing them.

Caroline focused on the gentlemen. They looked so civilized in their uniformly black evening suits, though Papa's was cut to accommodate his girth. He ate with the same robust passion he gave the rest of life.

"I'm wrong, am I?" he asked Jack, clearly warming to the debate.

Caroline's mother must have known that her window of opportunity for a dinner without Jack Culhane had closed.

"O'Brien, see that there's room at the table for Mister Culhane," she said.

The butler, who was an expert at appearing and disappearing with ghostly skill, left only to appear an impossibly short time later and announce that dinner was served.

They entered the dining room, which had been known to seat three hundred when Mama was having one of her larger parties. Their footsteps echoed all the way to the ceiling, with its frescoes of fat little cherubs, platters of fruit, and women who'd always looked to Caroline to be in some form of distress.

Jack was ushered to a spot just to Caroline's right. She glanced at her mother to see if a mistake had been made. Jack should have been seated far closer to Papa so that they could continue to converse. Apparently not, since her mother wore a content smile, probably at the thought of having quashed business talk. O'Brien looked pleased with himself, too. Caroline would never understand how the butler managed to read Mama's mind, but he was a master at it.

The family settled in, and wine was poured. Mama and the twins talked of the tea they'd attended in the afternoon while almost everyone else attempted to appear interested. Caroline, however, was too occupied by trying not to be so conscious of Jack.

Warmth seemed to roll from him. She caught a hint of wood smoke that must have traveled with him from his afternoon's adventures. She glanced his way and found that he'd been looking at her, so she pretended great interest in the silver of her place setting.

The first course was served: a little quail that had been stuffed with something or another. After a tiny bite, Caroline set her fork on the plate's edge. Good thing, too, because she was under extra scrutiny after this morning's fitting.

"We must improve Rosemeade's grounds and refurnish it immediately. It's entirely lacking in elegance. If we didn't need to be in residence no later than July first, I'd say to raze the whole thing and start over. But with both Bremerton and the season upon us, I shouldn't get carried away," Mama said to Papa after being sure Caroline had left her quail to languish.

"Do whatever you wish," Caroline's father replied. That was his stock answer for anything regarding the family's residences, which he left wholly to his wife.

Caroline wasn't feeling quite so calm. Their Newport summer cottage was her favorite. While it was hardly small at forty rooms, its Tudor-style stone-and-timber exterior gave it a sense of simplicity that this house lacked. Rosemeade also held memories of the many summer days when she'd chased after Eddie and Jack. Her heart would break if those were wiped away.

"Why would Rosemeade need improvement? It's perfect just as it is," she said.

"Perfect? Perfect to entertain a duke?" Mama asked.

Caroline could feel her hard-fought control evaporating.

"What duke?" she asked. "Bremerton's not a duke unless both his father and grandfather conveniently die."

Her mother couldn't have looked more shocked if frogs had sprung from Caroline's mouth.

"Caroline, really!"

"It's true, Mama. That's the one fact you have.

What you don't know is what sort of man he is . . . if he's kind or smart or has a good smile," she said, thinking of Jack's. "And—"

"Caroline, be quiet!" her mother commanded.

But Caroline's words might as well have been those frogs because she couldn't stop them. "And for once, could we have something that isn't made to look like something other than what it is?"

She waved her hand at the room's rosewood moldings that her mother had ordered covered in gold leaf. "Could we have wood and not make it look like gold?"

She pointed a finger at the marble fireplace that had been detailed to look like burled oak. "And stone that isn't painted like wood?"

She settled one hand against the half-high bodice of her silk-and-chiffon dinner dress, which, as far as she was concerned, was too fussy to be tolerated.

"And me? What about me, Mama? Couldn't we just agree that my hair is as straight as a pin and stop torturing it into curls? Couldn't we stop dressing me as though I'm royalty when I'm just me . . . plain, unremarkable me?"

Caroline's words caught up with her, and her anger passed as quickly as it had come. She'd never been able to hang on to it, which she supposed was a decent trait. A handier one would have been keeping her frustration to herself.

Her mother and father were staring at her,

aghast. Amelia and Helen looked as though they were about to burst into tears. And poor Eddie was gazing raptly into his wine goblet as though the secrets to life rested there.

Caroline didn't dare look at Jack. If she did, her humiliation would be complete. She pushed back her chair and rose.

"I . . . I think I'm feeling unwell," she said into the silence that hung over the table. "If you'll excuse me, I'll just . . ."

But because she had no idea what she planned to do, she simply turned and left. Her new shoes skidded on the hard floor, making her steps as wobbly as she felt inside.

She passed Annie in the hallway, but didn't stop to ask her what in heaven's name she was doing by the dining room. And instead of heading upstairs as she, too, should have done, Caroline rushed to the conservatory.

Once inside, she closed the glass and wrought-iron door that kept the room's warmth and humidity neatly trapped. She paused at the finch cage and shook her head.

"I know just how you feel," she said to the birds.

Though at least the birds couldn't see through the room's foliage to know that their kind flitted freely outside. Caroline had to watch Eddie being given full rein while she and the twins were groomed to be Mama's idea of perfect wives.

But that was not going to change.

The best she could do was work well within the cage that surrounded her, too. Caroline touched the tip of one finger to the pinkish edge of a delicate orchid blossom and watched it quiver. At least it was a very pretty cage, if over-furnished.

"I knew I'd find you here," said a male voice.